Ella Price's Journal

Ella Price's Journal

A Novel by
Dorothy Bryant

Afterword by Barbara Horn

The Feminist Press at the City University of New York
New York

Published by The Feminist Press at The City University of New York
311 East 94th Street, New York, New York 10128-5684

First Feminist Press edition, 1997

Originally published by J. B. Lippincott, 1972
New American Library/Signet edition, 1973
Ata Books edition, 1982

Library of Congress Cataloging-in-Publication Data

Bryant, Dorothy, 1930–
    Ella Price's journal / Dorothy Bryant : afterword by Barbara Horn—1st
Feminist Press ed.
        p.   c.m.
    ISBN 1-55861-181-9 (cloth: alk. paper)
    ISBN 1-55861-175-4 (pbk: alk. paper)
PS3552.R878E43   1997
813'.54—dc21   97-14405
                                                                                      CIP

The Feminist Press would like to thank Helene D. Goldfarb, Joanne Markell, and Genevieve Vaughan for their generosity in supporting this publication.

Printed on acid-free paper by BookCrafters, Chelsea, MI.
Manufactured in the United States of America.

05 04 03 02 01 00 99 98 97   5 4 3 2 1

To my husband

Ella Price's Journal

Notebook
NUMBER ONE

English R
D. Harkan
Journal Requirement

Use a 6x8 notebook. Paste these instructions on the inside cover. Fill at least one page a day, every day. Date each entry and concentrate on one incident or idea that is important to you that day. Don't worry too much about grammar and spelling but about clarity and honesty. I'll collect and check journals at least twice during the semester, and I'll grade solely on your persistence.

Suggestions for people who need priming

1. Your honest reaction to something that happened in class.
2. Your reaction to something you read.
3. A quotation—copy it and comment on it.
4. A problem you are struggling with.
5. A new word. Copy a definition from a big dictionary. Try some sentences using the word.
6. Description of an interesting sight or incident.
7. Suggestions for improving the college.
8. A summary of something you read.
9. A mistake or failure from which you learned something.
10. An idea you disagree with—tell why.

11. A question you can't or won't ask in class—leave room and I'll try to answer it.
12. A dream.
13. A favorite fantasy.
14. A description of a person.
15. An important experience.
16. When all else fails, a bit of your autobiography.

Monday, September 19

I kept a diary once (or journal or whatever you call it) when I was fourteen, exactly twenty years ago. I did it because I wanted to, not because it was required by a professor. And it was secret, nobody read it, not even my best friend, let alone a complete stranger. I don't understand how you're going to grade this. And I don't see what good it will do if we don't pay too much attention to grammar and spelling. You said not to worry. That's easy to say. Anyway . . .

My name is Ella Price. I was born in Nebraska and came here when I was ten. After high school I married Joe Price. We have a daughter, Louise (named after my mother), but we call her Lulu. She's almost fifteen. We live in Hillside Estates, just beyond the college. Maybe you've seen the billboards. . . .

Avoid distress in the lower tract
Move up to Hillside Estates

Isn't that funny? We moved there two years ago from Westside Manor, when Joe got his last promotion. Joe wanted to move all the way over the hill to someplace like Walnut Creek, but we couldn't. Joe's in the City Purchasing Department and makes a good living, but not that good. So we settled for Hillside Estates, which is sort of like Westside Manor, but windier.

This is my first semester at Bay Junior College. I always wanted to go to college, but I got married instead. Now Lulu is old enough so I have time to further my education.

I guess I look funny, so much older than the other students.

Tuesday, September 20

Today I was looking at the books I had to buy for my English class. One is the autobiography of a black nationalist who preached ideas that are tearing this country apart. One is a novel by a man convicted of marijuana possession. The essay book contains one essay by a rapist and one by a philosopher who's been in and out of jail all his life for refusing to support his own country. In glancing through the short-story book I found a couple of paragraphs I hope my daughter doesn't see. And the last book seems to be mainly on the subject that going to school is worthless because all the schools and colleges are no good. No grammar book is required, just a thin little handbook that gives some rules for punctuation and things like that.

I thought at first I was buying the wrong books, but I checked twice, and they're the right ones.

You said the class could choose two other books. I'll cast my vote for a grammar book and a good work of literature by someone like Charles Dickens.

Wednesday, September 21

I am taking three subjects at Bay Junior College—English, Psychology and Social Science.

Today I got up early, got Joe off to work and Lulu off to

13

school, and cleaned up the house a little before going to Psychology. I studied in the library until my English class. Tonight I made Joe's favorite dinner, steak and baked potato with apple pie for dessert.

Thursday, September 22

Same as yesterday, except the class was Social Studies. Last night watched TV for the first time in over a week.

Friday, September 23

I have been in college for only a week. It is all very new to me, and I have many impressions. My instructors seem to be very nice, but different from what I expected. One of them doesn't act like a college professor at all. I thought professors were more dignified.

Saturday, September 24

The younger students look through me, like I'm invisible. I wish I were.

Today will be very busy. Maybe time to write later.

Sunday, September 25

It's hard to write a whole page. What is there to say? I feel I'm wasting time I should spend studying. What's the use of doing this if it's not going to be graded?

Today is Lulu's birthday. She is fifteen. Last night she had a party for her friends. It was a very big party; over fifty young people came at one time or another, and we had to watch closely because some of them had been drinking. But everything went pretty well. Lulu had a wonderful time and received many gifts. She's popular, just like her father was at her age. She's only a freshman in high school and already a pompon girl. And she has many friends. That's so important for a young girl.

Tonight we'll have a family party. My mother and father will come, and Joe's family, which is much bigger. His mother, who is a widow. His brother (you know, Price Realty Company) and his wife and four children. Joe has four older sisters, but they live out of state. His mother says during World War II the Navy swooped down on the Bay Area and carried off her daughters. Anyway, they all married men who were in the service at that time and then went to live in other states.

That's the kindest thing my mother-in-law says about people who came here during the war—like us. I think Joe's family still thinks of us as Okies. But it's kind of funny because my parents look down on the Prices because they're Catholics. My parents really lost face when Kennedy was elected President. But Joe's family couldn't crow too much about a Catholic being President because he was a "nigger lover." I think they were all relieved when he was killed.

But it'll be a nice party. I'm awfully tired, and there's still a lot of baking to do, and Lulu has slept almost all day and won't be much help in cleaning up last night's mess.

But I managed to write a whole page. I bet you didn't think I could. Neither did I.

Monday, September 26

Today I walked into my psychology class and sat down. I was the first one there. Then other students started coming in. And they all did the same thing. They stepped into the room, looked around. Looked at me, then away quickly, and went to sit somewhere else. The room gradually filled up,

15

with students coming in and picking someone to sit next to, always sitting away from me, until there were no more seats and the last three or four had to sit near me.

It's because I'm older. Like a disease. I wanted to say to them, "I'm new here too, and I'm nervous, and . . ." but what's the use. They just feel I don't belong.

When I mentioned this at the dinner table Joe and Lulu made a joke out of it. And then Joe said, "That's not any different from when you were young," and I realized he was right. I wasn't popular in high school, the way he was.

Tuesday, September 27

I took Lulu shopping for a new skirt. She is a very wholesome, well-behaved girl (not like some of the ones I've seen at the college). I want her to be happy. After all, the teen-age years are supposed to be the best, before we have to take on responsibilities.

Clothes look wonderful on her. But she's very hard to satisfy. She may try on fifty things and just frown and shake her head, but when she hits the right thing—the effect is perfect. That's because in the back of her mind she knows exactly what she wants.

Wednesday, September 28

Today in my English class we discussed a story. I discovered I hadn't understood the story, or not the way you understood it. Tonight I felt so discouraged I had a third martini before dinner. It made me so dopey I played a terrible game of bridge with our next-door neighbors and couldn't concentrate because I kept thinking I should be studying instead. But I was too dopey to study anyway.

16

Thursday, September 29

Tonight we went to visit Joe's brother's family. My brother-in-law said I'm wasting the taxpayers' money because I'll never "do anything" with college. But Joe told him he should be glad to spend taxes on me instead of some dirty, pot-smoking, radical kid. Then my sister-in-law asked if it was true that all the professors were communists.

Friday, September 30

Today we discussed marijuana in class and you said that it probably wasn't as harmful as alcohol. I think that's a shocking thing to say. For one thing, you might have a lot of influence on the young people in the class, and because of your saying that, how do you know a lot of them won't go out and become dope fiends? You talked about alcohol as if it were some kind of poison. Of course, for some people it is. But for years my husband and I have been having two martinis before dinner. I don't see any harm in that. When five o'clock comes, I look forward to it, relaxing and talking about the day. It relieves tensions. It makes a nice relaxed glow that lasts all evening. You make it sound like dope addiction.

Saturday, Sunday

It's hard to write on the weekends. Joe wants me to spend time with him, especially since I'm always studying at night now. You assign so much reading. I have work to do for other classes too, you know.

And then there's the cleaning—and the ironing piles up. Lulu helps a little, but I don't blame her for not wanting to spend time on housework. She's young. Rather than argue with her, it's easier to do it myself.

Monday, October 3

Got up, made breakfast, first class at nine. Lunch and shopping. Studied till Joe came. Martinis and dinner. TV.

Tuesday, October 4

Just the same except for attending a different class. There isn't enough happening to me to write about every day.

Wednesday, October 5

I've been looking at this page for half an hour. I can't think what to write except what I wrote yesterday or the day before. I'm an average person with a nice home, a good husband and a lovely daughter. I lead an average life. I don't see how writing down the things I do every day will help me learn English. I need grammar.

Thursday, October 6

?????????????????????

Friday, October 7

Today I stopped you after class to ask what I should write in the journal.

You scratched your beard and said, "Whatever you are thinking—anything that's on your mind."

I said, "But I've done that, and I can't fill a whole page every day."

You laughed. "The problem is to select a fragment of your thoughts and compress it to one page. You could fill books every day." And when I said that my mind must be emptier than most, you gave me a funny look and said, "Just loosen up. That's all it's for. Loosening up. If you get desperate, write the alphabet or all the dirty words you know. To break the bottleneck."

You can laugh, but I'm worried because you said journals have to be turned in to be checked on Monday, and I know I'm not doing it right. So you'll probably give me an F because you'll say I wasn't persistent. But I'm really trying. If you'll just tell me what you want me to do. . . .

Saturday, October 8

ABCDEFGHIJKLMNOPQRSTUVWXYZ

DAMN   HELL

I guess your idea of loosening up is I'm supposed to write filthy words like the ones in the novel we're reading this week.

Sunday, October 9

I've been in this class nearly a month and I still don't know what you want, and tomorrow we have to turn in our journals and mine will get an F because I haven't written a whole page a day. I don't think I'm getting much out of this class anyway, so probably I should drop it.

Don't quit before you've really gotten started. So far you're too timid, covert, to write anything—too conscious of me as reader. I can't tell you what to write except what you really think.

D. Harkan
10/12

19

Friday, October 14

I looked up "covert" and it means something like sneaky. I think that when a person is really trying, and confused, and wanting to do a good job, you ought to encourage her instead of calling her names and accusing her of trying to hide something. I don't have anything to hide, or did you want us to write intimate details of our lives? Like the bedroom scenes in that novel?

Well, I'm sorry to disappoint you, but I don't live like that and I don't know anyone who does. My life is clean and respectable—what you call middle-class with such a sneer—and I'm not ashamed of it. I never thought I'd find myself in a situation where I'd have to say I wasn't ashamed of being respectable.

Evidently I'm not the only one in the class who couldn't satisfy you (so it's not just because I'm older)—otherwise you wouldn't have spent the whole period talking about the journals. I thought the student who called you a Peeping Tom was very amusing. That's the way I feel too. And when you said you only skimmed through our journals to make sure we wrote in them, I didn't feel any better. If that's all you do, what's the point of writing?

"You can't read and write well unless you can think straight, and you can't think straight unless you get in touch with your real thoughts." That's a crazy statement. You seem to think we're all stupid and can't think. I suppose you're so intelligent you can tell when we're "in touch with our real thoughts," whatever that means.

I'd like to drop this class right now, but I'm not going to "quit before I start." I've definitely decided to drop, but not before following your instructions to write *just* what I think. I'll go right down the list on the instruction sheet. Then I'll

20

turn this in and drop the class, which I'm sure isn't doing me any good anyway. Besides, when you read what I'm going to write you'll be glad to get rid of me.

Saturday, October 15

"1. Your honest reaction to something that happened in class."

This is supposed to be an *English* class—at least that's what the title is. That means we should study grammar. I used to be pretty good in grammar. I always got A's on the tests, but now I don't know a verb from a noun. When a student asked you why we weren't studying grammar, you said we studied it all the time. I think you're just sarcastic and superior. You try to make us feel like fools for asking questions.

"Doing grammar exercises doesn't have anything to do with reading and writing well. You've all been working grammar exercises for years, and you still can't write well." I think it's insulting to rub it in that we're all in "bonehead" English. Besides, I didn't *have* to take this class. I passed high enough on the entrance exam to take regular English, but after being out of school for so long I wanted to brush up on my grammar first. But instead of studying grammar we read stories and talk about all the deep meanings you say are there, but that I don't see at all. And we write in this journal, which I know is a waste of time. The only effect of all this is to make me afraid that I don't know what's going on inside or outside myself.

And then you get political, like bringing in that speech by the President and spending a whole hour analyzing three sentences to show how long words are used to lie or conceal or mislead. That was interesting, I'll admit, and maybe even valuable, but did you have to choose a speech by the President? I think you encourage young people to be disrespectful toward their elders and leaders. After all, doesn't disrespect for leaders account for most of the disrespect for law and order and decency in this country and in this college? Why, half the students here are just playing, and the other half are always marching and carrying signs and trying to stop the rest of us from learning anything.

If the students here had learned more respect for authority, more of them would do the assignments—half of them hadn't done the reading you assigned last time. You should give a test every time to make sure they do the assignment, maybe with a list of vocabulary words that we should all look up in the dictionary. Then you'd be teaching English. So far it's everything but English—philosophy, politics, psychology, but no English.

What you did to my first paper is an example. I worked hard on that. I kept the handbook next to me while I corrected every single error—not one misspelled word, not one comma out of place—and you wouldn't grade it. "Try again." As if I wasn't trying. But you ju?t said I went off the subject in the second line and that the paper "didn't say anything." You said you didn't care if every comma was in the right place; if the paper didn't say anything it didn't matter how well I said it, I said nothing. Well, I guess it wasn't brilliant, but that's none of your business. You're supposed to correct our grammar and not try to force your opinions on us.

That's what you'd really like to do. If we don't write something that you agree with, you say we haven't said anything. What you really want to do is to tear down all the things we believe in and make us believe what you believe.

And what you believe is that everything is bad, all the things our generation has worked for. I don't think that there's anything wrong with enjoying life and the things people have worked for, like new cars and color TV and a swimming pool (which we don't have, but I wouldn't mind having one) and martinis before dinner and—it's as if you looked into our lives and decided to tear them apart. Well, my husband has worked hard for all of these things, and there's nothing immoral about enjoying them instead of agonizing about all the people who don't have them. Maybe if those people had worked as hard as my husband, instead of collecting the taxpayers' money to support their illegitimate babies, they'd have those things too. But according to your ideas they shouldn't want them anyway, so why try to make us feel guilty about having them?

You seem to want to make women feel especially guilty. Last week when you said all that about America being a matriarchy where men work themselves to death to provide useless domestic frills for women, I wanted to speak out. It's easy to blame women, but it's not right. It's my husband, not me, who has to have a new car every two years, and color TV, and now he's talking about a pool—all for me, he says, but it's really what he wants, and I'm just the excuse. And I'm the one who goes to work at temporary office jobs to pay for these things when we get them.

But what hurt most was your personally insulting me in class last week, when you were talking about television commercials and how women dyed their hair and "plastered crap on their faces" trying to look like the "plastic women" in the commercials, "with the result that the streets are full of women who look like aging Barbie dolls." You didn't look at me when you said it, but I knew you were describing me. I've kept my figure and have always taken pains to make

23

up carefully and keep my hair pretty (yes, bleached and softly fluffed around my face!). I take pride in my appearance, and so does my husband, but now every time I look into the mirror I see an aging Barbie doll.

I can't see why the college hasn't fired you for saying some of the things you do—that a college degree isn't very important, and most of us don't know why we're here, and if we did know we'd quit. Maybe someone should notify the president of the college of what goes on under the title of English.

Sunday, October 16

*2. Your reaction to something you read."

The story about the woman raising daffodils—no, it was chrysanthemums. I can't get that story out of my mind. Maybe it's because this was the first time we read a story that I understood before you explained it, or maybe it's because I'm the same age as the woman in the story. I could feel how lonely and trapped she was, and how she could begin to think that the old peddler in the wagon was something special instead of just a greedy, dirty old man. I felt afraid for her when she was talking to him, embarrassed at the way she almost touched him, afraid she'd go to bed with him, not because she needed sex but because she needed—something like sex but not the same, something she didn't even know she needed. And then she'd feel ashamed. But she didn't do it; she gave him some of her flowers, and somehow that seemed a worse seduction. I wanted to say, "Don't let him touch those," because I knew he would just throw them away. But she was so alone (of course, her husband was a nice man, but that's not the point), and she wanted to believe that someone understood. I bet she knew all the time

24

the peddler didn't know or care, but she wanted to believe, and needed to so much, that on the top of her head she did believe, and acted as if she did. Because after she couldn't believe anymore, what did she have?

I wanted to discuss the story, but when that student called it "soap opera" I felt too embarrassed to speak up. For once I was glad to see you argue with a student and demand, "Is the human loss any the less important for being female and over thirty?"

Just what is soap opera? I always thought it was a silly, false story that idle women followed day after day just to hear human voices speaking in their empty houses. But the way that boy used it, it means any story where a woman is the central figure. The student argued back something about "larger issues," and you agreed with him, or seemed to. Aren't you contradicting yourself?

I told my husband about the story, and he said it was because she didn't have any children. I don't know. Children aren't everything.

Of course, I love my daughter and get a lot of satisfaction from watching her grow up. She's pretty and popular and is turning out just as we hoped. I mean, she's not moody or troubled the way I was at her age. She's well adjusted.

Monday, October 17

"3. A quotation—copy it and comment on it."

Of an apartment-building manager who had killed himself I was told that he had lost his daughter five years before, that he had changed greatly since, and that that experience had "undermined" him. A more exact word cannot be imagined. Beginning to think is beginning to be undermined.

Albert Camus

I took this out of that essay you assigned. It starts out just meaning that the man brooded about the death of his daughter, got depressed and killed himself. But the last sentence changes the meaning. "Beginning to think is beginning to be undermined." I think that's true. If you really think about all the things you do from day to day, and wonder about them, you can't go on doing them, just thinking of days and years stretching ahead, all the same. There are a lot of questions about life you just shouldn't ask.

But you want us to ask them. You say we can't begin to write well and read well until we can think straight, and that means questioning everything, letting ourselves think what we really think and saying it. But then you assign Camus to show that you realize we can't do this without tearing our lives open. Have you ever thought that while you are teaching people to "think straight" you might be weakening everything that keeps them going? Or don't you care? Who do you think you are, God?

Tuesday, October 18

"4. A problem you are struggling with."

Combining school and homemaking isn't easy. Time enough to study is a problem. I'm a slow reader, and I'm always afraid I'm not going to remember what's important. But I'm getting better—got an A on my last psych quiz.

My biggest problem right now is finding time to go to the beauty parlor—or should I give up looking like a Barbie doll? I don't have any real problems. I'm healthy. I have a happy marriage. My daughter is pretty and happy. No problems. No real problems.

Wednesday, October 19

I don't see that my problems are any of your business. Of course, I might have a problem, but if I want to talk about a problem I'll go to a qualified person, like a psychiatrist. Not that I've ever done that. I'm not so helpless that I'd lean on someone like that—a paid shoulder to cry on. I guess some people might find it fun to be able to pay someone to sit and listen to them talk about themselves. That's all right for people who don't have the guts to face life, and have the money to pay someone to listen to them. The rest of us cope with unhappiness more simply—by taking a drink, or going to a movie, or going shopping, or watching TV.

But you would disapprove of all these things, I guess. I suppose you want everyone to expose all the things that trouble her, like vomiting and studying what comes up. I don't have any problems I can't handle by myself.

Thursday, October 20

All right.

I said I was going to be completely honest, then throw this in your face and drop the class. I guess I should stick to what I said.

My problem.

There's something wrong with me. I was all right until about a year ago, but then . . . no, that's not true. I was never all right.

Sometimes, I'm doing something, just going through my normal day, and . . . but I'm not. Inside, I'm thinking things; inside, things are happening to me—I don't know where they come from. And they are starting to break out.

I'm not making sense. I'll just tell what happened last summer.

I was driving down El Alma Boulevard and all of a sudden I was lost. I mean, it all looked the same—the used-car lots with little flags flapping on a string, the hamburger stands, the four-rooms-of-furniture stores. I couldn't locate myself. I didn't know if I was near home or miles from home, and I had the feeling that I could go on and on, up and down El Alma, and never be able to recognize where to turn off to get home. It was like a bad dream, but I knew I was awake.

Then I started aiming at the parked cars. I'd come closer and closer, then I'd realize what I was doing and swerve away from them, but then all at once I'd find myself going toward one again, as if I wanted to hit it. I pulled over to the curb and stopped the car. Then I started to cry. But I didn't feel it—didn't feel as if it was me crying—I just listened to the sobbing and felt water running down my face, but I didn't seem to be doing it and didn't understand it. After a few minutes I was all right. I saw I was just a block from my turnoff, and I went home.

I saw the doctor the next week, but I didn't tell him what had happened, just said I was feeling a little tired and run down. He examined me and said I was all right, then asked me if there was something troubling me. "No," I said, which was both a lie and the truth—I knew there must be something troubling me, but I didn't know of anything that should be troubling me. I just couldn't seem to come right out with what had happened. If he'd insisted, if he'd kept asking, I might have told him about it. But he was busy and didn't have time to coax me. Finally he said something about my getting new interests now that Lulu was growing up. And that was how I got the idea of coming to college.

28

Friday, October 21

"5. A new word. Copy a definition from a big dictionary."
Educate: "related to Latin *educere*—to lead forth." This word isn't new to me, but the derivation is. To lead forth—it sounds like taking you by the hand and guiding you out of some dark place. "The systematic development and cultivation of the mental and moral powers. syn. train, discipline, teach, instruct."

The dictionary says to train is "to direct to a certain result powers already existing." Like Lulu's pompon practice. Discipline is "to bring into habitual and complete subjection to authority." And it says that to teach or instruct is "to impart knowledge, a part of education. Knowledge tells nothing of the mental development apart from the capacity to acquire and remember, and nothing whatever of that moral development which is included in education in its fullest and noblest sense."

I looked in the biggest dictionary I could find, but it only confused me. Those synonyms don't seem to have much to do with the word—a person could be trained, disciplined, taught and instructed, but not educated. And you could tell if a person was trained or instructed, but how can you tell if a person is educated?

Moral development? I'm not even going to *try* to tackle that one.

Saturday, October 22

"6. Description of an interesting sight or incident."
A giant stands on El Alma Boulevard. I don't know if he's fifty feet tall, or thirty, or seventy, but he's more than two stories tall. He stands in a gas station on the corner. I don't know what he's made of, but he's painted with some kind of

shiny enamel paint. He has big, thick black boots and bright blue pants. The pants are loose at the bottom, like sailor pants. He wears a big black belt and a white shirt, open at the throat, and with the sleeves rolled up. His arms are thick and pink and held out straight in front of him with the palms of his hands up and his fingers curved as if he's holding something. His elbows are bent too, so he must have once cradled something in his arms, not just holding it in his hands. But there's nothing there now. Once I asked the man who runs the gas station, What did he used to hold? But the man couldn't remember.

His face is pink and thick and fleshy looking. I don't like the pink look of his face and arms. He has black hair and a blue cap that matches his pants. His eyes are wide open, almost popping, and he grins all the time, big white teeth showing, but the paint is peeling off one tooth and part of the lip, leaving a slowly spreading gray blotch on his smile. His smile looks happy and menacing and cheerful all at once. But above all it's stupid, willfully stupid. That's what I hate most of all about it, the fixed stupidity of grinning over outstretched, empty arms and hands, the stupidity of permanent good cheer, the insistent stupid smiling through and over everything.

He marks the street that leads to my home.

Sunday, October 23

It's hard to write on Sunday, little time to myself. Joe asked what I'm always writing about, and I tried to explain, but he said, "What's that got to do with learning English?"

So I started explaining "You have to learn what's going on in your mind and try to say it clearly. Then you can learn to think straight, and then you'll learn to write better."

"And just writing anything at all in there helps?"

"I think maybe it does."

"Aren't you going to learn grammar?"

I started to laugh because I was beginning to sound like you, and he was sounding like me. But Joe thought I was laughing at him, so I put the journal away and only had a few minutes to write this while he's in the shower.

I don't want to hurt Joe's feelings because he's so good, not like some other men. There are two women on the block who went to the junior college once but don't dare go anymore. Their husbands won't let them. That's what one of them said to me. "My husband won't let me. He says if I want to go learn cooking and sewing that's all right with him, but I don't need to know anything else to be a good wife and mother." Can you imagine a man—in the twentieth century—talking that way? You'd be surprised at how many men are just like that.

After the woman told me that she said, "But it's best if I don't go; I wouldn't want to neglect my family." Of course, that was a slap at me. She's jealous. And now that I'm taking a psych class I have another term—displaced hostility. She's mad at her husband and takes it out on me. Of course, she has to. How else could she live with a man who is so afraid of her knowing something he doesn't know?

Joe's not like that. He's never minded my reading. And when I said I was going back to school, he said what he always says, "Anything you want, honey."

Monday, October 24

"7. Suggestions for improving the college."

Maybe the college would be better if certain selected teachers were fired. Short of that, I have some suggestions for improving the work of one of them.

31

Why don't you stop trying to brainwash us? I'm so disgusted with this class that if I hadn't promised myself I'd keep writing until I went down the whole list, I'd just quit right now. I've noticed quite a few young people have dropped out already. Maybe that's what you want—you want us all to quit in disgust. The truth is you think we're all stupid, except for a couple of Negro students that you always defer to as if they know everything.

I had a very interesting talk with one student who dropped your class last week. He is a veteran, only twenty-one years old, and minus one leg. He dropped the course for the very reason I said—brainwashing. He was shaking when he said that he couldn't stand you, that after all he gave his leg for his country and it was rotten to come home and go back to school to learn something and earn a living, and then find himself in a class where students were allowed and even encouraged to say that the war was purposeless. In other words he lost his leg for nothing. You just can't expect anyone to accept something like that!

He decided to drop the course, he said, at the point when you assigned the black militant's autobiography. He was sick and tired, he said, of being forced to listen to stuff about what a hard time black people have, because a lot of other people have a hard time too.

I agree with him. I'm sick of Negroes and Mexicans and this group and that group who are always yelling. They're not the only ones who suffer. If they only knew it, there are just two kinds of people in this world, the ones who howl and complain and the ones who suffer in silence. So why don't they keep still for a change.

Here's another suggestion for your improvement. Why don't you stop acting as if you know everything and we know nothing? The way you pick on us when we express an opinion is awful—it isn't teaching, it's bullying. EVERY-ONE HAS A RIGHT TO HIS OWN OPINION. There. You can't stop me from thinking that, and you can't stop me from writing it here, even though you stopped me in class. When I said, "I have a right to my own opinion," you jumped at me, embarrassing me in front of all those young students, saying I was just trying to evade the issue and that no one had the right to hold on to some stupid prejudice in the face of contrary evidence and then close her mind by saying, "I have a right to my own opinion." I almost died. The only way I could fight back was to refuse to talk when you tried to get me to go on. And don't think you fool anybody by smiling at us and saying, "Go ahead, argue with me, an A to the student who proves me wrong." You just enjoy insulting us.

Your grading policy is rotten. I thought I'd like getting a chance to rewrite things to raise the grade. But I'm getting sick of writing papers over and over again. I'm getting sick of seeing "cliché" written in the margin. I'm sorry I've got such a trite little mind that you're not entertained by the way I say things. I'm just an aging Barbie doll, you know.

The other phrase you are wearing out is "no support for this assertion." I'm getting to the point where I'm afraid to express any opinion at all on paper because you expect me to be some kind of walking encyclopedia, pouring out facts and figures to back up the least little thing I say.

11 p.m.

Well. I just read that over. Was I mad! I'm not anymore. I'm just ashamed. Especially about that I crack I made about you favoring Negroes. It's not true. I don't know why I said it. Does that mean I'm prejudiced? I don't think I really am.

33

I was just mad because you embarrassed me in class. And because you were right.

I was going to tear these pages out and throw them away, but I think I'll leave them, just to remind me of how stupid I can be if my ego gets bruised.

Tuesday, October 25

"8. A summary of something you read."

"The Other Side of the Hedge" by E. M. Forster

All his life a man walks on a hot, dusty road with high hedges on either side. Some people get ahead of him. Others fall behind and drop things. Finally he gets tired and falls. Through the hedge he sees light. He goes through the hedge, losing everything on the way, falls into a moat, and is fished out by an old man who shows him another kind of life on the other side of the hedge where people are happy and free, not dragging themselves along a dusty road to some unknown goal. When the man objects that struggling along the road is the higher purpose of life, the old man shows him that the road ends in the other side of the hedge.

This leaves out a lot, like the fact that he found his long-lost brother on the other side of the hedge. Actually the story is already concise, like a poem, and I can't summarize it, but I wanted to try because it meant so much to me. Because that's how life has always seemed to me, walking along a dusty road, with no scenery, just the same boring things from day to day, the exhaustion of keeping up, wondering if I'm getting anywhere and wondering why I shouldn't give up, always being at the point of giving up, so that every step is like the last exhausted one before dropping out and refusing to go on (although, like the man in the story, I would never admit how I truly felt).

You know what really shocked me? Not that I felt this way about the story, but that most of the young students in the class did too. That boy who said, "The road is life, and going through the hedge is dying, and the other side is Heaven." Isn't that a terrible way for an eighteen-year-old to feel about his life? Why should they feel that way? Most of these kids have more than I ever had at their age. They wear good clothes and drive new cars. When I hear them complain about money troubles, they mean they haven't enough money for some luxury I never would have thought of at their age. They ought to be happy.

They ought to be happy—I ought to be happy. "Ought to be" doesn't mean anything. Maybe I'm not crazy, or all these kids are crazy in the same way I am—all of us sharing the same craziness. Maybe other people my age share it too, but we don't admit it because we worked for so many years to get the things that are supposed to make us happy, and if we suddenly admit that all those things didn't make us happy, what are we going to say about all those years? How can we forgive ourselves for throwing them away? I don't know. Can you really be sure you don't want something until you've got it? And if that's true, then maybe the years spent getting something you don't really want aren't wasted, because you wouldn't know what you don't want unless you'd done all the things to get you to the place where you know.

I'm getting all tangled in my own words.

The real question is: Is there another side of the hedge? Did Forster just dream about it or wish it? Or has he been there and come back to tell us it's there, so we'll have the courage to go there? How do we get there? Do we really have to give up, lose everything? But if it's really there, you haven't lost a thing, giving up everything to get there.

Wednesday, October 26

"9. A mistake or failure from which you learned some-thing."

I think there are two kinds of mistakes, a mistake from which you can learn something and a mistake from which it's too late to learn anything that's of any use to you (like trying to swim across a river and miscalculating the distance and drowning—whatever you've learned from that mistake, you can't use, because you're dead).

The first kind of mistake is easy. I slam the door, and a cake falls, and I learn not to slam the door while a cake is in the oven. I use a colon where I should have used a semicolon, and you explain the rule to me, and I don't make that mistake again. Those are easy lessons to learn, and they apply to things that don't really matter much.

The really important mistakes, the ones you really learn something from—well, what you learn is so hard and so cruel that maybe it would be better to just go on believing it wasn't a mistake, or keep making it even if—I'm getting this all mixed up.

Suppose a person has the feeling she's done everything just the right way, and hasn't made any mistakes to speak of, and that her life should feel like a great success. But every morning she wakes up feeling uneasy. And then one day, she wakes up in the morning and she says, "Oh, no, this was not the way to do it at all. My whole life has been a mistake." But it's her whole life, and it's over, so wouldn't it be better not to know?

Thursday, October 27

"10. An idea you disagree with—tell why."

I disagree with just about everything you say. No, that's

not really true. I don't know if I disagree. I just wish you wouldn't say certain things. I'm not sure why, exactly, except whenever you bring up a subject for discussion I start to feel uncomfortable. You always quote some far-out writer or contradict what I always accepted with some new—well, no, it's not new, really. Some of the most far-out things you say sound like an echo of something I already know, but I don't think it's a good idea to say these things. I guess you scare me. Does that mean I'm afraid of ideas? How silly. An idea is just—an idea, not a real thing like a chair or a person.

Well, that's not the subject. There are certain things you say I definitely disagree with. I'll take my pet one first.

Standards of female beauty—your famous Barbie doll statement. And then you said that women past fifty, bleached and painted and hobbling around on high heels, look like female impersonators. Other men *like* women to fix themselves up and dress in fashion. But I can see that you prefer the way some of these odd-looking young girls dress—straight hair (or frizzy if they're black), no makeup, no bra, baggy clothes. It's as if they don't care at all. It's defiant. Defiance is charming in young girls, I guess. But after thirty a woman's got to do something if men are going to notice her at all, and half the time, no matter what she does, they still won't notice because they only look at young girls anyway.

It's not that I'm trying to attract men or something—I have a husband. But have you ever imagined yourself a woman? You know, if you're a woman you can be nice and decent and intelligent and well educated and all the rest, but if you're not attractive to men nobody cares what else you are; you're a failure. And to know that, after a certain age, no matter what you do you're not going to be attractive to men anymore—what do you have left, motherhood? That doesn't

37

last long, unless you keep having one child after another. Year after year you just move more into failure, with your child growing away from you and still half your life to live, and what are you going to do with it? Don't you see that women wouldn't look like female impersonators if they had something else to do?

Did I go off the subject! If this were one of those papers we turn in, it would be full of red marks. Back to the subject.

I think a woman should do things to keep up her looks. Now, I had to stop wearing high heels to classes because the gravel on the parking lot tore them up and I had a terrible time getting from one building to another. And I'm letting my hair grow out because I just haven't had time to get to the beauty parlor, and I've cut out makeup because there's so much dust blowing around here that it gets all streaked after a while. Besides, my face changed color, being outdoors more in the sun and wind. But if I had the time, I'd still—oh, I don't know. Enough of that subject. Other things are more interesting.

"Any truly human person is driven half insane by the kind of world we live in." I think you said that anyone who could live in this world and not be sad, let alone anxious, distraught or agonized, must be either stupid or evil.

That's just not true. There are lots of quite nice people who mind their own business and go through their lives without getting very upset about anything, and they aren't subhuman or stupid or evil. They might just be healthier than you are. Have you ever thought that being unhappy isn't necessarily a virtue, that maybe it's a sign of weakness or sickness? Is no human being acceptable to you unless he is miserable?

One of the best human beings I know is my husband, Joe. He is a very good man. He loves me and Lulu. He doesn't

38

have any bad habits. And he's always happy. His favorite saying is, "I'm happy if I can eat, drink and ———." Things don't bother him. He's always the same, always very patient with my anxieties and sicknesses. And with all of those, where would I be without him? He's no Bertrand Russell, but nobody can say he's evil. His needs are simple, and he doesn't concern himself about things he can't do anything about. What's wrong with that?

Sometimes when I come home from school, I'm all excited or upset about something. And we sit and have a drink and I tell him about it. And as I drink and talk, things get a little softer—like a pain getting dulled. And Joe just nods and smiles until I see I'm just all agitated about nothing at all, and he's being patient and letting me work it all out. I begin to feel as if I really am crazy or something, and he's gone on for years and years humoring me.

Friday, October 28

"11. A question you can't or won't ask in class—leave room and I'll try to answer it."

Why don't more people commit suicide? Although I have a nice home and husband and child and all that, I often think of killing myself. All of a sudden, with friends or in the middle of a party, when someone has told a joke and everyone is laughing, a voice inside me might say, "Why don't you cut your wrists tonight?"

Suicide is a thing you can't talk to your husband about because he would take it as a criticism of him. Maybe it doesn't have anything to do with him. But he'd see it as either an accusation that he'd failed to make you happy or just another sign of your craziness, and you'd be so busy reassuring him you'd never get back to the subject.

Cutting my wrists wasn't my real suicide plan. The real one involved the ocean. When I was a girl, about sixteen, I used to take the train (there were trains then) to San Francisco, then the streetcar all the way out to the beach. All alone. I'd take off my shoes and stockings and just walk along the water, letting it lap up over my feet as the waves came in. A lot of people did that; nobody thought anything of it. I'd walk further and further out, until the waves splashed my skirt. Then I'd stop. But I wondered what it would be like just to walk out and keep walking.

There are advantages. My family wouldn't find me. They'd hear it from someone else first. And it's not sudden, a big decision like jumping from the bridge. I don't think I'd ever get up enough nerve for that. I could work up to it gradually. They say drowning doesn't hurt either. The water's so cold, I'd be pretty numb anyway by the time I got to a drowning place.

And then I could rest. I wouldn't feel freakish or odd anymore. I wouldn't feel bored with all my friends, or ashamed of being bored. I wouldn't feel that I had to work so hard to be normal, at least on the outside. I wouldn't feel so tired. I wouldn't feel.

I just realized something awful. I got this idea from an old movie, a really corny thing where a husband walked into the ocean so he wouldn't "stand in the way" of his wife. He was a self-pitying drunk. Why is it when I get serious and brave enough to write down my real inner thoughts, I come out with something from a third-rate movie?

I just remembered something else. When I was out there knee deep in the ocean and looking out to sea, not seeing anything but the water, as if the world was gone and there was just me and the ocean, the suicidal thoughts would disappear. I'd still want to walk forward into the ocean, but

40

it didn't seem as if it would be death. I don't know what I thought it would be, something better than death or life.

Don't bother trying to answer this question. It's all too stupid.

Besides, now that I've written it all out, I don't think I really mean it.

Saturday, October 29

"12. A dream."

All my life, since I was a child, I have had a recurring dream. It comes every time I am sick and running a fever. The dream has no plot, no sequence of events. I am simply under something, not a blanket, something solid like a ceiling, but soft and thick. Above me I hear footsteps which become larger—that's right, not just louder, but larger. The feet, encased in heavy boots, grow larger and larger, until I am terrified and I begin to scream until I wake myself up.

I never know exactly what it is that I am afraid of—that the boots will come through the thick covering and trample me? There's a feeling of suffocation. That's caused by the fever, of course, and the footsteps are my own heart pounding. What is the covering over me? Blankets? No. Earth. Soft earth. I'm underground with feet walking over me. But I'm not dead. I'm buried alive.

Sunday, October 30

"13. A favorite fantasy."

On Sunday we buy the San Francisco and Oakland papers. Sometimes Joe and Lulu argue playfully about what section each will get first. Neither of them cares about the section I want. My favorite section is the want ads. They're used to this now, although at one time they'd ask me, "What do you want to read those things for?"

"I'm always looking for a bargain," I'd answer. And soon they stopped asking.

That wasn't the real reason. I don't read the ads for things to buy. I read the For Rent ads:

> Buena Vista, 2 rms,
> view, near bus.

Then I daydream. A little place in an old Victorian house. I'd paint it myself, white. I'd have lots of books in it. A big chair near the window where I could look out and see people when I wanted to. But I'd be up high. I'd hear the sounds of their talking and laughing, but I'd be too far up to understand the words. Maybe they'd speak a foreign language, several foreign languages, musical sounds with no meaning to me, just tones of feeling. That's all I can see, really. Just me, sitting in a chair, surrounded by a few of my own things, only my very own things, and hearing distant sounds of strange people.

I do this every Sunday morning. There we are, all three eating a big breakfast and passing around pieces of the paper, and secretly I'm imagining myself off alone in a room. Sunday morning is our best family time, and in my mind I'm sneaking away. I'm ashamed of that. Like secret drinking. A vice.

But I'm more ashamed of a fantasy I used to have. I haven't had it lately. I had forgotten this one, and when it came into my mind I wasn't going to write it down, but here goes. Up until I started reading the want ads, I had another fantasy which used to come to me in the middle of the night, when Joe and Lulu were asleep and I would wake up and lie there thinking. Then suddenly this thing would come: Joe and Lulu were home asleep, but I was out somewhere. I

42

came home to find the house in flames. I tried to run in, but people held me back. Everyone and everything perished in the fire. My husband, my daughter, and every single thing that was a part of my life with them.

I used to end up crying when I thought about that—but then I'd feel relieved. I've always wanted to ask other women, and men too, if they had fantasies like that, but I was too ashamed to admit that I did.

But the other day you quoted Shaw—"when a loved one dies we feel a little relieved" or something like that—and I could laugh at it, see it as a pretty ordinary fantasy of escape from responsibilities, fresh start, etc. I could even laugh at the idea that lots of other people have the same kind of fantasy from time to time, and no one admits it to anyone else. I think I'm beginning to enjoy reading now more than I ever have, because sometimes I find a saying that is something I've always felt but didn't know I felt it until I read it. It's exciting to find that a great writer had the same thought as I and was brave enough to say so. I've done a lot of reading, but mostly not very good books. Books that entertained me but didn't say things *for* me. Is that the difference between a good writer and a bad one?—good writers say your deepest thoughts for you? are braver and don't hold anything back?

Courage must be the most important thing in the world. A lot of things that seem like courage aren't really. You can't be brave unless you're afraid—can't have one without the other. So being brave has to mean letting yourself have that terrible queasy feeling of fear inside you. Of course, you can have that feeling anyway. Sometimes I think I feel a little bit afraid all the time, and I'm not sure what I'm afraid of, whether it's one thing or a lot of things. I've always wanted to ask someone if everyone feels afraid that way, but I was even afraid to admit I was afraid, and I'm sure no one I know would admit fear either. I used to think not admitting fear was brave. But that's not true at all. Real courage must be admitting fear, and going ahead anyway, and—and doing what?

Well, so much for another couple of mixed-up pages. I'm sure I'm getting more confused instead of less. And surprised at what I write. I wasn't thinking of these things—it's as if they come out of the pen, not out of me.

So you can see how lucky I am to have a sane man to take care of me. Every time I start going too far over the edge, he catches me and kids me out of it. Then, when I apologize, he shrugs it off, says don't worry, "I'm happy if I can eat, drink and screw," and laughs.

There's another joke he tells all the time, the only joke he knows—you know, how lots of people have just their one joke. He heard this one when he was in the Army.

It's about a soldier who walks around picking things up. Everywhere he goes, he picks things up from the ground, old candy wrappers, leaves, rocks, bits of paper, anything. Each time he picks up something, he looks at it and then says, "No, that's not it." After he does this for a while, the doctors certify him insane and give him a discharge for mental incapacity. When they hand him the discharge papers, he smiles and says, "That's it!"

Joe tells it all the time, and laughs and laughs because he hated the Army so much he loves to think of someone outsmarting them. It's getting so that he starts to laugh as soon as he begins the joke. And so do the rest of us. Joe laughing and happy makes everyone else laugh.

Monday, October 31

"14. A description of a person."
He is about forty—anywhere from forty to fifty—very tall.

44

I think he is skinny, but it's hard to tell because of his clothes. He wears shabby, brownish suits that look as if they were bought for someone else twenty years ago; they hang on him like secondhand clothes or the clothes of a man who has recently lost weight. Inside the clothes, which seem not at all a part of him, his body moves quickly, yet awkwardly, like a man who could run very fast and make great leaps but has trouble sitting still or walking slowly. His skin is an unhealthy yellowish color, the kind that would be a good deep brown if he spent more time outdoors. His hair is black and bushy, though not long. He has a black bushy beard, and his hands are covered with black hairs. I wonder if the black hair covers his whole body, like a wild man.

His face is always alert and wary, as if expecting attack. When he smiles, he seems only to jerk his lips back in a ferocious grin that bares his clenched teeth. His teeth are very white and even, but not pretty; they're small and sharp like weapons, like the teeth of a meat-tearing animal. His voice is hoarse as if he has been shouting. But sometimes, when he is very excited about something, it drops to a deep, full sound. But when this happens, he usually stops talking altogether. Only his eyes are soft, round and dark and so soft they don't seem to go with the rest of his face. Sometimes I wonder if he grew all that hair to hide his soft eyes. He succeeded. It takes a long time before you notice the eyes.

It sometimes seems that he is in the wrong place at the wrong time. I think he would be natural only if—I see him bare from the waist up, riding a bareback horse and waving a saber.

When he talks, he paces back and forth and seems to forget the students in the room. Yet if one of them begins to react, he turns and calls on him, even before the student has raised his hand. If the student is shy or reluctant, he keeps at him, bullying and threatening until the student blurts out what he was thinking. Then he rips the idea to shreds and challenges the student to fight back. After a while he doesn't frighten anyone because the students can see the soft brown eyes above the bared teeth.

At the end of a class, he seems to stoop slightly, and he drags his feet as he leaves, as if he is worn out. But next class hour he rushes in, tense and alert, like the bare-chested Indian raiding the paleface settlement.

Tuesday, November 1

"15. An important experience."
Nothing important has ever happened to me.

Wednesday, November 2

"16. When all else fails, a bit of your autobiography."
We came here during World War II when I was about ten. We came from Nebraska, not Oklahoma, but everyone called us Okies anyway. I don't remember much about Nebraska except that my father drove a tractor for some farmer, until he lost that job, and my mother did housework. (But she would never let me tell anyone that. I even feel a little guilty about writing it here.)

Both my mother and my father went to work in the shipyards. After school I stayed with a Negro lady on our block and played with her children until my mother got home. After a little while we moved a few blocks away (where all white people lived) but I still went to Annie's (the Negro lady's) house for a while.

I was an only child. My mother always said we might be poor, but we weren't white trash having one baby after another. She always said, "We've just got the one so we can do right by her." She often reminded me that she and my father were working hard to provide things for me that they never had. All kids hate that—I did—but there was no doubt that my parents worked hard.

After a while they saved enough money to open a little grocery store near our house. Then my mother ran the store, and my father kept working in the shipyards till they closed, and then in the oil company. After school I helped in the store. But I could stay in the back room and study or read until my mother got busy and would call me. She always said, "Go ahead, study, so you won't have to work like this all your life."

When my mother wasn't working she was going to church. She made me go too, and she talked a lot about sin. When I was about sixteen I suddenly stopped believing in God. It wasn't a loss of faith—not a loss at all, just a relief that God wasn't spying on me and planning to burn me in hell. I didn't say anything to my mother, but after Joe and I married, I never went to church again. I'm sure she attributes this to the "heathen Catholic" influence. (Joe says he got the same kind of upbringing from his mother, so both of us have no use for churches. Lulu is supposed to make her own decision when she's eighteen. You should see the two mothers competing for her, but she just laughs; I don't think she knows what it means to feel guilt.)

As soon as we could, we moved to a house that "wasn't so near niggertown," as my father always said. That was what they always wanted, to get away from "the niggers." My father isn't really a bigot. What he really meant, I think, was he wanted to get away from being poor, and to him that meant getting away from the "niggers," away from the flatlands.

And finally they made it and bought a house on the hill. The people who lived there (mostly Italians and Irish) called us Okies and were never very friendly. But we stayed there anyway. It was only about the time I married that the neighbors began to accept us. Then—last year, a Negro family bought the house next door. And my father is bitter now and keeps mumbling about not ever being able to get away from the niggers. It would never occur to him to compare that Negro family's move to the hill with our own. I started to say something like that the last time we were there, but my brother-in-law jumped all over me about property values, and for once the two families were united—against me—so I shut up.

What I remember most about growing up was that I didn't seem to be able to please anyone. I didn't seem to be able to do the right things. I was supposed to get an education so I wouldn't be poor, but I wasn't supposed to get so smart that no man would want me. I was supposed to be pretty so I wouldn't be an old maid, but I wasn't supposed to go out on dates too much because I might get "in trouble." I was supposed to study hard and get good grades, but I wasn't supposed to be stuck-up. (Anyone seen carrying a book was called stuck-up!) It seemed everything about my life was like that—contradictions.

Sometimes a teacher would take me aside and tell me that I must go to college. But then my friends would say, Why go to college when you're just going to get married and have children? Almost all my teachers were old maids. They didn't look as if going to college had made them happy.

Joe was just the opposite of me in high school. I knew him for a long time before he knew me. That is, I knew who he was, because he was two years older and played football and was so popular. He was in one of my classes once, but of course he didn't notice me. He just joked around with everyone, and the teacher gave him a C so he could stay on the team. Everyone liked him, even the teachers, although he didn't do much studying, because he was always funny and cheerful and kidding around.

Then he hurt his leg and couldn't play football during his senior year. But that didn't bother him, or if it did he didn't tell anyone; he just helped the cheerleaders at the games, horsing around and being funny and cheering the players on. One of the cheerleaders was a friend of mine, and through her I talked to Joe a few times. Then he graduated.

Later, when I was a senior, I met him at a school dance. He was just out of the army, and his brother knew someone who was going to get him a civil service job. He kept saying how he missed "our" old school days, as if I were an old friend. I wasn't actually attracted to him, but I felt awfully flattered. I thought we'd have a couple of dates and then he'd see that I was too serious, too quiet, and he'd drop me. But he didn't. Pretty soon we were going steady. And when I graduated from high school we were married.

Everyone said how lucky I was. My father said I was lucky to marry a man who worked for the city and had security. My mother, I think, was just glad to see me get marrried and off her hands—all she ever thought about after I was fourteen was that I might get pregnant and disgrace her. Besides, even though Joe's family was Catholic, they were Irish, not Okies, and owned property. She was proud of that. Only a couple of my old-maid teachers, when they saw my engagement ring, tightly closed their lips and looked more severe than ever.

But I've already told that. There isn't anything else to tell about my life. It's easily summed up in a couple of pages.

I didn't think I could do it, but I've filled a whole notebook, and I must admit it's getting easier.

Notebook
NUMBER TWO

Friday, November 4

Today I took my journal to Mr. Harkan. He shares an office with another English Teacher in the basement of the humanities building. It's a tiny room with stuffed book-cases, and piles of books and papers on the top shelf, looking as if they'll all fall down any minute. I could see him through the partly opened door, slouched behind his desk alone, sunk into that wrinkled brown suit, like a toad in his skin. When I knocked on the door, he jerked his head up and nodded for me to come in and sit down.

I'd made up my mind that I was going to make him read the journal in front of me, then tell him to his face what I thought of him and walk out. Of course, I was shaking with fear, but I wasn't as mad as I thought I'd be. In fact I guess I was finding it hard to stay mad at him. I asked him to read what I'd done since the last time he looked at it.

"Now?" he said.

"Yes. Now."

He shrugged and took it from me. He read fast, faster than I've ever seen anybody read, but I could tell he was really reading because of the change of expression on his face. A couple of times he laughed and raised a bushy eyebrow at me. Once he muttered, "Give'm hell," meaning himself, I guess. A few times he slowed down and seemed to be reading some parts over and over. Then he handed the notebook back to me and sat looking at me so strangely that I began to squirm. I knew that now was the time for me to get up and walk out, but I couldn't move.

"That's more like it," he finally said. "It's real and honest, I think, except for saying nothing important ever happened to you. That's not true."

"Yes, it is." My voice was a whisper.

"That's important! Your feeling that nothing important has happened to you. That's very important." He looked at me as if waiting for me to answer, but I couldn't. "You've come a long way." I guess I looked surprised. "Yes, you have. Remarkable. In the journal. And here." He ruffled through a set of papers. "The last paper you did. Here it is. Clear, straightforward, facts, even a proper footnote, all in less than 300 words and not a wasted one. Good. Gave you an A."

Naturally by this time I'd forgotten all about my intention to tell him off and drop the course. He mentioned a few things I could have done to improve the paper. I was too happy even to concentrate on his suggestions, but I could see he was eager to explain some fine points. I tried to listen.

He sat back and frowned at me. "Are you serious? You really want to work?" I nodded. "Okay." He sat up straight. "First of all, the journal. Keep it up, it's probably the most important thing. But strictly private—I won't need to check up on you—nobody should look at it. And you don't have to

54

write every day. Long, thoughtful, penetrating entries, on anything, right?" I nodded. "And reading. You've got to read and read. Do much reading?"

"Yes, but not very good things. Mostly assignments and some magazines."

"What magazines?" I named a few and he sniffed and started working his mouth as if he was going to growl. He started scribbling on a piece of paper and said, "Get all that crap out of the house and read some of these. Then when you get so you really know the difference between crap and information, you can read whatever you want—even the *Reader's Digest*—and find some good stuff among the crap, or learn something by studying what crap is fashionable at a given moment. But for now stick to these. Don't buy. They're in the library."

He handed me the list and stood up. He opened a file cabinet and pulled out some papers. They were mimeographed lists of book titles. "Check off the ones you've read and start anywhere you want to, reading the rest. See how many you can check off in the next year or two. For the present, quantity—depth later. Come in and talk about them if you want to."

He stayed on his feet, so I thanked him and got up to leave. He said, "See you," in that hoarse voice of his, and slumped back into his chair.

I could hardly wait for Joe to get home tonight so I could tell him what had happened.

"I thought you were going to drop that class. I thought that guy was a nut who wasn't teaching anything."

"I was wrong," I said. "I think I've learned a lot. Just writing in the journal has almost changed my life."

"How?"

"Well, sometimes I put down thoughts that lead to other

55

thoughts I didn't know I was thinking. And trying to put things into words. . . . " I went around and around for a while trying to explain.

"I don't get it. Let's see it."

"Well, it's kind of private." He was quiet for a minute, and I could see he was hurt. "I don't have any secrets from you, Joe; it's just that if I knew someone was going to read it—anyone—I couldn't feel really free."

"He reads it. The professor."

"He's not going to anymore."

I don't think that answer made him feel any better. For a long time he didn't say anything. Then he started to laugh and make silly jokes, and we had a few drinks. I felt so guilty that I'd made him feel left out. Pretty soon he was grinning and hugging me, that little curl of black hair falling over his forehead the way it always does. He looked like a boy.

Pretty soon Lulu came in. She had been rehearsing with the pompon girls and still wore her short red skirt and carried the big red puffs of shredded paper. She showed us a new routine, with high kicks and hip swings, and I couldn't help but remember Mr. Harkan saying something about pompon girls being teen-age chorus girls who after this training needed only to go topless to be sexy enough for a nightclub.

Up until now I've just been grateful that Lulu was happy and slim and graceful and popular, not awkward and frightened as I was at her age. I was so afraid I'd pass my problems on to her. But I didn't. She's just like Joe—she even looks like him, cute freckled nose and black hair that falls in the same curl over her forehead.

Now I have conflicting feelings about her pompon dancing. Maybe I'm becoming too much influenced by Mr.

Harkan. At first I hated him. Now I've swung over to believing anything he says. I have to learn to think for myself.

Saturday, November 5

Tonight I took out my short-story book. While we were sipping our martinis I made Joe read the story we talked about in English yesterday.

When he finished, he put the book down, then said, "It's stupid."

"No, not really, Joe."

"It's about a bunch of people in a little town, right? They all draw lots to see who to throw rocks at. That's not stupid?"

"Yes," I said. "Throwing rocks is stupid; that's what the author is saying."

Joe just shrugged. "I know throwing rocks is stupid. Why do I have to read a story about it?"

"It's an allegory. That means that it doesn't mean literally what it's saying. It means something else."

"Then why doesn't it say what it means?" he asked, and poured another drink. I put my hand over the top of my glass, feeling I was going to need a clear head. I wasn't getting anywhere at all. What was so exciting in the discussion in class was just falling flat and Joe was looking uncomfortable—or just patient, the way he is when I get upset about something.

"The story tells how they stoned her to death to please the gods, so the crops would grow, the way primitive people do. Only the story is set in modern times, so it's symbolic. In class yesterday Mr. Harkan asked what does it mean? And someone said the story means we're barbaric, killing people by lottery. Or we're doing things without thinking, like the people in the story, who didn't know why they still did this every year. We think we're civilized, but we don't even question doing terrible things to one another—in an everyday sort of way."

"Like what?"

"Well, Mr. Harkan said, like capital punishment."

"Capital punishment. You mean if a guy kills somebody and they execute him it's like he lost the lottery, just by chance, and got killed? That's a lot of crap; he killed someone."

"That's exactly what I said! But then Mr. Harkan read us some statistics on who gets executed. Mostly poor people, illiterate, black, ignorant people who never had a chance. It's as if they lost the lottery the day they were born, and things happened to them that made them inefficient crooks."

"Inefficient crooks?"

"Mr. Harkan says efficient crooks don't get caught." I realized how often I was saying "Mr. Harkan says," so I tried to switch to one of my own ideas. "Or like war." Joe just waited for me to go on. "We teach our kids you can't settle anything by violence, and then whenever countries can't get along we go out by the thousands and kill each other—even though we know the last war, or the one before that, didn't change anything."

"We can't just let the commies come and take over." I was about to challenge that with one of Mr. Harkan's attacks on parroting slogans, but I stopped myself. "I served my country and I'm not ashamed of it," he went on. All of a sudden he was defending himself. How did this happen? I wasn't attacking him. "I guess I just don't get it."

"Never mind. It's not important." I held up my glass for another drink.

58

"I don't like things like that. I like a story to be real."

"But it is r—" No, this was all wrong. This wasn't what I meant to do.

Then he grinned. It was a heartbreaking grin. "Honey, I'm just too dumb."

"No! No, you're not." Suddenly I started to cry. He put his arms around me and kept joking about how thickheaded he was, until I thought I'd die of shame for making him feel so inadequate. I wished I'd never seen a book. I wanted to share with him, not make him feel bad. I dried my eyes and said, "I'm such a stupid neurotic, how do you stand it?"

But he just grinned the way he always does. "Lean on me, hon, I'll take care of you."

"If this is all school does for me I should quit."

He didn't answer at all, just poured my drink.

Sunday, November 6

I feel better this morning. I was ready to quit school, but that's not the answer. I really love it now. But I mustn't ever try to force any of it on Joe. He says he doesn't care what I do as long as I'm happy. Is there any reason why I can't be happy and make him happy too?

Monday, November 7

Yesterday I sat down with the list Mr. Harkan gave me. I went through the whole thing, but I'd never even heard of most of the books. I was able to check only a few, like *The Scarlet Letter,* which I read in high school but can't remember. I didn't know where to start, so this afternoon I dropped into his office again.

"What kind of reading have you done?"

"When Lulu was small, murder mysteries. I used to sit up

59

at night feeding her and reading. Then historical novels —oh, not good ones, those things they make into bad movies. After that science fiction. Then best sellers."

"Nothing on this list interests you?"

"It's not that. The list doesn't mean anything to me. They may be all great books, but I never heard of them. I don't know one book from another. I don't know what would interest me." Each sentence was like a tooth pulled out. It really hurts to admit such ignorance.

But he gave me a big smile, then frowned and stared at the ceiling for a minute. "Why don't we pick out some books with female protagonists?" That sounded like a good idea. We decided I should start with *Madame Bovary.*

Wednesday, November 9

The two-martini habit is lethal. It used to be good to pass the time getting slightly numb and talking. But if I'm going to do this much reading, it'll have to stop. Tonight I drank fruit juice instead. Somehow that seemed to shorten the cocktail hour, though I'm not sure why it should. Do I talk more when I'm drinking? No. In fact I'm just starting now to become really talkative.

It's getting easy to speak up in class. It's impossible not to. Mr. Harkan says things that start so much whirling around in my head that I'm almost dizzy. Sometimes I feel I could talk for hours about just one thing he mentions in passing.

But when I raise my hand, I'm usually the only one. Today I started hearing little snickers around me when I responded to something he said. It reminded me of when I was in high school and I learned to keep still, because when I raised my hand to volunteer anything I'd be called teacher's pet. But I thought it was supposed to be different

60

in college. This "college" is a really strange place. I'm just beginning to get an idea of how strange.

Today Mr. Harkan assigned a film and lecture at the university—said he'd made arrangements for us all to get in free. Someone asked if it was an assignment.

"Yes, it's assigned," Mr. H said. "I'm even going to give a quiz on it to make sure you go." Everyone groaned, and he gave a tired sigh. "I hate doing that—treating you like prisoners—but I learned my lesson long ago. If I don't hold a club over you, you won't go. Last year a student said that the most valuable thing I did was to force him to go to lectures, films, art exhibits; that these things were the best, the most interesting, and that he wouldn't have gone to them unless I had forced him to; and that—get this—now that the class was over he wasn't sure he would again, without me to push him. Why? I don't understand it. You've grown up near one of the greatest universities in the world, near one of the liveliest and most beautiful cities in the world, and you live as if you were in Kansas!"

Everyone was quiet for a while. Then a Negro girl in the back row raised her hand. "I know why I don't go," she said. "Cause I don't feel right—I don't feel welcome; like, this isn't my place, it's for white people."

"That kind of segregation ended before you were born."

She shrugged. "I still feel . . . something. I don't know—a concert, a lecture, that's for white people. They let us in, but—well, I just don't feel right, not comfortable, like I do in a drive-in movie or something."

"I know, I know." I was nodding and talking without even raising my hand. "It's not race. I feel the same way. It's as if you have to be born in it, like being part of a different world, where people talk about books and go to the ballet when they're young. That's what the division was to me

61

when I was a child: the big line between the kids who went to the ballet and the ones who didn't. Only a few did—and they didn't associate with me."

"You're talking about class," said Mr. H.

"I guess. I think if you don't do these things, have these things, when you're little, you never quite feel comfortable in that atmosphere. I feel as if someone might come up to me at any moment and say, 'Oh, no, you'll have to leave, you don't belong here, sorry.'"

We started talking about class structure, about America never admitting we had different classes but having them just the same. But it was only me and the Negro girl and Mr. H talking. The others just sat there, and pretty soon I heard a rustling sound. I know now what that means—it means three minutes to the hour. Is that all they can do, sit and wait for the time when they can leave? Why do they come to college? No one's forcing them.

As class ended some of us stayed in a little group, finishing our talk, then walking out, drifting down toward the cafeteria. Mr. Harkan, the Negro girl, an older boy just back from the war and me. We sat down and talked more about our shyness and fear, and none of us were shy at all.

The Negro girl's name is Georgia. She has hair that sticks out eight inches around her head, and big gold loop earrings, and she wears tight pants and a tight sweater all the time. The sweater is covered with buttons and badges, and she's always passing out leaflets. I was afraid of her. I thought, the way she looked and acted, she'd be tough and hostile and anti-white.

When I got close to her I saw that her eyes were crossed. I don't know why, but this touched me, made me see her as a real person, an individual, a kid with cross-eyes, that crossed more when she concentrated to understand what you were saying.

I'd never been in the cafeteria before. It was one huge room, lined with windows on one side. Metal and Plastic chairs and tables sprawled across the plastic floor. Against the wall stood rows and rows of machines, gleaming with brightly lit pictures of the food they dispensed for a coin or two. We walked around looking for a clean, empty table, walking carefully to avoid globs of spilled food. We finally found a small one, littered with spilled sugar and potato chips. I guess I looked repelled, because the veteran sneered and said. "What do you expect? This is no college—it's a high school with ash trays. You should study this cafeteria. It's very instructive. Look around you. Let me show you how it breaks down. Up there's the black section."

It was true; several tables were entirely filled with Negroes.

Georgia interrupted. "They don't go to class much, you see them here all the time at that table. They sit and talk about how they're discriminated against, and play cards, and gossip about all the black people who've sold out—they mean people like me who'll sit and talk with you."

"But you sit at the black tables too. I've seen you."

"Sure. I'm black," she said. "And they could be right. Sometimes you don't know you're a sellout till you're sold." She frowned and stopped talking.

The boy went on with his description. "That big table is the jocks." He pointed to a large crowd of heavy-looking boys. "And over there's the biggest crowd—the saddest—the frat boys and sorority girls, trying to imitate something that doesn't even exist on the four-year campuses anymore. The closest those kids ever came was a bad college movie musical with Bing Crosby and Doris Day. Over there's the hard-core gamblers. In that corner, near the door, a small nest of politicals; next to them, a few grotesques. And we—whether you know it or not—are sitting in the smallest group of all, the so-called intellectuals, which means we actually mention books and ideas while we drink coffee."

"You're so hostile," I said.

"There's no school here, no atmosphere of learning. Oh, there are a few grinds in the library, but even that's mainly a pick-up station, and grinds have nothing to do with live ideas."

I felt ashamed to admit that, compared to my life up to now, I found the school bursting with ideas, so I just asked him why this was so.

He looked suprised. "You know why. The live ones get into four-year schools. How many students here do you think chose Bay Junior College—I mean, as their first choice? We're here because we couldn't get into a good school."

"I disagree. I think this is a very good school," I told him. "Some of the faculty are very good, and I've already learned a lot."

"You're different. You're older."

It was as if he'd slapped my face. "Well, I can't help that!" I said.

Georgia's eyes had been crossing more severely at me. She rejoined the conversation. "Why do you come?" She waited for me to answer, and when I didn't she said, "I mean, you don't need a job or anything. You got a husband to support you and you're up on that hill; what else do you want? You got everything you need."

The way she said "up on that hill" she must think we're rich like the people who live over in Walnut Creek or

64

Orinda. How could I explain what a short way we'd climbed? When I lived on the flatlands, did I feel the same way about "hill people"? Probably.

I caught Mr. Harkan looking at me with a slight grin, as if he was enjoying waiting for me to think of an answer.

"I come here to learn."

"Yeah, but what *for?*"

"Just . . . just to learn."

The two young people looked at me as if I spoke a foreign language. To fill the silence I said, "Well, what do you come here for?"

"To-help-my-people," Georgia said, too fast, I thought, too pat. Then, as if she felt she should do something to prove her sincerity, she got up and left, moving over to the black table.

I turned to the veteran, who sneered at me again. "I can't afford the luxury of 'just learning.' I have a family to support, and a degree will get me a good job." And he left too.

"Those two," I said, "make me feel that there's something immoral about learning for its own sake."

But Mr. Harkan was laughing soundlessly as he watched the veteran cross the room. "That guy. You know how long he's been here? More than ten years."

"Ten years!"

"Not steadily. He comes and goes. Probably he's completed a few units by now, but he's never managed to finish one of my classes. *This* time he's on the G. I. Bill and it's his wife (his second, I think) who works to support that family he talks about."

"Then all his talk was just—"

"No, he's quite right. And sincere too. That's what's so funny. He's furious at the quality of this place, but he's part of it too." Then he started to laugh again. But his laugh was bitter. His laugh is almost always bitter. He never expresses satisfaction with a laugh, but only with a look of wide-eyed surprise. He seems to laugh at the things that bother him most.

There were shrieks from the black tables that everyone pretended not to hear. The shrieks of laughter, the jumping up and down, had the look of a performance—unrestrained gaiety with underlying threat. We watched Georgia giggling, walking away from the table, shouting good-byes, leaving the cafeteria.

"She's torn, terribly torn," said Mr. H. "But I'm afraid we've lost her already."

"Lost her?"

"To thinking. To becoming a real student. The pressures are too great, the slogans too easy—and the rewards, financial and otherwise, too clearly earmarked for racial blackmail."

I didn't understand what he said, but I think I've copied it correctly. I never got a chance to ask him what he meant, because at that moment someone else joined us.

"Hi, Dan."

I looked up and saw a woman standing behind Mr. Harkan. She was very tall and thin, elegantly thin. She had deep black hair and very white skin, like Snow White in the fairy tale. She looked older than I, with deep lines around her eyes. She must have been beautiful as a young girl. She looked familiar, but I couldn't place her and assumed I must have seen her around the campus.

Mr. Harkan turned and looked up at her. He smiled at her in a way I'd never seen him look before. I don't know quite how to describe it—gentle, impersonal, kindly and yet with a tiny bit of hurt in the smile, hurt and forgiveness. But that

66

doesn't really describe it at all. The look reminded me just a little of the way Joe smiles at me sometimes. It had—patience in it; I guess that's the word. And patience is something that I'd never seen on Mr. Harkan's face before. "Sit down. Join us."

She sat down next to him and looked at me. She smiled at me, and for a moment I didn't like her smile. There seemed to be something ironic in it.

"I thought you'd be gone to the Big U by now," said Mr. Harkan.

"Almost," she said. "I'm accepted for the winter quarter, so I won't be back after Christmas vacation. I've arranged to get my work in early, so I'll have all the units I need."

"Now here's a real student. Laura's one of our successes."

"I get the prize for endurance," she said, but her smile was friendlier now.

"How long has it been?"

"Nearly six years. I came here to . . . to pass the time. Got hooked. It's taken me all this time to get my lower division units."

"Don't let her kid you. She's one of the best students I ever had. You two ought to know each other."

"You look familiar to me," I said. "My name is Ella Price."

"Laura Wilkens. You look familiar too. This your first semester?"

"Yes."

She was quiet for a moment. "I remember every bit of mine. The insecurity, the excitement. I wonder if it's really worse for us than for the young ones."

"Follow her advice," said Mr. Harkan. "Laura can be a great help to you."

"I wish we'd met sooner," I said.

67

"Yes, I'll be gone in a few weeks, I'm happy to say."

"Place is getting to you," said Mr. Harkan.

"Oh, not that bad, it's just that—"

But just then a loudspeaker began to blast out loud, crashing music. I jumped at the sound. I looked around expecting everyone to cringe as I did. But no one did. I thought, I suppose the young ones like it. I looked around to see if some would tap their feet or nod their heads in time to the music. But they all sat without any response at all, except that all conversation stopped, of course, and people sat at the tables like figures in a wax museum.

We all three got up and walked out. We seemed to be stricken permanently dumb by the loud noise. None of us commented on it when we got outside. We just gave each other a little wave and went off in three different directions.

Monday, November 14

Spent an hour in Mr. H's office arguing about Emma Bovary, who I think is a very stupid woman who created most of her problems. I said, "I really don't see why you thought I'd enjoy the book or identify with a woman like that."

"I don't see why you can't," he said. "I can identify with her; with all her illusions and silly fantasies and ridiculous love affairs, I like her."

"No, she was wrong. She had a good, secure life, a nice, loving husband, a fine—"

"So you think that every woman who has a secure middle-class life, with a nice husband and nice children, is fulfilled and happy?" I could feel myself getting red as he started to laugh hoarsely, then pounded the desk and said, "It's not enough, is it? It's not enough for a human being, and Emma Bovary is the only person in that narrow, mingy little town who knows it. That's why I dig her."

"But look at the stupid things she does," I told him. "If you're going to be a nonconformist . . . "

"What else does she know? She's read a few cheap novels, seen a glimpse of fancy balls and finery. Her vision is narrow, granted, her rebellion is tawdry, but she rebels; she's got life in her, and she rebels."

"You may be right," I said, "but I really couldn't understand or forgive her for her attitude toward her child, turning her face to the wall after she gave birth. And never paying any attention to her daughter. That's unnatural."

"How many kids do you have?"

"Just one, a girl."

"Why? Why just one? You sick or weak?"

"No. I . . . we just . . . " I could feel myself turning red. I would have gotten angry, but he was already laughing so I couldn't.

"So having kids isn't the most 'natural' thing in the world for you, not the greatest, or you'd have a flock of them, right?" I didn't say anything. "Now, I'm not saying you're Emma Bovary—maybe that's a bit exaggerated—but think for a minute: how did you feel, how did you really feel, when you had your kid?"

I started to answer him but stopped. I made two or three false starts before admitting, "I'm really not sure just what I felt—a mixture of things. I'll have to think about it."

I've been thinking about it throughout the day—thoughts and feelings from so many years ago.

I don't remember the pain—I think the pain is too great to be imagined, even right afterward. I remember how I felt about it, though. First, shock that it was so great. Surprise and shock. And then I was resentful, angry that I was to be torn apart in this way as part of the normal course of events. But I didn't blame Lulu because of it—I looked at people in the street, all the people in the street, for a long time afterward, and thought, Every one of you arrived here by tearing someone up that way. That continued to astonish me for a long time. Then gradually I forgot.

Last week in my psychology class, the instructor talked about the trauma of birth and said maybe we never recover from the shock of being born. I wonder why no one has ever discussed the trauma of birth for the mother. Has anyone ever written a book about the effects of this experience on women? I asked my psychology teacher about this, and he just gave me a funny look and said he didn't think so. Then he changed the subject as if I'd said something in bad taste, or something that just didn't interest him. That seems strange to me. Books are written about the effects of comparatively trivial experiences—deep, lasting effects, supposedly—but discussing childbirth is taboo.

I remember that when I had Lulu a lot of women were having "natural childbirth" (as if there's any other kind), and I read some articles that said women only felt pain in childbirth if they were tense and neurotic. It seemed as if, if you couldn't hypnotize yourself into believing it didn't hurt, you were a nut. Such a profound experience for so many women—and you can't even be honest with yourself about it, much less talk about it.

Right after Lulu was born, when I looked at her, I felt afraid. I felt, A part of me has been cut away from me. It can get into danger, it can drift off from me into the world, and what happens to it happens to me, but I can't control what will happen. I felt helpless and vulnerable in a way I never had felt before. And I knew I would always feel that way. I didn't like the feeling.

70

And I remember that when I got pregnant I was angry. I pretended to be happy and all the rest of it, but I wasn't. I hadn't decided—it had happened to me, in spite of being careful. And my first thought (I'd forgotten until this minute, because I was so ashamed of it) was, "Now, Joe's got me." I didn't like being dependent.

And I remember my mother always saying, "Well, raising a baby is the hardest job in the world," and that sentence was full of meanings. It meant, "I worked so hard raising *you.*" It meant, "Nobody could ever be as good a mother as I was." It meant, "Now you must sacrifice yourself as I did."

And Joe's mother was the same, except she, being Catholic, thought I should have a baby every year. The two of them are really alike in being martyr-mothers, and each feels superior to the other, Joe's mother because she had a lot of children, my mother because she didn't!

But Joe had had enough of big families. In fact, he hardly looked at Lulu for years and years. At first, when she was little, I thought it was because he wanted a son. I said we should try again, for a boy, but he didn't care about it. He missed going out when Lulu was small. I think he was glad when she started school and I could work off and on so we could have a few luxuries. I tried to make up for Joe's indifference. But Lulu never really was close to me—Joe was always her favorite.

And after a while I started to have another feeling (which is another reason why I didn't have more children), a nagging feeling that there was something else I should be doing instead of doing things with Lulu. But I have that feeling while I'm doing most things—a feeling that there's something missing, something else . . . but I don't know what. (I don't feel that way while I'm studying.)

Of course, all these thoughts were mixed with others, with

71

great rushes of love for my baby. But some of Emma Bovary's hatred for it all was there too. But I've never admitted it before now.

I still think Emma was a stupid woman who would have done better to stick to her dull husband than to get herself in such a mess she had to swallow arsenic. Isn't some kind of life better than death?

Sunday, November 20

This week it's been *Main Street,* and Carol isn't much better than Emma. But I think I feel more sympathetic to Carol because the people in her town seem so much worse. Maybe it's because they're Americans, and maybe I recognize their kind of narrowness and nastiness more easily. She doesn't do the kind of stupid immoral things that Emma does; she tries to improve herself and to bring some kind of culture to her town. And the people laugh at her and make fun of her. Some of the things she does don't seem worth doing. But they treat her like a freak.

Anyway I can identify with her because I just went through something that reminded me of her experiences: my two neighbors, with their little digs about not neglecting their families by going to college. We used to have coffee together a lot, but now I never have time. But last week they were so insistent that I met them one day for lunch. What did we talk about? Gossip (about neighbors or famous people), shop talk (cooking and sewing), clothes and competition (I've-got-more-than-you talk).

Then one of them started complaining about her children. They were defiant. They were ungrateful. They were unpatriotic. I pressed her to be specific, and finally she admitted that her son was talking about going to Canada rather than be drafted. It was the first interesting thing any of us had said.

"Well, I can understand his feelings," I said. I even wished Lulu would be more like that, so that when I talked to her about some of the issues we discuss at school she'd do something besides yawn and turn the radio up louder.

They both looked at me as if I'd said something obscene. I tried to explain how I felt. And somehow—I'm not sure how—we got into an argument about China, of all things. I was really getting warmed up when I saw them exchange a look. It was like the looks exchanged by the apathetic students sitting near me when I raise my hand. Only it was tighter, more assured.

"Well, we can certainly tell you've been out at the college," one of them said, with the nastiest smile I've ever seen. "I found that fun for a little while too, but I just couldn't neglect my family any longer."

"Or take classroom space away from some young person," the other threw in.

I don't think they'll insist again on my meeting them for coffee.

Friday, November 25

No school today. Yesterday was Thanksgiving. It was a mess. I got into an argument with my brother-in-law—about the war. Was I stupid! I could have avoided it, but I was too busy showing off what I'd learned in the reading I did for my social science class. But I wasn't just showing off. I was sincere. The things I read were so different from what I had heard—well, I thought that all I had to do was tell him these things and, hearing them, he'd want to read those books, too, and find out all these facts that were left out of the

73

newspapers. I should have known better. After all, think how mad I used to get whenever Dan Harkan confronted me with something I didn't know. There it was, a perfect example. It didn't matter what I told him, he didn't want his ideas shaken. He started yelling all kinds of stupid things and ended up saying that a couple of months in college had turned me into a smart-aleck communist and that was enough proof for him that he was right and that all he'd heard about communist brainwashing in the colleges was true and he'd stick to the things he knew in his heart no matter how anyone tried to confuse him.

I looked around the table at everyone to see their reaction to this. I expected them to laugh, or at least to look at him like the fool he was, but they were all looking at me, resentful of me, as if he had spoken for them—no, resentful of me as a troublemaker. Even Joe kept looking down at his plate as if he were ashamed of me. Lulu too. So I shut up.

Then Joe began joking—he told his old army joke, I guess to make everyone forget how awkward I'd made things —and soon everything was back to normal.

Later the men played cards while the women did the dishes. (Lulu stayed with the men, sitting on Joe's lap.) My mother was tight-lipped and severe as if I were a child again and had misbehaved. Her mouth has a way of going thin and turning downward when she disapproves, almost as if she's about to cry. The other women talked, without noticing the silence between my mother and me.

Finally I couldn't stand it anymore, and when my mother and I were alone for a minute, putting away the silver, I said, "I'm sorry if I upset everyone, but if I had a son, I certainly wouldn't want him in this war."

She kept her tight-lipped face turned away from me. "But you don't have a son, and your first duty is to your family, not to get mixed up in other people's problems." I was about to say that the war was everyone's problem, when suddenly she turned a furious face on me and said, "You were always like that!"

Like what? I tried to get her to explain, but she refused to speak to me. I had to stop asking, so the others wouldn't notice that my mother wasn't speaking to me. But I still wonder what she meant.

Today I start *Anna Karenina.*

Monday, November 28

Sometimes I feel awfully bitter about being a woman. Maybe it's just these books I'm reading, but I don't think so. I think I've always felt this way. But I never said anything because I was afraid of what people would think. If a Negro complains about the problems of being a Negro, people are sympathetic or at least willing to admit there are problems. But if a woman complains about being a woman, it's taken as a sign that she's a failure as a woman, as if any woman who's dissatisfied with being a woman ought to be too ashamed to admit it—it's a sign she's a bad woman—as if there aren't any real reasons for being dissatisfied.

I don't mean complaints about biology, like menstruation and menopause and childbirth pain and all that. I guess there isn't much that can be done about these things (but has anybody really tried—medical people?) so there's no point in being bitter. But what about the other things? Inferiority. Age-old inferiority. Always there. Sometimes you don't notice it, but it's there and every once in a while, when you least expect it, it pops up and hits you. Or you just don't know. You don't know if you're being discriminated against because you're inadequate or because you're a woman. I swear there's a look my psychology teacher gives me every time I disagree with him. But if I challenged him on it, he'd use it as proof that I'm neurotic—which I am, I guess, but I still say he has that look.

Wednesday, November 30

Dan Harkan admires Anna K even more than he does Emma B. I don't like either of them very much. I'm not sure why. We talked about identification with a character, and he says he can identify with them. But I can't. Maybe it's because they were ruled by their passions. They let go- —they go after what they want, even though it leads to unhappiness and misery and destruction. I guess Harkan is a passionate, impulsive man, and he likes these characters as struggling passions, not as people. But I see them as real people and I told him, "Real people just can't let go and follow their feelings."

"Why not?" he said, and I got annoyed.

"Well, because you know very well you can't just do whatever you want to do."

"Why not?"

"It's all very well to talk this way about a book, but what if we followed our emotions and just did what we wanted to and to hell with everyone else? If my feelings told me to shoot my husband I should just go ahead and do it!"

He laughed. "Why use an example like that? Why shouldn't you assume that your feelings would tell you to embrace every old lady you saw on the street?"

"Those women," I said, "weren't impelled to embrace old ladies but to escape their responsibilities."

"What responsibilities? The responsibility to let them kill you—to keep still while they crank the rack slowly and

76

break your back with their rules for you, their duties, their responsibilities? Your first responsibility is to be yourself! Why assume this means hurting others?"

"But if I have to go against others in order to be myself . . ."

"That's not hurting them, not if you're right. Might be good for them."

"Well, I always thought—"

"There are a lot of things you always thought, eh, but did you, really?"

I guess he's right. I say that in the last couple of months I've changed my mind about a lot of things. But it really wasn't a change. It feels more like opening a door, the door of a closet where I'd hidden a lot of things that didn't seem to fit into my life, a closet stuffed so full that once I'd opened the door just a crack, I couldn't push it closed again, and things started tumbling out. At first I tried leaning against the door, but that was too tiring. So I started to relax, just letting it slowly open. If I had more nerve I might just swing the door open and let it all out.

I guess I'm afraid that if I let that stuff out it'll make a mess of my nice, neat little house. But it's too late now.

Wednesday, December 7

Finished *Anna Karenina.* Doesn't anyone ever win? Emma swallows arsenic, Carol goes back to her dull life, and Anna jumps in front of a train. Are women like these always destroyed?

Dan Harkan says, "You miss the point. Destruction of the protagonist implies indictment of the society." He says I'm just being sentimental to want the survival of the character as if she were a real person, instead of an invention of the

77

author; that I just want a happy ending. I don't think that's true. If you destroy the rebel, aren't you saying that rebellion is useless? If a writer puts a character into a trap and says, to the reader, Look, this is the trap this person is in, it's intolerable, it's killing her . . . does the writer's responsibility end there? Only if he assumes that his readers are just observers, outside the trap—like men reading about poor Anna Karenina, shaking their heads and pitying her but not really seeing themselves in her place.

But if the reader *is* an Anna Karenina? If she sees herself in the book, and the author shows her being destroyed one way, then rebelling only to be destroyed another way . . . what does that do to the reader? I think it destroys the reader a third way—it teaches despair.

Monday, December 12

It really helps to have someone to talk to about the books. Harkan scares me sometimes, because, of course, he's way ahead of me in understanding them, but after we've talked I sometimes go back over the section we talked about and I can see what he means, and where I missed something important. That's real learning, just talking with someone who knows more than I do about something. Not that I don't enjoy my classes. But I get much more out of sitting with Dan Harkan, talking or just listening while he rambles on about a book, mentioning other books in comparison. "They're all the same," he said one day. "Every book is amplification of every other one. Every author keeps expanding, filling in, trying to get the message through to us, the one, single message, which, when we finally get it clear . . ."

I didn't understand what he was talking about, but I don't like to interrupt when he goes on that way.

78

Today we talked about all three books, and he asked me what the three women had in common.

"A thing," I began stupidly. "A kind of spark—no, more like an irritant—that made them restless. Boredom? I guess they had a depth of boredom that couldn't be covered over by gossip and martinis or things like that. None of them could get wrapped up in children, though Anna certainly loved her son. They all rebelled. They all failed."

"Go on."

"They couldn't really make the rebellion complete. They all died or gave up."

"Why?"

"They weren't strong enough, I guess. Anna had the best chance. But she couldn't live outside the conventions. It was all too much for her. She wasn't strong enough."

"Society destroyed her."

I started to nod, almost obediently, just because I thought he must be right about everything, but then I shook my head. "No. It's because they were men."

"Who?"

"The authors." I'd got an idea, and I had to go very slowly to find it, dig it out. "These men, the authors, didn't really want the women to succeed. They liked their heroines, but being men they were prejudiced about what a woman ought to be. Soft and weak and all. So they couldn't make their women strong enough to make a go of the rebellion. They couldn't imagine a woman like that. They couldn't go on liking them as women, feminine, you know. So they had to destroy them."

"No." He sat and thought a minute. "No, I can't go for that."

"But you're a man."

He laughed and shrugged. I felt proud because for the first time I'd gotten something out of a book that wasn't already obvious to him. But then he recovered and said, "What about *The Red and the Black? Native Son?*" And he named some other books that, of course, I haven't read. "Male rebels, all destroyed by male authors."

So I'm shot down again. And a few more books are added to my list.

I'd hoped for more reading time during Christmas vacation, but it doesn't look as if I'll get it. We've already accepted invitations to three parties, and I haven't done a bit of shopping.

Friday, December 16

Last day of school before Christmas vacation—quiet, sunny. I almost hated to leave the campus.

Saturday, December 17

We went to a movie tonight, another Doris Day thing. She's Joe's favorite. After it was over, I said, "God, I thought it would never end."

Joe looked at me as if I'd slapped him. "I always thought you liked Doris Day."

"So did I. But I don't."

He was quiet for a while and then said, "You don't like a lot of things anymore." I started to tell him about the film series at the college, but when I mentioned a couple of movies he said, "I don't understand French."

"Neither do I. They have subtitles." But he didn't answer.

When we got home he wanted to make love, but I didn't feel much like it. "You never feel like it anymore," he said. "You'd rather read a book or something." His look made me feel terrible. I told him how sorry I was and that we had a

80

whole two weeks now, and I'd devote more time to him and Lulu while I was on vacation from school.

Then we made love and he fell asleep right away, but I can't.

Thinking about it, I realize that it isn't true, what he said, "You never feel like it anymore." We make love once or twice a week just the way we always have. He sounded as if going to school or reading books made me stop being affectionate. I felt so guilty when he said that, I didn't think about whether or not it was really true.

Any time that I don't enjoy sex much, I feel ashamed of myself for feeling that way. It's like the way I felt when I finally had to give up breast-feeding Lulu because there wasn't enough milk to make it worth the trouble. I was so ashamed. But my mother says that when she had me women were ashamed of women who nursed, "like cows." I guess things change from one generation to another. Once women were ashamed if they enjoyed sex. Now women are ashamed if they don't. In one way or another the shame is there, but the rules change.

How I hate contraceptives. I still, after all these years, have a terrible time inserting the diaphragm—half the time getting all smeared with jelly and never feeling sure if the thing is in right. Not to mention having to leave it in for hours afterward. They say you can't feel it—that is, male doctors say so. I can feel it, like a fist squeezing my insides while jelly and semen ooze out of me for hours, because I'm not allowed to douche.

I tried the pills once. I gained a pound a day, my ankles swelled up, and I got so depressed I could barely drag myself around. Back to the diaphragm. And the fear. Sometimes I think it'll be a great relief to be old and sterile and not wait from month to month for the sign of blood.

It seems to me that with all the "marvels of science" this could be easier. But the only progress I can see is that now *some* women in *some* places can get an abortion—*sometimes*—legally, without risking their lives. Some progress! Is it because most of the doctors are men? So we have things like organ transplants, like boys putting new parts in a hot rod, but we still don't have painless childbirth and simple and safe contraception because men say to women, "That's your problem," and don't worry about something that'll never affect them, at least not directly.

There must be plenty of indirect effects on men, if they would only recognize them, if they could see the bitterness I feel as I write this, if it only would occur to them that women would be much easier to get along with if a few simple things like this were taken care of. But maybe they don't want us to be easier to get along with. Maybe they prefer us neurotic and emotional—so they can look down on us.

And, of course, if I ever said any of these things to a man, it would only prove that I'm a sick, bitchy man-hater.

Maybe I really am a poor sex partner. (I make it sound like being part of an athletic team!) I can't help it, sex seems overrated. I guess men want sex more than women (not more than Emma and Anna, though!) After I have an orgasm, I really don't care much about sex for another week or two. It's a kind of bodily function that serves a purpose, makes you feel relieved, but in itself it isn't so pleasant. Well, yes, it is, I guess. I just don't seem to have a very strong sex drive.

I did when I was younger. I remember when I was in my teens I used to have fantasies of being raped. I think the reason was that no "nice" girl could have intercourse with someone she wasn't married to—it was all right to want sex, you weren't supposed to be frigid, but you weren't supposed to want just sex. You were supposed to be in love. Well, I just wanted sex, I was as frustrated as any boy, but I couldn't admit it, even to myself, because I was a girl, so I used to daydream that someone tied me up and I was completely helpless and couldn't stop him from doing whatever he wanted. I was a little vague on what he did, but mostly touching.

When I started going with Joe, the fantasies stopped, I guess because Joe and I petted a lot, just like my fantasies, always stopping short of intercourse because we were afraid I'd get pregnant. I always told myself I was going to marry Joe anyway, so it was all right. If I hadn't married Joe I would have lost my nice-girl self-image! I was so sexually stimulated and frustrated for a couple of years before we married that I could hardly think straight.

I had my first orgasm about a week after we were married and right then sex fell back into place—or into the background—and became less important. I still remember my sense of relief. And I thought that was fine. Now I'm not so sure. I don't think I know anything at all about sex, and all the talk about it only confuses me more. They say experience is supposed to be the best teacher, but I was never supposed to make use of that teacher—and it's too late now.

Maybe young people are freer than we were. But I don't know. When the subject comes up in class, a few students talk a lot about how free they are, and I think they have had sexual experience. But somehow they don't really seem to know any more than I do.

4:40 a.m.

I still couldn't sleep, so I started reading *Washington Square.* I just finished it. Why did this book mean more to

83

me than the others? It's not supposed to be such a great book, and if I told anyone I liked it better than *Anna Karenina* they'd think I was crazy. But I do, whatever it means—if it means I'm stupid or ignorant or unable to appreciate good literature, too bad; *Washington Square* meant more to me. Why? Nothing very special or dramatic ever happens in it. A dull young woman turns into a dull old maid. But she's not really dull, she's invisible; no one sees her as a human being, as a real person. Her father sees her as a disappointing substitute for the mother who died giving birth to her, her aunt sees her as a prop in soap-opera fantasies she makes up, and her fiancé sees her as money. But nobody sees *her*. And so she can't be herself, and she never finds out who she is. The three of them easily stifle her because she's—weak? No, gentle, loving. She needed their love so much that she couldn't fight.

It happens every day. We don't get chopped down like redwoods, we wither. There's no big rebellion crushed. And we don't jump in front of trains. We just keep going. Not dead but not alive. And nobody ever knows. That's what's so awful, that no one knows. And that's why this book means more to me, I guess, because the author says, "Yes, I know, I know."

Tuesday, December 20

Christmas shopping. How I hate it. I never realized before how much. I just blamed myself for not being able to get into the "spirit" of Christmas fun. Here I am with a huge list and not one of the gifts a pleasure to buy. Because they are all for strangers—all duty gifts for relatives. I wander around the stores asking myself what my mother and father, my relatives in Nebraska I've never seen, Joe's dozens of nieces and nephews, what do they want, what would please them?

A gift should be something you give freely any time, to whoever it belongs to—it belongs to the person who'd be pleased by it, and you give it when you find it and say, "Oh, so-and-so would love that!" Like that new illustrated Blake. Dan Harkan would love it. A gift for someone I know. I don't know the people on my list.

And then there was that awful scene with Lulu. It used to be that every Christmas season I'd get a temporary job in a department store to help pay some of the bills—we seem to spend hundreds of dollars during this time! I used to get Lulu a whole new outfit, and maybe a party dress, and give her some money—and then I'd get some kind of surprise to put under the tree for her, so she'd have something to open Christmas morning, the way she did when she was little.

I told her that this year I wasn't working, so we'd have to cut down, but I guess she didn't believe me. When I took her shopping she went straight toward a rack of expensive dresses. When she finally got it straight that we couldn't buy that way this year, she was furious and said, "Never mind, I don't want anything!" Then she stopped speaking to me and dragged along behind me as I went through the stores.

When we got home she crawled onto Joe's lap and sulked until he got it all out of her. Then he looked at me, as if appealing for money.

At first I felt terrible. But when I saw Lulu curled up on her father's lap, looking not like a little girl but seductive, wheedling, manipulating, I was furious.

We've spoiled her, that's all. It's not her fault. But I see how spoiled she is. And I don't know what to do about it.

I think Joe must have given her some money, because after I left the room there was a lot of laughing and horseplay, and Lulu was nice as pie for the rest of the night, with a slightly sly smile all the time.

But if he did give her money, that means we'll be getting behind on the bills again, and how can I go to work and school both?

Wednesday, December 21

Did a great mound of ironing this morning, while baking cakes and pies for Christmas dinner. Then I felt I needed a walk outdoors. I never used to walk at all, but since being at school and walking around the campus, I miss the exercise. Nobody walks around here. We just get into our cars and go down to the supermarket. There's really not much place to walk, just narrow sidewalks past houses that look all alike. The trees haven't grown beyond stubby sticks yet.

But I went out anyway, and I'm glad I did, because I discovered why Laura Wilkens looked so familiar to me. I was coming round a corner when I saw a woman pushing a lawn mower in front of a house that had a FOR SALE sign on it. She looked familiar, and as I got closer I saw it was Laura. No wonder we looked familiar to each other when Dan introduced us—we're neighbors! Only she's been here since the first houses were built here, much longer than we have.

As soon as she recognized me, she stopped the lawn mower and invited me into the house. Her house is exactly the same as ours, of course, but how different! There are books all over, and drawings tacked to the kitchen wall (she draws too, very well), and papers she's been working on spread across the front room—and more than any *things* a feeling, a spare, clear feeling of this being a house where interesting people are doing interesting things.

She pointed to the papers scattered around. "I have to get

everything in this week," she said. "Then I start the winter quarter at U.C."

"It must be exciting."

"I'll be glad of the change."

We sat in the kitchen and drank tea and talked—about books, imagine! We talked about *Madame Bovary* and *Anna Karenina*. She told me about other books. Before I knew it, three hours had gone by. It seemed like ten minutes.

She lent me *The Golden Notebook* and a collection of Ibsen's plays. As I was leaving, I looked up at her (she's almost as tall as Joe), and I said, "You don't know how wonderful it is to know that I have a neighbor like you, someone to talk to." Then, as we crossed the lawn, I saw the FOR SALE sign again and said, "But it looks like we won't be neighbors for long."

"I want to move to Berkeley," she said, "near the campus if I can."

"How does the rest of the family feel about that?"

"You mean my husband? I'm divorced. Got the final decree last week. As for the kids, my older boy graduates from high school in June; he'll go away to college. My daughter brags to everyone that she's going to live in Berkeley, where the action is." She laughed. "And the little boy—well, Teddy's not little anymore, he starts junior high next fall, so it's a time of big change for him in any case." The lines around her eyes deepened. "It can't be any worse, anyway." Then she made her mouth smile and waved at me as I walked away.

Thursday, December 22

I'm still addressing cards, but at least the tree is finally up. I've squeezed in *The Golden Notebook* whenever I could during the past two days. It's written as a journal, just like mine, but what a difference! I don't know anything about women like this—free, independent women who earn their own living, raise their own children, sleep with whoever they want, make their own rules. But in some strange way their lives don't seem to be much different from mine. The main difference I see is that no one cares about them, no one takes care of them at all. They're not really in a position to use influence or power, and no one gives them any protection either.

They remind me of what my history teacher said about slaves in America. After the civil war they were put to work doing the same old things, at a wage that didn't buy any more that what they had before. And when there was no work to do, they were laid off. At least under slavery they had food and shelter in the winter too, because the slave master wouldn't let his property die. But now they didn't belong to anyone, and for some of them being free meant just being free to die.

That doesn't mean slavery was better than freedom, and it doesn't mean women ought to go back to leaving votes, money and everything else to male control. But the women in this book are used and hated by men. Anna keeps saying, We are the new women, but where are the new men for us?

Monday, December 26

It's over. I behaved myself. Throughout Christmas dinner I didn't start one argument. I avoided any subject that would lead to trouble. That means we can't talk about anything interesting. Bored, bored, bored!

This time I sat back quietly and asked myself, Aren't they

88

bored too? Here we sit, around a huge table made from sawhorses and planks and covered with linen and china and loaded with food that most of us can't eat (reducing diets, diabetes, hypertension), and we talk about some other Christmas ten or twenty years ago, and everyone laughs together like a chorus and we look like the December cover of an old Saturday Evening Post. It's as rehearsed and formal as a dance.

What's wrong with that? Maybe it's just a ritual, a ceremony of love, people sharing good feelings; that's what a family dinner is all about. You don't have to have an intellectual debate, you just have a ceremony. That's all right.

Bull. It's all false. The truth is that I look around the table and see that these people don't even like each other. My mother and my mother-in-law still bear old grudges, starting with their disagreement over my wedding arrangements. (Joe's family expected a big Catholic wedding, and his mother always tells him—but not in front of me—that he never seems really married because we were married by a judge rather than choose between her priest and my mother's Baptist minister.) And, of course, our having only one child is too obscene for words.

But my mother is even worse. Catholics are heathens, idol worshipers. And the Irish drink.

But worse still are Joe's brother and his wife, now up to five children and with all the moral superiority of being such superparents. And constant talk about big real estate deals, into which they always manage to use the term "little Arkansas," the part of town where we "Okies" lived when I was a child, and where now there's a lot of speculation for business property.

I just keep smiling and nodding.

But I can't be as good as Joe. He's not just being polite. He has a good time, no matter what. He laughs and jokes with everyone and makes everyone happy. The more he has to drink the funnier he is. I think people would feel like terrible wet blankets if they didn't laugh along with him. He makes me feel petty and mean about thinking the things I'm writing now.

Tuesday, December 27

Antigone. What a play! This would sound silly to anyone who was educated—that I'd just discovered something that everyone else knew was great and I was running around saying, It's great, it's great, like saying, "Mount Everest is high!"

Why did I get so excited? It's that Antigone faces a problem that's not a woman problem, it's a human problem. A female character whose conflict is not men as men relating to her as a woman. It's a conflict that could be faced by anyone, man or woman. If the law is wrong, do you break it? She's heroic by any standards, and feminine by any standards. She's not trapped in sex; she's the hero in a story about loyalty and integrity and courage and freedom and lots of other things.

That's what I really want. I don't want to cover pages in my journal secretly griping about "woman's hard lot." I want to get above that. That's what's awful about being a woman or a Negro or whatever, you're stuck to the tar baby; you push with one hand and that gets stuck, you kick and your foot gets stuck, and you want to get loose and get on with other things but you can't. You have to just take that tar baby along with you wherever you go—and everyone sees only it and never notices you.

90

Saturday, December 31

Today I walked over to Laura's house to return her books. We got into a discussion of *A Doll's House.* I said I didn't see how two people could live together so long and not really understand each other, not understand the basis of their marriage.

She gave me a crooked smile, and said, "Oh, I can."

"You, personally?"

She nodded. "I lived with my husband for nearly twenty years without knowing the real basis of our relationship."

"Which was . . ."

"I'm not even sure now," she said. "I'm still working it out in my mind. But it wasn't what I thought it was." She gave a little shake of her head, as if she didn't want to get onto personal subjects. "The real flaw in that play is the ending. It's just absurd. You can't do that. Just walk out, without a job, without any knowledge of the world, leaving the children. It just can't be done."

We didn't have time to talk much about it. We promised we'd get together more often; then I had to hurry home to get ready for the last of the big parties, New Year's Eve. "Yes," she said, "on New Year's Eve we can celebrate the ending of the holiday season." I could see that we agreed perfectly about the whole mess. She waved to me from the door as I walked away, and though she was smiling she looked terribly sad. A car drove up to the house and she turned toward it. A lanky boy got out—her older son, I guess.

8 p.m.

Joe's shaving. An added note on Laura. I told Joe about her, and he said he knew her husband. "Salesman, big

91

building-supply outfit. Regular supplier of ours for years. Last time I saw him was while they were going through the divorce. He said she started playing around so he left her."

I thought and thought. "Wasn't he the one you said was always asking you to go to bars and pick up women?"

"He's the one." Joe laughed. "Old Tom, always had a hot one on the line."

"You think that's funny?"

"Well, I never took him up on it. What are you so serious about? He might have thought it was good business, to keep on my good side. You know how it is."

"Nothing. Never mind." I thought it best to drop the whole thing. This was no time to get into a discussion of the double standard.

And I'm almost out of pages. That's nice—came out even: new year, new notebook.

Notebook

NUMBER THREE

Tuesday, January 3

It was like coming home. Yesterday I left the house early in the morning. I decided I'd have breakfast in the college cafeteria, noise and all. But it was quiet and almost empty. Dan was there. I must have talked like someone just let out of solitary confinement. Then he told me about his vacation. He and his wife hate the whole thing and always vow to ignore Christmas, but end up making compromises for their three children, who want a tree and presents like their friends. He was glad it was all over too.

A little after eight the loudspeaker woke up and blasted us out of the place. We left the reverberating building and walked out behind the science building where the arboretum slopes down to the creek bed. There was a little water in the creek; I guess there will be for a month or two before it dries up again. It was cold but sunny and sheltered down there. We walked back and forth in the little valley where there was only the sound of trickling water.

Dan was very quiet. He dug his hands into his pockets and looked at the ground. Little gray streaks in his beard shone in the sun.

"Are you tired?" I asked him.

He shrugged. "Christmas vacation was depressing enough, but the alternative . . ." He made a sweeping gesture with his arm, taking in the whole campus.

"I don't understand," I told him. "I envy you. Most people would envy you."

"Why?" His grin was ironic and hard.

"Because of your job. Because yours is a hard job, but it's honest and valuable. Yours is one of the few professions with integrity. How many people can earn a living doing something they know is right?"

He grinned even harder, then sat me down on a bench like a child. "Let me tell you a story," he said.

"There is a man. A man who has had a lot of bad luck, failed at a number of things. He has been oversold on possibilities that never really existed, not for him. He's down to his last fifty dollars, and he decides to go to Reno and gamble. This is his last chance, and he's desperate. He goes to the crap table, and within a few minutes his last fifty dollars is gone. It represented his last feeble hopes, and it's gone.

"Then a guy standing behind him taps him on the shoulder and says, 'I've been watching you. That was a lousy run of luck. Let me buy you a drink.' He buys the man a drink and encourages him to talk. He buys him a second drink, and then a third, while the loser tells the story of his disappointed life. 'Let's have dinner,' the guy says, and he listens and sympathizes for two or three hours, until all the anger is dissipated and only quiet despair is left, resignation mixed with gratitude for the guy's friendliness. Finally the two men shake hands and the loser goes away quietly.

"What he doesn't know is that this sympathetic man is employed by the house to watch for losers who might become desperate and start tearing the place apart. His job is to ease them out quietly so they won't endanger the whole system. Understand?"

I shook my head.

"That sympathetic man," he said slowly, "is the junior college teacher."

"No."

"Yes. Do you know what the dropout rate at this college is? Something like eighty percent. They all plan to transfer to a four-year college. Do you know how many do? Maybe fifteen percent. They're not going anywhere from here, but they get a chance to dream awhile, hang around for a year or so, getting used to the idea that they're going to spend the rest of their lives outside—outside the places where money is made and jobs are fairly easy, or at least not totally dehumanizing.

"They come to me, asking to learn how to read and write better so that they can get a place in the system. But there is no place for them. It was all decided, a long time ago, who was getting a place and who wasn't—not them, or they'd be in a four-year school to start with. I try to tell them the truth, tell them the way it is, but they don't want to hear it. You notice that in class, don't you? How hostile they are toward real thinking? Because down deep, inside their guts, they know they haven't got a chance. But they want to believe a little longer; they want me to play that game with them . . . just a little longer. They are hostile toward me as an obstacle between them and a 'decent' life. But they are even more hostile when I try to help them see what the real obstacles are.

"They are the staunchest supporters of all the lies that they're victims of: that competition is great because it weeds out the unfit, that if everybody got an education they'd all have good jobs, that they're free, that if they could just learn grammar rules. . . . Oh, the poor bastards.

"You know what happened once? Once I said to a class . . . I told them the percentage of transfer to four-year colleges. You know how they reacted? They pitied those *other* poor sods who weren't going to make it. Each was sure *he* was going to make it—this in a class where the reading level was about fourth grade. They wanted to get away from that subject and learn speed reading!"

"You're cruel," I said, almost choking. "If a person is dying, why tell him so? Why take away his hope?"

"False analogy!" he snapped. "The only way these kids are going to come alive is to know the truth, to see where they are. And when they do see, the sign of their brains coming alive, the sign they're becoming educable"—his voice had become so hoarse he was whispering—"is that they'll tear the place down." Then he gave a short laugh, like a bark. "And, most likely, me with it."

We just sat quietly for a long time, and finally I told him, "You don't have to ease me out quietly. I can be told the truth."

"What are you talking about?"

"What you said. About the gambling house, about being a loser and all that."

He started to laugh. "You silly ass. I didn't mean you. You can keep going till you get a Ph.D."

"I can?"

"Sure, if you're crazy enough to want one." Then we talked about my plans, and he just kept smiling at me and shaking his head when he saw how happy I was.

That's the good part. The bad part started when Joe got home last night. As soon as he got in the door I said, "Guess what? I'm getting an A in English. He already told me."

"Harkan?"

"Yes. He thinks I can get a degree if I want to. It'll take a long time, but I'm capable of doing it."

"Sure. Sure you are. I always said you were smart."

"Yes, but that's not the same. . . ."

"Yeah."

"What's the matter, Joe?"

"Nothing." He opened the cupboard and took out the bottles. "We'll drink to it."

"I'd better not. I have to work on that term paper tonight."

He nodded, put ice in a glass and poured the glass nearly full of vodka. "Here's to your A in English," he said, and took a big gulp. I put my arms around him and kissed him. Then I tried to draw back, but he wouldn't let me. He held me tightly and said, "Let's celebrate. Let's go somewhere."

"One night next week, after—"

"No, I don't mean one night. I mean a real vacation, a second honeymoon. Things are slow right now. I could get away for a few days."

"Now? I couldn't."

"Why not? Lulu can stay with my mother. Look." Joe reached into his back pocket. "I got these today." He handed me two plane tickets. I just looked at them for a while. I couldn't understand.

"What are they?"

"You can read. Tickets."

"To Hawaii. When?"

"The seventeenth. Surprised? Honey, it'll be great. You deserve it, after all this—"

"But, Joe, I can't. Final exams start that week."

"Hell with final exams."

"No, it would be wonderful, but not right now. If I miss finals, I'll flunk, and all this will be for nothing."

"What does it matter? You proved your point. What do you care about grades? You said yourself about a million times last month, all you cared about was learning; you didn't worry about failing anymore."

"But, Joe . . ."

"Never mind. Forget it. It was a stupid idea. You're right. You couldn't leave now."

But I couldn't forget it. And something else bothers me. He couldn't have paid cash for those tickets. Lately the mail has second and third notices for bills. And every time we get into the car, he complains about the way it sounds or looks. I know what that means—time for another new car.

We've never had any arguments about money. Just the thought of married people arguing about money sickens me. I've always let him handle it because I think it humiliates a man not to be in control of the money. I never criticized when the bills got ahead of us, though it did worry me. All I ever did—from the time Lulu was in school—was to take a temporary job until we got the bills paid off. We never talked about it, one way or the other. I just did it.

But that was when I didn't have anything better to do. I just couldn't quit school now. Maybe I should try to explain to him that we mustn't take a trip or buy a new car because then I'll have to quit school and go to work to pay for it. But I couldn't say that to him. That would hurt him.

100

Friday, January 6

Coffee with Laura today. We talked about Doris Lessing and *The Golden Notebook*. I said Lessing's comments on relations between men and women were devastating.

Laura gave me a kind of weary smile and said, "Nothing she said has been contradicted by my experiences in the two years I've been on my own."

"Do you go out . . . on dates?" The phrase sounded so silly.

"I used to. Now I hide. Until the loneliness becomes unbearable. Then I venture out . . . find the manhunt unbearable, or the men unbearable . . . and run home to hide again."

"I thought . . . with all the divorces . . . I thought single people had a good time. I guess I'm naïve."

"Yes, you are," she said. I waited for her to go on, but she wasn't eager to talk about herself or her experiences. I liked that. I liked the way she changed the subject and we talked about books some more. I like to think that two women can have a friendship that isn't based on gossip or girlish confidences.

Saturday, January 7

Last night I dreamed of the giant in the gas station. I stood at his feet looking upward at his arms, which held something now, but I couldn't see what. Then I noticed there were small handholds running up the side of his body. I began to climb up his pantleg, clinging to the small grooves with my hands, the full weight of my body hanging and swinging slightly. I began to feel dizzy. Afraid of falling, I kept my eyes on the grooves, which opened in front of me but seemed to close behind me, so I had no place to put my feet and no way to get down again. The color of the grooves changed, and I realized I was now climbing up the white shirtfront. I tried to turn around to see what was held in the arms but got dizzy again and clung to the shirtfront. There were no more handholds. I was clinging to a real shirt. And I heard a great thumping, the beating of a real heart under me as I climbed. As I reached the throat, where the shirt was open, I could hold on to the thick black and gray hairs that sprouted like tall grass.

Getting a good grip on the hairs, I turned to look at the outstretched arms. They were empty. It had all been a trick to get me to climb up there. As I realized this, I felt, rather than saw, the head above me begin to move. I clung to the thick hair, afraid to look at what I knew was coming down on me—his huge, open mouth. I would either be swallowed or, if I let go, fall and fall.

The dream didn't really end. It just melted into another one that I can't remember.

Sunday, January 8

Today Joe handed me the tickets to Hawaii and asked me to take them back. He smiled and gave me a kiss. I felt terrible. He went on being especially affectionate, trying to let me know it was okay. But I just felt worse.

Read Shaw's *Candida.* I don't like her much, but I understand her. She chooses her husband instead of the poet because that choice gives her some place to put her energy and ability. I can't figure out whether she has more or less choice than most women today.

Anyway I'm much more interested in "the secret in the poet's heart." Shaw never explains that; he only says it's there, and that the poet goes off alone and content knowing he has it. Does he just mean his talent? I hope not. I'd like to think there's a secret for all of us, even if we're not artists.

Monday, January 9

Today we had the most exciting discussion ever in English. Kafka's *Metamorphosis.* Most of the time it's hard for Dan to get a discussion going, but this time people were fighting to talk. Who would have thought that a crazy thing like a man waking up in the morning and discovering he was a cockroach would mean anything at all as a story?

Most of all I enjoyed watching Dan lean back, looking relaxed and delighted while people talked excitedly. After class we went to have coffee, and he talked for a while.

"I use that story with my most sophisticated classes—and I've used it with people who were barely literate. Once a man came up to me after a few days' discussion of it in class and said, 'You've just changed my life—seven years in therapy, and it took this story to make me see.' See what? I don't know. He couldn't make it clear to me; whatever it was, it was his, privately, his realization, at a deep, intimate level."

"You look so happy," I told him.

"It's a breakthrough. You struggle along for months to get one day like this."

"And then you've won."

He shook his head. "This is only a teaser. Gives you an idea of what real teaching could be like. I used to think, when it happened, Now we're over the hump, now we can really get going. But the next class time, they were back in it again—wrapped in the blanket of hostility-apathy."

"Always?"

"With a few exceptions. But even those exceptions—when

the change is permanent, look, it's the end of the term! In a couple of weeks I start again with a new batch."

Just then a blast of music came over the loudspeaker system, crashing down on us like the roof falling in. We looked at each other silently, got up together and walked out.

"There's hostility for you," he said, when we were outside and could hear each other. "The sickness of this place shows there, like a boil, that building, with its little ghettoes of aimlessness, seething. If I could reach them, if I could channel that energy, that—"

"Our class is down to about ten people," I said. "Is that where the rest of them went?" I pointed back toward the cafeteria, but Dan just shrugged.

Thursday, January 19

Took my first final today. It wasn't so bad. I needn't have worried so much. Dan says finals are anacronistic (sp?) and a waste of time and energy. We're not going to have a final in his class; we're just going to meet and talk about the class, evaluate it and him, and talk about where we each go from here. There are only a few of us left, and we have a good time now. Too bad class is ending. But I'll have Dan for English again next semester.

Sunday, January 22

I'm so stupid. Today I mentioned the last book we read in Dan's class, *The Autobiography of Malcolm X.* Joe was quiet for a couple of minutes, so I went on talking and got carried away. I guess I still hoped I could draw Joe into the things I'm learning. I started feeling happy, chattering like an idiot, until he interrupted me.

"I still don't see what learning English has to do with

reading about a convict, dope peddler, pimp, anar—anarc—whatever he was."

"Well, I thought that's all he was too. The newspapers—here, let me read you . . ."

He sighed.

"Don't you want to hear it?"

"Sure, if you want, go ahead."

"But don't you, for yourself, want to?"

He sighed again. I kept looking at him and waiting until he said, "I don't see the point of reading about guys like that."

"Like what?"

"Like I said."

"But what if you find out you're wrong? Wouldn't you want to know that?"

He shrugged.

"What are you afraid of?" Each time I spoke I thought I should stop now, drop it, not push him. But I couldn't help it. I thought, Stop it, but I went on arguing. "Are you afraid to find out the truth?"

"What good would it do? He's dead, isn't he?"

"You can find out why he died, what he really was, why we didn't know the truth about him, why . . ." But he just shrugged again and this time turned away from me. "Look at me, Joe. Let me ask you something. Do you believe what I've been saying about him, that we were told lies about him, that if we'd listened to him maybe there wouldn't be so much trouble now?"

Joe was quiet for almost a full minute. "Maybe."

"Even without reading the book you're willing to believe that, but you don't want to read it, don't want to know."

Joe nodded, and it was my turn to be quiet for a while. He started to turn away again, as if the discussion was over, but I couldn't let it go because I was getting hold of an idea.

"Then teachers like Dan Harkan are wrong. Dan thinks that people have been fed wrong information, and that if you contradict this, keep hammering at them with facts—if you shake them up and make them think—once they start thinking they get rid of prejudices and lies because they demand the truth. But that's not right, is it?"

"I don't know."

"I mean, Joe, deep down we really know already. We know a lot of our opinions are based on lies, don't we? Just like you don't want to read that book because you already know what's in it, and you believe what's in it, although what's in it is the opposite of what you say."

"Well, there's nothing I can do about it, so why—"

"How do you know that?"

"Look. I just want to enjoy life and be left alone." He got up and turned on the TV. "I'm happy if I can eat, drink and screw. That asking too much? At the end of the day I want a little rest, a little fun. Why should I suffer the world's problems?"

"But you can't be happy. You can't be happy and afraid at the same time, afraid of knowing things. Oh, not just you, Joe. Me, too. Everybody. We're afraid to think about things we know are true, and—I'm getting this all mixed up, but what I mean is we always talk about being free, but we're not free at all, we're scared."

"I'm not scared!" he shouted. Then he rubbed his head, shrugged and said, "I don't know. I guess I'm just not the intellectual type. I can't talk about these things with you, —just tell me what you want. . . ."

Of course, by this time my excitement over the idea had subsided, and I saw that Joe was hurt. Saying I was sorry didn't help much.

Why can't we live together and love each other and let

each other be what we are? Why do I make him ashamed of being what he is, and why does he make me ashamed of what I'm doing, my studying that means so much to me, and ashamed of making him feel. . . ? Oh, hell.

Joe works all day and comes home tired. Probably if I had a full-time job my mind would be occupied with that for eight hours a day, and I'd come home tired too. Tired of thinking. Maybe our minds can only work so many hours a day, and after hours of thinking about a job there's not much thinking energy left.

So what? Does that mean I'm supposed to go back to one of those stupid typewriters all day long so I'll be too numb to have any thoughts? That's like saying primitive people are too busy surviving to become neurotic, so we should throw away technology and go out to live naked on roots and berries.

Well, if the way to keep women from bugging their husbands is to keep them working all day, then somebody had better do something fast and invent a lot of jobs, because there must be a lot of women like me with time on our hands. Of course, it's all right if we use that time to gossip or drink or fuss over children or chase someone else's husband. But we mustn't start thinking!

Cool down. Suddenly I'm so mad I'm almost pushing the pencil through the page. Maybe I was wrong to think I was less neurotic. Maybe I'm as bad as ever, but I'm taking it out on Joe in a different way.

Wednesday, January 25

Took my last final today. I'm sure I did well on it. It's all over. I stuck with it and accomplished something. And I know I can do even better now. It's wonderful to have goals, something to look forward to. I'll get a degree. Maybe I'll major in English. There are so many tremendous books to read and talk about and write about. Maybe someday I'll even teach.

No reason why I can't if I just remember to keep my stupid mouth shut at home.

And I'm determined to do that—especially after what happened today.

I stopped to see Laura, expecting to find her all excited about being at the university. I rang the doorbell, but no one answered. I saw her car parked outside, so I kept ringing and waited. Finally the door opened, just a little bit, and Laura looked out at me. She had been crying; her face was all red and puffy.

"Oh, it's you, Ella, come in."

"I'll come back another time."

"No, no, it's all right. I'm glad you came."

I followed her into the kitchen and sat down while she made coffee. She didn't say anything and seemed to gradually compose herself, but when she sat down, her eyes filled with tears again.

"What is it? Can I help?"

"It's nothing, really. Just Teddy." Teddy is her thirteen-year-old boy. She has a boy seventeen, a girl fifteen, and Teddy. "He just says awful things to me sometimes. We had a row this morning before he left for school. And I was feeling a bit down, a little tense about starting Cal and trying to sell the house, and my job's been hectic, and if things go on this way with the children I don't know how I'll . . ."

She shook her head as if to clear it, then took a deep breath and seemed to pull herself together by a great effort. "My marriage was pretty awful. We had to get married. And my

108

husband chased women a lot. I always knew. I realize now that he wanted me to know. But at first I didn't realize it, so it had a peculiar effect on me—made me feel ashamed, inadequate—I was just his wife; other women were attractive, not me. Of course, he occasionally reminded me that he had to marry me.

"It made me very protective toward the children. I wanted to protect them against hating their father, against feeling contempt for his drinking and running around. So I made sure, even more than he did, that they never found out. I built him up, made a hero of him.

"Then, when they were all in school, I decided I needed some other interests, to take my mind off the whole humiliating mess. I started taking classes at the college. Of course, I soon realized that I'd been a masochistic fool. I did well at school. I even gained some understanding of why my husband needed to chase women. Pretty soon I really didn't care whether he did or not. It was his problem. I wasn't interested. My interests were elsewhere.

"And then all hell broke loose. He was suddenly jealous. He kept track of my schedule, called home to see if I'd arrived within half an hour after classes were out, forbade me to study in the library, accused me of going to the college to meet men, interrupted my studies every way he could. And finally demanded I quit school.

"It took me a long time to understand what had happened. I'd changed, and he was afraid. I guess because he couldn't or wouldn't change. So I got a divorce, but not really on the grounds I gave, not for the reasons everyone thought. It was ironic—I divorced him because he was jealous.

"I expected problems, but"—her eyes filled again—"I'd done my work too well with the children. Their father is an abused hero, thrown out of his home. He only sees them once or twice a month, so it's easy for him to keep up a front. He's always behind on support for them, but he takes them to expensive places or buys them things, while I worry about keeping them in shoes. Now, of course, if I tell them the truth, they don't believe me.

"Teddy has really declared war on me. Whole days go by with him refusing to speak to me. Then, when he does, he—" She choked up again and shook her head. "What with school and working and all . . . I just get tired." Then she gave a little smile, shook her head again and asked me about my final exams.

I talked for a while, not thinking much about what I was saying, just trying to take her mind off her troubles. And all the time, I was thinking, Whatever problems I have, they're nothing like this, and I should remember how lucky I am.

Saturday, January 28

Joe wants to take me out tonight to celebrate finishing my first college term. Dinner and nightclubs in the city.

Sunday, January 29

I wonder if there is anything so boring as a night of "fun." We started by drinking three martinis. Isn't a bar a funny place? Dark and soft and some people talking too loud and others whispering and everything—just weird, if you look at it like you'd never seen it before, like the man from Mars asking himself, "Now what are these people doing?"

Then we had dinner. Poor sweet Joe insisted on all the courses, climaxed by a big steak. There was so much I felt sick; great piles of food, but none of it tasted very good.

The nightclubs were depressing. In one of them a naked girl sat on a swing. Bored. In another all the people sang old songs they didn't really know and pretended they were

110

sentimental about them. I said to Joe, "They're all laughing, but nobody looks happy." He was in the middle of a laugh. He stopped and looked around the room, as if I'd told him there were devils floating over the heads of the people.

"Everyone's just trying to have a good time. Relax, honey. Enjoy yourself. Take it easy." All I could think of was that in one of James Baldwin's essays he says people were always driving him up the walls, saying, "Take it easy, Jimmy."

But I tried. I really tried. But how can you *try* to relax? Anyway I laughed and sang and pretended that naked girls were fun and noise was relaxing. My headache grew until I thought my head would explode, but Joe had a great time. I didn't spoil it for him, so I felt I accomplished something. After all, if I expect him to accept and adjust to what I like, I have to be able to do the same in return.

Tuesday, January 31

Saw Laura today. She was feeling much better, excited about the university. Our schedules leave us both free on Tuesday afternoon, so we're going to meet every week.

Thursday, February 2

"You have learned something, and that always feels, at first, as if you had lost something."

G. B. Shaw, *Major Barbara*

Strange how my reading ties into my life. I learn a new word and immediately begin seeing it and hearing it everywhere. Or I run across a quotation like this one and immediately see it acted out—in an incident Dan told me about.

It involved one of the art teachers.

"He hung an exhibit of student work in the cafeteria—one

111

more effort to change the atmosphere there—seen it?" I shook my head. "Well, most of it was good student effort, pretty ordinary stuff. But one of the paintings was striking. An American flag, flat across the canvas, nothing else. Except when you get up close you see that about half the stars are swastikas.

"It's not terribly original—I've seen the device in other protest art. But it does hit you the way this kind of thing should, the wordless warning, or accusation, depending on how you want to see it. The art teacher was kind of pleased, not especially at the painting but at the kid's awareness of what's being done in art and his serious intention. I was interested because the kid is one of my students too. This is his third semester of remedial English, and we felt it was significant that, as he started exploding with paintings like this, he was beginning to write coherently too. Coincidence? That kid couldn't complete a sentence before!

"Yesterday the painting disappeared. Vanished. Nothing else was stolen. At first they thought a student had taken it, but one of the cafeteria workers said he saw some teachers take it down.

"The artist went straight to the president's office. Threatened pickets, demonstration—I think he could have done it. By that time all the art students had heard about it, and they were mad. The president swore he didn't know a thing about it and asked for a day to investigate.

"Gradually the story got pieced together. A couple of faculty superpatriots (who shall remain nameless) took the painting down. Another faculty member saw them do it, and he talked to some of his friends. Somebody called the local newspaper. Local paper called the president to ask if it were true that the students had burned the American flag and run up a swastika. In the meantime two different petitions were

112

going around the faculty—one to bar subversive art and the other to ensure freedom of expression. There weren't many signatures on either, because most of the faculty's afraid to sign anything but their paycheck. Art students organized a demonstration. But they were picketed by counterdemonstrators—black—who were circulating a petition condemning 'effete white protest.' In other words, saying nobody has a right to speak or demonstrate on anything but race."

"What's going to happen now?" I asked.

"Nothing. The president got the painting, put it back up." He started to laugh, that deep hoarse laugh that sounds like a growl. "The kid is stunned. He thought the college faculty represented enlightenment. He thought oppressed blacks were all freedom fighters. He thought . . . he was just beginning to think. I hope all this won't be too much for him." He sat there glowering until I changed the subject and we talked about Shaw's heroines. I said I wished I had a little bit of St. Joan in me. But he just said, "We've all got a bit, just enough to know that God has plans for us—not enough to follow through."

Monday, February 6

Androcles and the Lion. Shaw makes the early Christians a bunch of misfits and oddballs, like hippies; maybe he's right in saying that people who start a new movement always appear to be freaks and misfits.

There's one of his great women again—Lavinia is beautiful and intelligent and brave. I cried when I read her speech refusing to save her life by accepting the old gods.

> . . . do you think that I, a woman, would quarrel with you for sacrificing to a woman god like Diana, if Diana meant to you what Christ means to me? No: we should kneel side by side

113

before her altar like two children. But when men who believe neither in my god nor their own—men who do not know the meaning of the word religion—when these men drag me to the foot of an iron statue that has become the symbol of the terror and darkness through which they walk, of their cruelty and greed, of their hatred of God and their oppression of man—when they ask me to pledge my soul before the people that this hideous idol is God, and that all this wickedness and falsehood is divine truth, I cannot do it, not if they put a thousand cruel deaths on me.

But all I do is cry . . . as if I were watching a cheap soap opera. There's nothing of Lavinia in me—no guts.

Wednesday, February 15

Today was one of those blooming, sunny days we get in February, the best part of the year, before the grass turns brown and the smog gets thick. Dan and I sat on the lawn outside the library. (We never go to the cafeteria anymore; too noisy, too depressing.)

Classes are smaller now and the campus seems quieter. Dan says it's because so many drop out during the fall semester, and there are more jobs in the spring too.

"That's too bad," I said, and he jumped on me again.

"The ones who drop out are the ones with sense!" He was off into one of his attacks on the college. I wasn't going to tell him again how much it meant to me. I just listened till he stopped for breath.

Then I said, "Maybe you're right. Maybe we should just close the place down."

He laughed. "I wouldn't teach in any other place. Because this is where it has to happen."

"What."

"The change. Not in the universities. They create a

114

moneyed elite who really can't tolerate change. Even the rebels they create aren't very effective. You know why? Because here is where it is—in the mass man, the guy who takes a crack at junior college and then drifts back to work in some ordinary crummy job. These are the people. Ignorant, bigoted, narrow, frightened, greedy, hedonistic, materialistic, boring and bored. Unless you change them, you can't change anything. You can have small factions fighting each other, but it's going to be nothing but struggle and shifts of power until you change these, the majority, until they become decent, moral, thinking people. Hitler didn't take over Germany; Germany, and all the rest of us who made Germany what it was, produced Hitler. It's the people who decide what they want. They've *got* what they want, that's what is so intolerable to face. We can't bring ourselves to believe it. They have to change so they want something better; we have to keep at them, any way we can get to them. My chance to do it is here. Every fundamentalist, racist, closed-minded, opportunistic clod who comes along, passing briefly through this place, is an opportunity." He grinned. "I keep telling myself."

I felt like applauding; it was the kind of speech that called for some response. Then he said, "Rhetoric, all bullshit rhetoric," and I couldn't figure out whether he really meant what he said or had just let his words run away with him.

I saw his eyes shift and followed his glance. There was a girl walking around, handing leaflets to people sitting on the lawn. A group of black students glanced at the leaflet, then pushed it back at her and turned away. I heard one of them say "Honkie protest!" and laugh. The girl moved toward a group of white students on the oppposite side of the concrete path, but they wouldn't even look at the leaflet.

One of them said loudly, "None of that communist trash." Then they all laughed.

By the time the girl reached us, I felt so sorry for her that I took a leaflet. Dan took one too, glanced at it and said, "Good girl. Thanks."

The leaflet announced an antiwar march Friday night, March 2, in Berkeley. It'll leave from the campus and go all the way to the Oakland naval station.

"Are you going?" asked Dan.

"No, of course not."

"What do you mean, of course not?"

"Well, I'm against the war, but I don't think things like this accomplish anything."

"What makes you say that?"

"What good does it do to make a fool of yourself, marching down the street?"

"Is that what you're afraid of—making a fool of yourself?"

"I didn't say that!" He made me so mad, the way he kept grinning at me and stroking his beard. "It's just . . . "

"Just what?"

"Well, if I could be sure that it would do some good . . . "

"Oh. What are you sure of? What do you do whose effects you're absolutely certain of?"

"You said yourself that, with all the demonstrations of the past few years, Negroes were worse off than ever. There's an example of what marching and demonstrating do."

"Sure, but they might be still worse off if they hadn't demonstrated. Who knows? You're evading my question."

"What question?"

He grinned again and spoke slowly. "What do you do that you are absolutely sure will have good effects?"

"Well . . . "

"Aside from brushing your teeth, and—"

116

"All right, all right. I'll agree, we can't be sure about the effects of anything we do, so if we believe in something we ought to do whatever we can. Is that what you want me to say?"

"Why so hostile?"

"I'm not hostile!"

"Then stop yelling."

"I'm not"—I lowered my voice—"yelling." I pulled the leaflet over and put it between us. "Look at some of the groups that are sponsoring this. You know those are communist groups." He didn't answer. He seemed to be waiting for me to go on. "I suppose you think it's all right to join in this with communists. But if you do, everyone just says you're a communist too."

"Is that what you're afraid of?"

"I'm not afraid. I just don't think it's a good idea."

"Okay." He was quiet then, but I couldn't seem to stop talking. Mostly I talked about hotheaded kids who can only think of dramatic things like marching and demonstrating, and about the psychological and political misfits who march in protests against anything at all. I got more and more angry, but Dan didn't tell me to stop shouting; he just listened without commenting. Soon it was time for my anthro class, so I left.

Later

I can't get it out of my mind.

I'm still angry. Why? Nobody insulted me or hurt me. The only thing that happened was that I was invited to demonstrate and then invited to say why I wouldn't. Maybe if I list all the objections to demonstrating, I'll be clearer in my mind about it.

117

1. Demonstrations don't do any good.

I guess Dan demolished that one. There are a lot of acts which we can say surely, in certain conditions, are bad or good, but there are a lot more about which we can't be sure. And if we never did anything but what we were sure would be effective, we'd never do anything at all.

2. Communists, drug takers, freaks, misfits are in it.

I can't help that. If communists are against murder, I'm not going to come out in favor of it, just to be different from them.

3. I'm afraid.

Afraid of looking silly. Afraid a heckler will throw something at me. Afraid I'll be called a communist and my neighbors will point at me. Or that I'll want to teach some day and won't be able to get a job. Afraid a policeman will hit me. Afraid I'll be arrested and disgraced. This is getting wild—none of these things is going to happen, except that I may feel like a fool. So maybe it's just the fear of looking foolish and feeling ashamed. I ought to feel more ashamed of feeling that way. Lavinia had more pride than that; it never occurred to her to worry about what people would think.

4. Joe.

Tuesday, February 21

Laura talked about nothing but the rallies at Cal, organizational meetings for the march.

Friday, February 24

A lot in the newspapers about the coming aemonstration. It seems that Oakland denied the march organizers a parade permit, which means they can't go into Oakland. Dan says this is completely illegal, but by the time it gets to a court it'll be too late. "But what those idiots don't realize is they probably are tripling the amount of people in the march. I know plenty of people who'll go just to prove the Oakland police don't have a right to tell them not to."

Tonight was the first time we—Joe and I—ever discussed a demonstration. We were driving to my parents' house when Lulu asked about it. I tried to explain, at least what I knew about it and what Dan had said about the constitutional issues involved. Before I was through, I could see that she had lost interest and had her transistor radio glued to her ear again. My voice trailed off into silence. Joe hadn't said anything at all. I looked at him. He still said nothing, just started whistling under his breath as if he were a million miles away.

But he wasn't. There was a silent dialogue going on between us. He was saying, I know you want to go to that march. And I won't tell you not to, because I never tell you what to do. But I don't want you to go.

And I was saying, I'm not sure whether I want to or not. I'd like to talk about it, but I can see how upset you are already at what little talking I've done. I know if I say I want to go you won't stop me, but you'll feel hurt because I'm doing something that I know you don't want me to do, even if you won't say so.

And he was saying, I'm an easygoing fellow and not the kind who tells his wife what to do.

And I was saying, And because you're so easygoing I don't want to hurt your feelings.

And he was saying, My whistling shows I've forgotten all about it because it's not important, and things will be so much better if you just forget about it too. It's not worth all this thinking and troubling. Relax, be happy, take it easy.

119

And then he wasn't saying anything, even silently, and I was all alone and feeling stupid to be so obsessive about a stupid demonstration that I don't want to attend anyway.

Pretty soon I began to hum along with his whistling. He turned and smiled at me and I smiled back. I felt I'd narrowly escaped causing unnecessary tension again. After all, I've got things pretty well organized now. In school I can have all the intellectual stimulation I want, all the talk about issues I need. But I must leave all that in school, not bring it home with me. It's like good housekeeping—a place for everything, and everything in its place. (I used to go crazy when my mother said that to me.)

Saturday, February 25

Today I'm thirty-five years old. A very important birthday. It's halfway. I have another half of my life to live. Until recently life was over at thirty-five—in some parts of the world it still is. But I've been handed the equivalent of another lifetime, like a second chance.

How did I spend the first lifetime? Doing nothing. That's not quite right. I had to grow. And I produced a child, and all that's a lot of work and takes a lot of time, so the first thirty-five years weren't a total loss. But that's all I did. Now I have this second lifetime, and I'm grown up, and so is my child, almost.

That first lifetime was decided for me by other people, or outside forces. But I have to make the second one—make it up as I go along.

Six months ago I believed this second half of life would be like a prison sentence, locked up in life with nothing to do. But now I know that just because no one has any "use" for me, no one has any plan for me, no one has taken account of my presence because I'm invisible,—well, that's not such a tragedy. Maybe it's a form of freedom. Maybe I have to decide what to make of the rest of this life. I can make it up day by day, not like a cake by the recipe but like making a statue come out of a rock by chipping at it. No one knows what statue is hidden in the rock. So no one should tell me how to do it. I don't even know what's there. That's great. That's frightening too.

Joe says get all dressed up and be ready at seven for a birthday surprise. I guess he's taking me nightclubbing again.

Tuesday, February 28

Again, Laura could talk about nothing but the peace march. She suggested we meet and march together; she just assumed I was going. I said I wasn't sure. Then I was silent, looking into my coffee cup and thinking. When I looked up, Laura was looking at me, and I could see she understood. I asked if the children were going along and she said, "Probably not. Lately they generally refuse to go anywhere with me."

I guess we all have our problems.

Wednesday, February 29 (why is it called Leap Year?)

Today Dan passed out dittoed copies of "The Man with the Hoe." Then he said, "How many of you have ever seen this poem before?" I raised my hand. Then I looked around the room. I was the only person with my hand up. I started to say something, but I could see Dan wanted to read it first. He took us through the poem, line by line, word by word.

He's wonderful at that, getting at all that's there, more than you ever think could be there. It took almost the whole hour, and by the time he finished I was really excited.

"It's not the same poem I remember. It's different, stronger somehow."

"It's the same. Maybe you're different."

"Who wrote it?" asked a girl. "You didn't put down the poet's name."

"Who do you think wrote it?" Dan waved at me to be quiet.

"Has it been translated from another language?"

"No, it's American," Dan said.

There was a silence. "Revolutionary," said a boy. "Is the poet black?"

"No."

It went on like that, a guessing game, until there was no more time and Dan said, "Okay, Mrs. Price, want to tell the class how you happen to know this poem?"

"Why, it's an American classic," I said. "We all had to memorize it when I was in school. Edwin Markham. In the front of my sixth grade classroom was a reproduction of the painting that inspired it. I thought everyone knew the poem. It must have been in three of the books I used in school."

"You mean it's that old?" said one girl.

I winced but Dan just nodded and grinned. "Modern, isn't it? Lines like 'When whirlwinds of rebellion shake all shores,' and the warning to 'masters, lords and rulers in all lands.' The waking up, the rising up of the dumb man with the hoe, no longer content to be 'brother to the ox.' It's what's happening. So how come the poem isn't in the schoolbooks anymore. How come none of you had to memorize it in school?"

A girl in the back row giggled. "It sounds subversive. You

122

know, it's the kind of thing my father would say, 'What kind of commie propaganda you bringing home now?'" Everyone laughed.

"When that poem was written," Dan said, "it was an indictment of European imperialism. Remember the statue of liberty—'Give me your tired, your poor.' The man with the hoe came here, we are the children of the man with the hoe—we identified with him. But"—Dan leaned back against the desk—"obviously we no longer identify with him. Otherwise the poem wouldn't suddenly stop being a classic, not because it's dated and irrelevant, but because— can it be that the accusing finger of the man with the hoe no longer points so clearly at Europe? How embarrassing. Can't allow that in the kids' books! Maybe it isn't really an American poem anymore. Maybe some starving peasant in South America, working for a U.S.-controlled company, is carrying around a copy of it; maybe it's the first thing he'll learn to read as soon as he's literate. Maybe he doesn't have to learn to read it—it's his anyway; unknown and unread, it's still his. Not ours anymore." Then he mumbled something that sounded like "Way things are going never will be again." He slumped a little against the desk. "We're overtime. What're you hanging around for? That's all today." And he shuffled out of the room.

For a moment, no one moved. Then, a nervous giggle and the spell was broken, the mood shattered. But not for me.

Not for me.

Friday, no, I guess Saturday morning, 1 a.m., March 3

I stood on the corner of Bancroft and Elsworth for about twenty minutes. I could hear the loudspeakers up on the university campus. People in twos and threes, sometimes in

123

larger groups, brushed past me, going toward the sound of the loudspeakers. It was already dark. I didn't know what to do or even why I had come. Finally I started to walk, following the movement of larger and larger groups on both sides of the street, walking toward the sound of voices and applause, toward the lower plaza of the campus where the marchers would assemble.

The air was cold and damp, and most people had covered their heads with scarves or knitted caps. It was hard to see faces.

But on the campus the faces were all lit up by the bright lights above the playing field where the speeches were still going on. The faces looked happy, or at least calm and content. I don't know what I expected, but not so many smiles. People walked back and forth to keep warm and, I suppose, to look for familiar faces. The field was so crowded that I couldn't walk without brushing against people who constantly murmured, "Pardon me," or who just smiled as I brushed past. That was the first thing I noticed. I'd never been in a crowd of people who seemed so—is friendly the word? Not really, because no one spoke to me or tried to strike up an acquaintance. They were easy, relaxed, gentle. I can only think of the word "happy," and I know that's not right. I don't know a word to describe them. I don't think they were a special kind of people—they were just people. But maybe for tonight they had left behind their pettiness and discontent with the small details of life. They were all there for the same purpose, and each was glad that all the others were along. The larger the crowd, the more happy and polite they became, because each addition was more support and more reassurance. I was amazed. I didn't think there could be that many people against the war in the whole country.

The speakers stood on a platform surrounded by a few

124

hundred people who stood still, listening. But beyond that cluster, many hundreds more walked back and forth, searching the faces of others, talking to friends, stopping occasionally to cock an ear toward the speakers' platform. Beyond them, on the edges of the moving crowd, were tables, a ring of tables labeled by various organizations, selling buttons and pamphlets and books. I went up close to the tables titled for communist groups. The young girls sitting behind them looked exactly like all the other young girls. Some boys walked around handing out leaflets; others carried cans, collecting money. A hot-dog stand was almost unidentifiable behind the mob that surrounded it. It was like a carnival, yet not like one. Here the atmosphere was warmer, closer.

I'd thought I might feel uncomfortable, but I didn't. I was completely anonymous—there was no chance of being seen by my family or neighbors; they wouldn't have been caught dead there. And there was the feeling of closeness. Everyone who was there belonged—the act of coming there made a person unquestionably a part of it all.

Inwardly I didn't quite feel a part of it. I didn't see how I could go through with it, especially alone—how I could actually get out into the street and march along with people looking at me, let alone heckling me. I couldn't do it, that was all, but maybe I could watch—and breathe in some of this unexpectedly good air, this free air. Was it the absence of fear that made the air so good?

Then people were moving out to the street, and I heard the speaker calling for monitors, the young people with ragged orange armbands. I followed one of them, knowing she would take me to where the march would start, where I could join spectators on the sidewalk and then decide what to do next.

The intersection at Bancroft and Telegraph was a thick

mass of people, with policemen trying to clear a path for the escape of a couple of cars that had made the mistake of coming down Bancroft. The police were keeping all the people on the sidewalk and wouldn't let me cross the street. Finally I walked down Bancroft, threading my way through the crowds, went around the block and came up to Telegraph one block below the starting point of the march. The sidewalks were full of people. A boy crouched near a lamppost, beating on a long drum. A tall, long-haired boy making soft, reedy noises on wooden pipes was walking by. He stopped and stood leaning against the lamppost above the drummer and began improvising a melody to the rhythm of the drum. The drummer nodded without looking up. After a while the piper moved on. Then I saw people moving toward the curb and turning their heads toward the campus. It was starting. I moved forward and stood behind a brown-suited Negro policeman.

First came a red truck full of sound equipment. One boy drove, one sat with him in the cab and another hung on outside. Behind the red slats fencing the truck bed, young boys and girls stood, three or four of them, looking out at the people who looked at them from the curb. The only older person on the truck was a fat, bearded man in white shirt and pants. He was shaking bells and chanting.

"Who's that?" someone behind me said.

"Poet."

"What's he doing?"

"Getting rid of evil spirits, I think."

"But will it work on the Oakland cops?" I heard laughter.

About twenty feet behind the truck came the first line of marchers, five abreast, keeping to the right side of the street near the curb. They were all boys, one of them black. He looked at the Negro policeman and said, "Brother, what you doing in that uniform?" A few people laughed, including the policeman.

I began to look around at the people on the sidewalk, wondering why they were there. Most of them didn't look hostile, and I saw one of them move off the curb and join the march, then another and another. There were yells, "Hey, Jim" and "Lucy, wait up," as people recognized friends and moved into the march. I guess there were many people like me who had come alone and were looking for a familiar face before they joined in. I could wait until I saw someone I knew—that was one way of postponing action indefinitely.

In the meantime I began to enjoy watching the people go by, all kinds of people, moving in all kinds of ways and with all kinds of expressions on their faces. There were plenty of young people dripping with beads and hair, but even more families, middle-aged fathers and mothers with groups of youngsters who must have been their own children and those of their friends. A lot of older women alone, open-faced, matter-of-fact, intelligent-looking women. There were some quite old people, two or three in wheelchairs. Some of them talked among themselves, as if they were taking a casual stroll. Others walked silently, with a look of determination. A few of the younger people stared defiantly at those of us lining the curb. One little blonde girl (straight hair down to her hips) kept swinging her arms in a gathering gesture and saying to the spectators, "Come on, come on, what are you doing out there, come on along!" Most of the marchers didn't often look at the spectators and when they did, turned away quickly. There was a touch of embarrassment in it for most people. That comforted me. They seemed to feel just as I would in their places.

I began to envy them. I leaned over the curb, longing to step off and join them, but I could not quite do it. I began walking along the sidewalk, moving with the march but not in it, afraid to join it but wanting to be part of it. There were others doing the same thing, the ambivalent, drawn along the edges as if by a magnet.

I stopped behind some men who were arguing loudly. "Bunch of cowards, send them to Russia; go to China, traitors, draft dodgers!" one of them kept yelling.

"If you're so hot for this war," said the man next to him, "why aren't you over there? They'll take volunteers—even your age." A few people laughed, and the first man looked around as if he wanted to hit someone. Then he turned to me, sizing me up quickly and evidently deciding I was respectable.

"What do you think, lady, it's a disgrace, isn't it, what this country has come to?"

"Yes," I said. "I think it is."

Then I took a deep breath and stepped off the curb.

The little blonde girl was coming by again, and she cried, "Peace!" as her arm swept me into a place next to her. Then she floated off again, still exhorting people to join.

My first feeling as I walked along was fear, a deep, cold blast of panic chilling my insides while I asked myself, What are you doing, you idiot? Now you've done it, stupid!

Done what?

Gotten out in the middle of the street to make a fool of yourself as publicly as possible. Why are you doing this?

Because I'm against the war.

Why?

I'm not sure. I never even thought about it until a couple of months ago. I still don't know much about it. But I think it's wrong.

And you're marching in the street because you tried

everything else—letter to your congressman, etcetera—and none of it worked?

No, I didn't try anything else.

Nothing else?

No.

Never written a letter? Never worked to elect someone who'd change things? Never even licked a stamp?

Never.

Oh, those things weren't dramatic enough?

No, it wasn't that, it was just that I never thought much about such things.

Never thought. What makes you think you're thinking now?

I kept looking at the ground. I couldn't seem to raise my eyes; I just watched my own feet taking slow steps forward. Then I thought, Don't walk like you're ashamed of yourself. Straighten up, raise your head, look people in the eye. Now's no time to look sheepish. I raised my head and looked as steadily as I could at the people lining the streets. The faces were friendly, a little uncertain, a little sheepish as I looked at them, and a little envious. They were out, and I was in.

Someone handed me a candle and a paper cup. A man walking beside me showed me how to light the candle, drop a bit of wax in the bottom of the cup and make the candle stand up in the cup. I felt better carrying the candle. It seemed to add dignity to our shuffling along, bunching up behind red traffic lights, being herded close to the curb by monitors.

I noticed men running back and forth along our sides, snapping pictures as fast as they could. They didn't look like newspaper men, and they seemed to be photographing everyone and everything as fast as they could. The man next to me shrugged toward one of them. "You are now in the files of the F.B.I." I started turning away whenever I saw one of the men—there must have been dozens of them—snapping pictures. But then I saw it was futile and tried to ignore them.

"Candles out. Candles out," said a monitor. "We didn't issue those candles. Candles out."

"But I like carrying it anyway," I said.

"It lights up your face," said the man who had spoken before, "so they get a clearer picture of you."

"Don't be so paranoid," said a woman behind us.

But we all blew out our candles and walked silently for a few seconds until a girl on the end of my row said, "Nobody'd better publish a picture of me—my mother doesn't know I smoke." We all burst into laughter, a loud release that took away my tension and made me see how funny it all was. At that point I stopped feeling afraid, and a whole new mood came over me, like the feeling I first had in the crowd, but different. I felt calm and peaceful. And pure. Pure in the sense of being concentrated, free of distractions and anxieties. I felt right—not self-righteous, not smugly correct, not right while others are wrong; I don't mean that. Just right, like a piece of tile dropped into place, perfectly fitting its place in a design. And warm with closeness to the people walking beside me, not physical closeness, something more. Something I had missed all my life without knowing it existed.

The crowds along the sides of the street thinned out as Telegraph Avenue widened into a thoroughfare and cars went by, slowing down briefly to look at us, then speeding up again. Now it was just a cold, dark walk on the side of the street near the gutter. We moved slowly. I could hear the sound truck up ahead but couldn't make out the words. I saw some people leaving the march and hurrying along the sidewalks, probably to rejoin it nearer the front. I decided to do the same thing. As I reached the sidewalk I looked back toward the campus. As far as I could see there were more and more coming, five abreast and thickly crowded.

I went back into the ranks of marchers about seven rows from the front.

"You don't think they'll let us through?"

"Hell, no, they'll stop us at the Oakland line. They say there's a hundred police up there."

"They can't do that, we got a right—"

"They still going to crack your head. Then three months from now some judge'll say you had a right. But you still got a cracked head."

"Anyone hits me going to get hit back, cop or no cop."

"I'm not afraid."

I am, I thought. I almost ran away then. I was still only a few blocks from my car and could have been home within a few minutes. I moved back onto the sidewalk, that step up the curb now separating me again from the demonstrators. I could be just a spectator, or an uninterested woman merely walking to her car. I moved toward a side street, but then I stopped and looked back. I didn't want to leave yet. People were starting to sing, some were walking arm in arm, some were clowning and showing off for the TV cameras. But underneath was a hum of fear as we got nearer to the Oakland line. Everyone had read the newspaper. Everyone knew the police would be waiting there. And nobody knew what would happen. I think that, except for the boys in the front, everyone felt the way I did.

I decided to move ahead, as I had before. I could walk on the sidewalk, up to the Oakland line, and see what was there. If it looked dangerous, I would turn off and go to my car. If not, I could rejoin the march. I began to walk fast, past the first line of marchers, past the red sound truck, past the television car moving slowly in front with cameramen perched on the trunk and facing back toward the marchers. I thought there would be fewer people up ahead, but the streets and sidewalks were becoming more and more crowded. After another block, I was moving from one side to the other, getting nowhere, picking my way around people on the sidewalk who were looking into the street. The street was packed with what looked like hundreds of boys—I couldn't figure out what they were doing there—just milling around. Finally I could hardly move at all, in any direction. I managed to get to the corner, went down a side street, then along a parallel street for two blocks; then I was in Oakland, and I turned back up toward Telegraph Avenue, beyond the Oakland line.

I came up behind the Oakland policemen, standing three deep in a row which stretched across the street where the sign said ENTERING OAKLAND, forming a human barrier. They stood with their hands behind their backs, grasping clubs and facing toward Berkeley. I could see nothing beyond those broad backs. All around me people were hanging out of windows. Some boys had climbed poles and clung, facing Berkeley. Others stood on top of cars. Everything was quite still as everyone watched.

"What's happening?" I asked.

"Fighting, I think," someone said.

Who fighting who? The police were just standing there, and the marchers were still two blocks back. I went up behind the police, but twenty feet from them I was stopped by a policeman who was walking back and forth, keeping everyone clear of the backs of the police.

"What's going on, officer?" I asked, with my most respectable suburban matron's manner. But he just gave me a disgusted look and waved me back. I didn't fool him. If I were a respectable suburban matron, his look said, I'd be home where I belonged.

I moved back again, looking at the rows of blue-shirted backs, unable to see a thing past them. Finally I saw someone slide down from the hood of a parked truck. I took off my shoes, scrambled up on it and stood up.

For a full block beyond the rows of policeman, the street was thick with boys and men. Some of them carried sticks, and others held objects in their hands that I couldn't see. They too faced toward Berkeley, toward the red truck which had stopped in the intersection just beyond them, facing them. Down nearer to the truck I saw hands raised as if the boys were waving or throwing things. All were shouting. Beyond the truck I saw the crowds of marchers, stopped and spreading out behind the truck, some shouting back. The police stood in a stolid line. The TV cameras had vanished.

I finally understood what was happening. Hundreds of boys and men, hecklers, filled the streets between the marchers and the police. The police watched them throwing things at the marchers but did nothing. They would let these rowdies attack the marchers. Their only concern was to hold the Oakland line. Boys were rushing toward the truck, throwing things and waving long sticks. The blue line never wavered. I could hear the sound truck now. "Hey, you guys, don't you know we're doing this for you?" This only brought on an angry shout and more throwing.

Then the sound truck began addressing the marchers. "We're going to turn. We're turning off." The roar from the front rows was as angry as the one that had come from the hecklers. The loudspeaker went on. "I don't care what you call me. You may be all ready for a fight, but we've got

133

thousands of people behind us there, people who never hit the streets before; they're still leaving the campus. Still leaving the campus! You want a bloody mess or you want to build a movement? Build a movement? Turn off. This march is turning off here. If you cannot turn off here, you are no longer a part of this march. Turn. Turn off here. Turn." Then I could hear the poet chanting into the microphone.

The sound truck stayed where it was, repeating its message to turn off, shielding the marchers from the hecklers who were now moving on them. "All monitors up front. The march will turn off here. All monitors up front." The orange-armbanded boys and girls formed a line across the street, holding hands, to hold off the hecklers. They made a strange contrast to the blue line. I saw the little blonde girl in the midst of the line, her arms stretched outward in a position of crucifixion. A young heckler ran toward her and raised a club. "We love you!" she yelled, and I held my breath as he shook the club over her head, but he did not bring it down and finally walked off, swearing and shaking his club at the line of monitors.

I got down from the truck and walked back around the block, retracing my steps until I could rejoin the march, now turning west, down a dark side street, where windows opened and black faces appeared. All tension was gone. Even ranks had loosened, and marchers spread out, covering the entire street and sidewalks.

"Ella?"

I jumped at the sound of my name. It was Laura. She was smiling and said, "If I'd known you were coming . . . "

"I didn't decide until the last minute."

"You alone?"

"Yes."

She put her arm through mine and we stepped back into

the march together, walking along, saying nothing. Someone started singing "We Shall Overcome." Others joined in. Everyone sang softly, but the hundreds of soft voices combined filled the dark air. Timidly, I joined too, humming along, feeling again the closeness, the clear, pure rightness.

Then Laura laughed. "I was just wondering what the neighbors would say if they saw us now. Well, they won't be my neighbors much longer. The house is sold."

"I'm going to miss you," I said.

"Why? Berkeley's not that far away."

"It's light-years away!"

She laughed. "But only a few miles. We'll still be friends."

Then we were quiet again until we reached the civic center where the march broke up. Laura's car was parked nearby. She drove me to my car, and we parted with a laugh and a peace sign, like the old victory sign Winston Churchill used to give.

I was back home by eleven.

Joe asked, "How was the movie?"

And I answered, "A little dull. I can't think why Dan assigned it." I was surprised at how normal my voice sounded.

Then we went to bed, and I waited until Joe fell asleep so that I could write all this down before I forget. The feeling is already slipping away, but even if I can't feel it anymore, I want to try to remember it.

Notebook

NUMBER FOUR

Sunday, March 4

And now the reaction has set in, like a hangover. The peace march did something to me, changed me. I'm not the same person anymore. Why?

It was an act, not a thought, not an idea safely written down in a notebook and tucked away in the drawer. An act. Now I begin to understand the importance of moving the body, walking from here to there or even just standing—maybe that's why we call taking a position "standing for something."

And so I wrote it all down, went to sleep and woke up behind enemy lines again.

I don't mean that. It's guilt. Every time I look at Joe I feel guilty because I lied to him.

Lulu told us some of her football boy friends phoned and said they went to Berkeley Friday night and "threw eggs at the commies."

And she and Joe laughed. But they didn't mean anything.
They just weren't thinking.

Tuesday, March 6

I thought it might help to talk to Laura. But I found her in
terrible shape again. Her daughter was picked up yesterday
for shoplifting. Laura had to go to the police station to get
her and will have to appear in court. The girl showed not a
sign of remorse. When Laura asked her why, she said, "I've
been ever so depressed since Daddy left."

Laura said, "But she timed it. She saw how high I was
after the march. She had to bring me down." I asked if she'd
called her ex-husband. "Right away. All I got was a cursing
tirade. He refused to go to the police station. But as soon as I
got her home, he was on the phone, all sweetness and
sympathy. By the time she hung up, she was worse than
ever."

"What about your family? Isn't there anyone who could
talk to her, make her see what she's doing?"

"My maiden name was Locatelli. Does that tell you
anything? My family is so shocked at having a divorced
woman in it that they hardly speak to me. They wouldn't be
a bit surprised to hear that my daughter has turned to a life
of crime." She managed to smile.

I tried to sympathize. "Lulu loves Joe so much, I can
imagine how she'd act if we ever split up." There was a
silence as Laura looked at me.

"Don't," she said.

I laughed. "Don't what?" She just looked at me. I laughed
again, but the sound was hollow. Laura walked into the
front room and I followed her. There were packing boxes all

140

over; books and clothes covered all the chairs. "When are you moving?"

"Next week." She sat down on the floor and waited until I sat down too. "You're where I was a few years ago." I started to protest, but she waved me silent. "Don't make the same mistakes I did.

"When I reached the point where my husband couldn't humiliate me anymore with his infidelity, when he began to interfere with my efforts to develop, to find some satisfaction—I thought, I've already learned to live without a husband. A divorce won't make much of a change. He'll just be officially gone, instead of unofficially, and I'll be free to do what I want—maybe even free to find someone else.

"I was wrong. First of all, the children. The shoplifting incident is just one in a long list of things my daughter has done—not just done but got caught at. She always gets caught. That's the real object, you see: to keep me in a state where each time the phone rings I'm not sure if it's the school saying she's not there, or the girl friend she said she was staying overnight with—who hasn't seen her for a week—or a parent saying my daughter gave her daughter a marijuana cigarette, or . . . it's a reign of terror. And wherever I turn I find blame, not help.

"Don't say it. I know you're going to ask if I've gotten professional help. Parasites, that's what they are—the psychiatrists, family counselors, all of them—trotting out their little labels and clichés: 'increase communication with your children' and all that. Let me tell you something. If there's something wrong with you and you go to a psychiatrist, he'll say, Let's find out what's wrong with you. But if there's something wrong with your children and you go to a psychiatrist, he'll still ask, What's wrong with *you?*

141

"Kids are very smart. They catch on right away. Here's a chance for a double punishment of me. So they get into trouble (or, like Teddy, they're just beastly to me) and then we go to one of these professionals—and I get another dose of punishment, which I have to pay for!"

She was standing up now, walking back and forth. Her long strides covered the width of the room in three or four moves; she was like a caged animal pacing.

"Maybe your older son could talk to them."

She laughed. It was the most awful, choked, sick laugh I ever heard. "Marty," she said. "Handsome, bright Marty. He got a scholarship to Stanford for next fall, did I tell you?" She stood still and faced me. "Shortly after my separation Marty confided to me that he believed himself to be homosexual. He swore me to secrecy; I was the only person he told, and of course I mustn't tell his father. *He* wouldn't understand. And he asked for help. I sent him to a psychiatrist. For the past two years he's gone to him. I borrowed money on the house. The sale will just cover the loans. That few thousand dollars was all I had. But that loss wasn't the worst thing. The worst was *my* occasional session with his psychiatrist, because, of course, if a boy is homosexual, we all know whose fault it is, don't we?

"And what's Marty gained? A lot of jargon. He's very glib. His recent stance is that homosexuality is perfectly natural. However, at the same time he says it's my fault. Pointing out the contradiction in these two statements doesn't penetrate his armor of—of virtue, I guess I'd call it. He's extraordinarily self-righteous.

"Last month I told him, The money's all gone; you'll have to stop therapy. He didn't say a word. A few days later he joined the gay liberation movement. He's trying desperately

142

to get his name in the papers. Having exhausted financial punishment, he's found something else. Can you imagine the reaction of the neighbors? He was furious when I told him we'd found a buyer and were moving—he hoped I'd still be here when he became a celebrity."

"Have you challenged him? Told him you think he's doing it to spite you?"

"Anything I say proves that I'm a reactionary who discriminates against nonconformity. But in the back of my mind, I know, I know that whatever other factors operate in this, my son has chosen this *at least partly* as an ingenious method of torturing me. But no one believes that. If I say it, it stands as proof of my paranoia, my neuroticism—proof that I did ruin my children."

She sagged at the shoulders and sat down on the floor again. "But it can't last forever. It'll all play itself out sooner or later. I tell myself, If I just wait, and do my best, and be a decent person, sooner or later my children will see that I *am* a decent person. Maybe it'll happen tomorrow, or next week. And I will have won. And if we're lucky, they won't have damaged themselves too much by then."

She sat there very quietly, breathing deeply, as if she'd run a long way. I tried to think of something to say, but I couldn't. I thought she was through, but then she took a deep breath, and I saw that she was starting again.

"Let me give you some other facts on the single life. I was ready to start fresh, make new friends. I was naïve. Wives make social arrangements—and wives don't invite single woman to their homes. The few couples we know dropped me completely.

"No, not completely." She swallowed. "In the past two years, of every couple we knew, some of them on this block, the couple has dropped me—but the husband hasn't. Every one of them has made a pass. Late at night, or on a Saturday afternoon—when he's supposed to be out at the hardware store, I guess—one of them appears, on some flimsy excuse. Usually drunk. And they all act the same, as if they're doing me a favor, or as if they're tourists in a foreign country, where no one who counts will ever hear of their behavior.

"And here's the worst part. At first I acted outraged and angry. But after a while, when you've been alone long enough—when the only adult who calls, who speaks to you at all, who acknowledges your existence, drops in looking sad and sheepish and sorry and almost as miserable as you are and nudges you toward the bedroom—quite often, you don't resist anymore." I must have had a terrible look on my face, because she said, "Don't worry, your husband wasn't one of them."

"But, Laura, surely there are lots of single people, with so much divorce. . . . "

"I could spend hours telling you about that jungle. It's unimaginable. The men are . . . God, the naked sickness of the—" She shook her head. "I've met some nice women, but single women my age always seem to be looking over their shoulder for a man to rescue them from this . . . this ghetto, this awful status. The loneliness—after the first year I thought it would get better, but it gets worse.

"Finally"—her voice was deeper and stronger now, as though talking had relieved her—"there are the more mundane problems, like money. And working part-time and going to school and keeping house and . . . I've got twice the work of a married woman and none of the advantages. When I finally get my degree I'll be well over forty, and God knows if I'll be able to get a better job even with a degree."

144

For a few minutes we both sat silently. I couldn't think what to say, and she didn't seem to expect me to.

"I don't know what your situation is. I'm not asking; I'm just guessing. But for what it's worth, if I had it to do all over again, I wouldn't, not this way."

"You wouldn't have divorced?"

"Not until I had someone else to go to. I know that must shock you. It would have shocked me a while ago. It would have meant doing what my husband did—well, not quite—but it would have meant cheating. I'd have called it cheating. But I've learned a lot since then. I've seen the underside of a lot of marriages, seen people sending out these feelers, these trials—affairs that usually fall apart but sometimes don't. I've met a lot of divorced people, and in almost every case the one who ended the marriage had already prepared the territory ahead, had someone. That's what a lot of these married men do—play around for years, never losing the nice domestic nest to come home to, unless and until they find something better. Then, and not until then, they walk out."

"And that's what you'd have done."

"If I had, I'd have avoided all this wear and tear—emotional and financial. Why, if I met a nice man now I probably wouldn't know how to act. I'm so defensive and hostile and afraid and tired and . . . "

Her voice trailed off and the lines deepened in her face again. She looked so defeated that I didn't say what I was thinking—that I couldn't be that calculating, that I couldn't live with a man that way from day to day, coldly making plans, looking for a new husband before giving up the conveniences afforded by the old one. And I like to think that she couldn't be that way either. I felt sorry for her, but I

145

like her so much, and I don't think I could like her if she were like that.

Tonight Joe and I had a long talk. I was going to tell him about the peace march. After the second martini, I was sure I could. But instead we talked about Laura. I told him about her problems. We both said how sorry we were. And had another drink. And pitied her. And had another drink.

Now I feel guilty—no, worse. I feel dirty. We kept saying "poor Laura," and the more we said it, the more more we used her misery—to achieve an intimacy that we lack? There was something cannibalistic about it. I feel sick.

Monday, March 12

"Somehow I feel that the peace march is the most real thing that's ever happened to me."

Of course, it was Dan I said that to—who else is there? He only looked puzzled, said that demonstrations were becoming so routine that he attended them more out of habit than anything else.

I tried to describe how I felt, why, from the moment I stepped off the curb, something—happened—as if I were stepping up to a different level of experience.

As I saw him smiling more and more broadly, I began to feel like a fool and stopped.

"No, no, go on! I love to watch you react to things. There's something very fresh, young—something new in your way of responding to . . . " Then he sort of cleared his throat and said, "Well, you've certainly had a lot to talk about this week."

146

"I don't dare even mention it!" I blurted.

Then all at once I was in tears, telling him everything. I must have gone on pouring it out for an hour. I kept repeating phrases like "behind enemy lines."

When I was all through, he sank back, all wrinkled up in his chair, and stared at his hands.

"Change is mysterious, isn't it? Some people change very slowly, adding things to a basically unchanging temperament. Their change is like the slow laying down of sediment. Or like slow erosion, shaping patterns that get deeper, more pronounced.

"Then there are earthquakes, the sudden, shaking realignment of material. That's you. Your change . . . was volcanic. Like a quiet mound. still and silent for years until the moment comes when the pressures have built up and then—bang!" He clapped his hands together, swinging them upward as if to imitate an eruption. I think he was trying to make me laugh. "You even look different. You've got a real face now."

"That's fine," I told him quietly, "but it doesn't really help me much with—"

"When one person changes, a lot of other things change, have to change." I sat waiting for him to give me some advice, but he only grinned. "I don't have any answers. All I'm good at is raising questions."

"That's very easy for you to say! You opened up all kinds of things; you played a big role in this. And now all you have to say is—" I was appalled at the sound of my own voice. What was wrong with me? I got up and ran out.

Now where am I? More guilty than ever for saying these things to Dan about my personal life, about Joe. And after lashing out at him that way, I've probably lost the last friend I had, the only person left that I could talk to.

147

Friday, March 16

It's all right. I went Dan's office, acting as if I had a question about the assignment, and he acted as if nothing had happened.

Sunday, March 18

Put away all books for this weekend, trying to devote my time entirely to Joe. (Lulu's always off with her friends.) One more week till Easter vacation.

Friday, March 23

Oh, my God.

If I write it down will I know what's happening?

Last day before vacation. Campus quiet.

Dan and I sitting his office correcting my last paper. Laughing. Arguing.

"What time is it?" he said, and reached for my watch. He clasped my wrist to turn up the watch face, and I felt something like a hot pain flash from the point of his touch through my body—to my womb. It felt like that. I must have reacted. Something must have shown in my face. He moved his eyes from my watch to my face. His grip tightened and he pulled.

I tried to pull my hand back. He held on. I stood up. My purse fell from my lap and spilled things all over the floor. We both dropped to the floor. I started picking things up. He just watched me. I stuffed everything into the purse, pulled open the door and left. He was still crouched on the floor, watching me go. I ran all the way down the hall, out of the building, down the slope to the parking lot.

I had to sit in the car for a minute. I was dizzy and hot. I felt as if I must give off a steady, hard heat, like a blush rising continually from my feet to my head. I could feel each of my sex organs—my vagina ached, my womb churned, my nipples tingled. They still do when I think about it as I write this down. Like an animal in heat. Disgusting. But I don't feel disgusted.

I drove home very slowly and carefully, feeling—this is crazy—feeling as if I gave off enough power to move the car myself.

I've been lying on the bed for a long time trying to figure out what happened. I feel as if I have a fever, but my temperature is normal. I look in the mirror expecting to see that I give off sparks. Every cell of my body is alive—I can feel each one. I look at my hand, my arm, my knee and wonder what is happening that I can't see.

I've fallen in love. I'm thirty-five years old, and for the first time in my life I've fallen in love. I never understood what it meant. All the stupid songs, all the poetry, all the junk written, I understand now, I excuse it all now. It's all an attempt to explain this feeling, it's all a hope to have this feeling that I can't even describe, but that makes everything else seem pale, a substitute, a way of keeping busy in emptiness. All this sounds stupid. All right, it's stupid.

I can't do this.

I know what I have to do.

I have to tell Joe. I can do it very simply. I'll just say, "I've got a crush on my teacher, just like a young girl; isn't that silly?" And we'll laugh about it, because that's the silly sort of thing women do; aren't women always falling in love with a teacher or a minister or something? And I'll say, "I wanted to tell you so I wouldn't make a fool of myself, and if you know about it, we'll laugh about it, kid me out of it."

Tonight when he comes home I'll tell him. We'll sit and sip drinks and I'll tell it, like a joke. Telling Joe will kill what I feel, like pulling a fish out of water, and it'll bring Joe and me together again.

2 a.m.

I didn't tell him. It can wait. I haven't done anything wrong. I have a whole week before I see Dan again. By the end of vacation the whole thing will have passed, like a bad cold. Let me just enjoy the feeling for a little while. It's not as if I plan to do anything about it.

Saturday, March 24

I can't write about anything but the way I feel. But it's hard to find the words. I struggle and write stupid things.

Every one of my senses is sharpened. Colors brighter, textures deeper. I imagine I can see the vibrations given off by colors.

Shapes are surprises. My finger explored the can opener today. And smells. Smells fill me and pass through me. Especially out of doors I inhale the world. Music is almost unbearable. Touch is not only in my fingers but in all of my body.

> To brush my arms against a bush
> > to feel wind flapping my skirt against my legs
> > > to grasp the ground with bare feet

I want to taste—not food, everything. I'm like a baby who puts everything into her mouth, not to chew or eat but to taste, to feel.

150

Last month I read an article on drugs. If this is how they make you feel, I can understand why people take them.

Sunday, March 25

All the old trite symptoms, can't eat, can't sleep, don't hear what people say—I have them all. But it's not "can't." It feels more as if I don't need food or rest. I feel so strong. But I wish I could concentrate better, so I could study. No, I don't care.

I'm not hurting anyone. I'm good company for Joe. Tonight he told his old army joke, and it seemed marvelously funny and meaningful. I'm very turned on sexually, and Joe is benefiting from that. How strange I can write this without shame.

Monday, March 26

fire		fearing		
	aching	light		
searing		shimmer		
	knowing	burn	glow	
filling		scorch	shine	
			consume	

Tuesday, March 27

Cheap love songs almost make me cry. How stupid. Last night I dreamed I had another baby. A girl.

Wednesday, March 28

Walked over to Laura's house, but she's gone. House empty. Just as well. What would I have said to her?

Thursday, March 29

Now I know why poets have used a fire image so often for love. I feel as if I must glow. I do. Joe can't keep his hands off me, and Lulu said today that I look pretty and young. (The first time she's spoken directly to me in how long?)

I'm afraid. I'm afraid to go back to school Monday. Maybe I shouldn't go back at all. I'll tell Joe I've decided to quit school. I'll tell him. I will!

Good Friday

Maybe Joe's mother is right about being Catholic. I wish I had a religion and could fast all day and meditate on the agony of God suffering for me and pray for guidance and do penance for my sins and feel absolutely sure what was a sin and what wasn't a sin, because, if you were absolutely sure, it shouldn't be too hard not to sin.

Saturday, March 31

sin
   adultery   fornication
     betrayal   liar
   cheating   immoral
                     selfish
                            dishonest

Monday, April 2

When I got to school I went straight to Dan's office. The door was open and he was sitting over a set of papers, jabbing at them with a red pen. I just walked in and stood there. The pen stopped moving. Then I saw him raise his head, but it took me a long time before I could look directly into his face. He was frowning at me.

He stretched out one leg to kick the door shut, reached out and took the books and purse from my arms and put them on the desk. Then he stood up and gripped my arms, hard, just above the elbows. He kissed me as if tasting me, first with his lips, then with his tongue along the outside of my lips, then inside my mouth.

I just stood still with my arms hanging at my sides. I think I was almost too tired to feel anything. His grip tightened and his mouth hardened on mine. He flattened his body against mine until we weren't kissing anymore but just pressing ourselves together.

There was a noise in the hall, and we both fell back into chairs. The door rattled, opened, and Dan's office partner came in. He's used to seeing me there and hardly glanced at me. I got up, picked up my things and left. We hadn't spoken a word. But it's all settled.

I made up my mind. It was almost a simple question. Is it worth the lying, the guilt, the trouble, and without any idea of what it will lead to, if anything? And the answer was a simple yes. Everything else is important, but everything else comes after this. I disapprove of myself for feeling this way, but I'm not sorry I do. If any woman had said such a thing to me last week I'd have considered her silly and selfish and cruel, if not insane. That was before I understood how it feels, and no one who hasn't felt this way can understand.

Wednesday, April 4

Today after class   stayed until the group of students around Dan gradually drifted away. We walked alone down the hall, finishing our discussion—or Dan was talking, as casually as ever, and I was listening and hearing and not hearing. When we got to his office door, he stopped in mid-sentence and said, "Where'll we go?"

"I . . . I don't know."

"Where is your car? Go down and wait in it. When you see me drive by, follow me. We'll find some place where we can talk."

I did what he said. After I had sat in the car for about ten minutes I saw his little red car. I followed him off the campus, around to the hill behind and up to the top. There was a bulldozer up there, and the top had been leveled, but off to the side there was a small clump of trees shading ivy-covered ground. He parked here, and I pulled up behind him. He got out of his car and came back to mine, and I slid across the seat as he got in behind the steering wheel. He was grinning at me, a hard grin that looked almost menacing, and he kissed me more roughly, pressing my head back and then pulling away abruptly to look at me.

Then he kissed me more softly, gently, sweeping his lips across mine in wider and wider arcs until they went across my face nearly to my ears and back. "God, you're wonderful to kiss. But so serious. Guilt? Always been a faithful wife?"

"Yes," I said. "And you?"

He looked at me severely. "No!" I kept my gaze steady on his. "Look. Maybe you want to forget the whole thing. Technically you're still a good, faithful wife, and you can go back to—"

"No, I'm not going back."

"Back where?"

"Back to—wherever I was."

He smoothed my hair back from my forehead and said,

"Remember the old fairy tales. They're all true. Sleeping Beauty. Snow White. All the evil spells are broken by love's first kiss." He shrugged. "Well, I shouldn't assume too much. Not quite love's first."

"Yes," I said. "The first."

He looked a little taken aback, even uneasy. "Weren't you in love with your husband, at first?"

"I never felt like this."

"Why'd you marry him? Because everyone gets married and raises a family and all that?"

"I don't know. I don't know why I ever did anything. I don't know why I'm doing this."

"Using me to console yourself? Doesn't he give you much attention?"

"Oh, no. Joe loves me. At least I . . . "

"You're not sure."

"I'm not sure if he ever felt like this. No. I can't believe he ever did."

"Like what?" He was grinning again, teasingly, but then as he looked into my face he began to look puzzled, as if he didn't understand whatever it was he saw there. "Well, you're using me for something." I started to protest, but he said, "Oh, it's all right. You're using me—to grow. I don't mind. I'm using you too."

"What are you using me for?"

He put his head down between my breasts, and his words were muffled but sounded like ". . . survival."

I felt afraid to tell him I didn't understand, afraid he'd realize I'm not as intelligent as he thought I was and would be disappointed in me. It's silly for me to begin to feel that way, but I can't help it. I guess the trouble is that I don't understand why anyone as brilliant as he should be interested in me. If I were one of the young girls who run after

155

the professors, I could understand it, but what do I have that he could want?

After a while he raised his head and said something else that bothered me. "You waited a long time, didn't you?"

"I . . . I didn't know I was waiting. It was all a surprise to me."

"Liar," he said, but he was smiling. "It's always the woman who decides. When did you decide?"

I just shook my head, dizzy with the implications of what he said. I didn't even want to think about that. I won't.

"Where will we make love?" I just sat numbly for a moment. "Where can we go? Any ideas?"

I didn't know what to say.

"Your house?" he asked, and I shook my head. "Mine's out too."

Then we just sat for a while.

Finally, trying to keep my voice light, I said, "Haven't you some immoral friend who'll let you use his place?"

"You're the only immoral friend I have." He laughed.

"A motel?"

"Oh, Christ!" he exploded. "Are you willing to go to a motel?"

I shook my head. "No, that would be awful." But I was lying. I don't care where we go, but I was too ashamed to say so after his outburst. For all my respectability I lack his fastidiousness. He's right to be revolted. One day I'm shocked at what Laura says, and the next day I'm ready to throw everything aside and go anywhere, any place where we can be naked to each other.

How self-righteous I was with Laura. I couldn't cheat, couldn't live day to day with Joe while . . . not me. Well, I'm worse than a woman who's looking for an alternative to an unhappy marriage. I'm married to a wonderful man and I'm . . . I don't know what I'm doing.

156

Each time I flip back a few pages and read earlier entries in my journal, I almost want to scream. It's as if twenty different women wrote it, one succeeding the other, contradicting the one before her.

And none of them very nice women . . . fearful, petty, narrow . . . and getting worse—devious, selfish. That's what I am now.

At the same time that I'm in this wild state, very practical thoughts come into my head. I've got to be sure that I don't get pregnant. The thought of it sweeps into my head like a poison that could paralyze and petrify me. It must come from my upbringing. I think if someone had told my mother I was dying of leukemia it wouldn't have bothered her as much as being told I was going to have an illegitimate child or even that I was pregnant when I got married. I can't remember ever talking with her about it, but somehow I came to believe that this was the worst thing that could ever happen.

I know there are a lot worse things that can happen and that are happening to people every day, like being bombed or starving or having a terrible disease, or being unloved, or uncared for, or—I won't make a long list. I know this in my head. But in my guts I still believe getting pregnant is the worst thing that could happen. Of course, I'm always afraid of getting pregnant. But this fear is different. It's all mixed up with my mother's attitude, with my guilt at being unfaithful to Joe, with all the fear that's mixed in with my determination. Crazy determination . . . determined to do one thing one day and the opposite the next day.

I called my doctor, but he can't see me for about three weeks. (Is it an emergency? No.) I'm not sure what to do except that I've got to be more sure. Aren't there some new contraceptives? Even if I were to go on using a diaphragm, I can't carry the thing around in my purse wherever we go.

What about Planned Parenthood? I once sent them a contribution. At least I could get some information from them, without telling them who I am. They have an office in Oakland—nobody knows me there.

I just called and they said they have a class they want me to come to; then they'd make an appointment with a doctor for me if I want, but first I have to come to the class. "What kind of class?" I asked the girl.

"Oh, just informational—tells you the various methods of family planning."

Monday, April 9

I went to the Planned Parenthood Clinic today. It's a small, low building that looks very temporary. It's so bare inside it looks as if someone must be moving in or moving out, or as if everyone there is prepared for a quick getaway.

I was sent to a little room with about twenty student desks facing a table. The wall behind the table was covered by a blackboard that was quite clean except for small eraser marks, as if the board was seldom used. About ten women sat in the room, and they all turned and looked at me as I came in. Then they turned away quickly and I sat down. The room was absolutely still. No one talked to anyone else.

The women were all very young. I was the oldest one there. About half the women were white and half black. Four of them held babies on their laps. The white women were thin and pale, the black ones plumper (except for one tall, lanky girl), but they all wore the same anxious look, like little girls who had suddenly been told some very bad news. I imagined that they were very poor, very young girls, with probably more than one child and the haunting fear that there would be more—and more. The silence, among such young girls, was unnerving. Even the babies were quiet.

Except when someone entered the room, they all kept their eyes on an object on the table. It looked at first like a big transparent plastic bubble. Then I could see the transparent plastic was in the shape of a woman's hip and buttocks. Through it we saw approximations of female sex organs. An opening in the bottom became a plastic tube curving upward—the vagina. It stopped where a pink wrinkled pear jutted off from it—the womb. Two little tubes ran off from that to end in balls the size of olives—ovaries? We all sat and stared at it together.

After a few minutes a woman came in. She was very thin and wore glasses and a white uniform. But I don't think she was a nurse. She reminded me of my high school cooking teacher. She carried a little box that she set down on the table next to the plastic model.

"Today," she said, "I'm going to explain some contraceptive techniques to you and answer your questions. This is to give you a chance to find out about all the methods and choose the one that suits you best. Then you can make an appointment with one of our doctors, who will examine you, confer with you and prescribe one of these methods, according to your preference and needs. Please feel free to interrupt me at any time if you have questions or if I use a word you don't understand. All right?" She got no response at all; if anything, the silence was deeper.

She began her speech, naming one contraceptive technique after another, pulling samples out of the box. After describing each technique, she gave an estimation of its effectiveness. Sometimes she picked up the plastic model to demonstrate, as when she pulled a little vial out of the box, shook it, touched the end of it to the "vagina" and sent a stream of white foam gushing up the tube. I wondered who washed the model out after each demonstration.

After each type of contraceptive she paused and asked if there were any questions. No one spoke. I felt an air of expectancy, as if all the girls waited for her to get through talking so that they could see a doctor and get something, now, right now, to ease the anxiety, something before the next time their men touched them. They reminded me of a group of the hungry in *Major Barbara* who must sit through a sermon before being fed.

She had started with the least effective method, rhythm, "about forty percent effective," she said, wrinkling her nose. The diaphragm was better, about eighty percent, and the foam was as good, maybe a little better. The IUD was even better, ninety percent, a little coil the doctor put into the uterus (she couldn't demonstrate on the model very well; it was full of foam), but the pills were just about one hundred percent if you remembered to take them every day and could tolerate the side effects.

"Just about?" murmured an anxious, thin white girl next to me. Those were the first words spoken.

"Well, nothing is absolutely perfect, but the pills are just about. . . . " The woman shrugged and moved her hands, smiled and shrugged again.

No one smiled back.

"Finally," she said, more briskly, "you should know that abortion laws are changing rapidly. The law now reads, 'if dangerous to the mother's health' instead of 'fatal.' It is now possible, in the case of contraceptive failure, by a rather complicated process . . . "

I sat there until we were dismissed to make appointments with doctors. I didn't make an appointment. I just left.

I wished I could just forget the whole thing—Dan, everything. I hated it all. I hated Dan. Why should he be exempt from all this? I imagined us sitting together in this class, sharing responsibility. Ludicrous, ridiculous. We couldn't do that—it would kill the romance. It was up to me to take care of all these indelicate things, to be practical, so that our love affair could be safely impetuous! What a great beginning to the great affair.

Friday, April 13

Joe knows. He hasn't said anything, and I don't say anything, but he knows. I can tell. He sits and watches me when he thinks I don't notice. And I pretend I don't see him watching me.

I always thought of Joe as not being very sensitive or aware. There were times when we would disagree or he'd say something that hurt me and I'd lie awake at night while he fell right asleep, completely unaware that I was upset. So there was nothing for me to do but get over it, not be nagging or mean or sulky. Or other times, when I'd worry about Lulu or the state of the world or something, and I'd see that he just couldn't hold a worry in his head for five minutes.

Yet last night I was awake, with my mind in a turmoil, and Joe was awake too. I could tell from his breathing—and I guess he was listening to mine. There we were, side by side, awake and silent.

Wednesday, April 18

In the cafeteria, Dan peeling an orange, as if he were undressing it, looking at my face all the time. Impossible to talk, of course, because of the blaring music—a few students throwing food at each other. Aimless hostility. Like sitting in the midst of a battlefield. Of all places for lovers!

Still, it was a happy few minutes.

There's so much I know about myself, my life, that I didn't know before.

I know the answer to Dan's question—why I married Joe. It wasn't just that everyone else was getting married. Among the people I grew up with I was considered a freak, because I was "too serious" and read books and "brooded." I thought they were right, that something was wrong with me. By their standards I was sick and Joe was healthy—always cheerful, happy, unthinking. Well adjusted.

If I had ever gotten away from those people, gone away to college or something, I'd have found out that to feel passionately about things is not freaky or neurotic. I'd have found people who felt as I do about things. I'd have met someone like Dan—at the university or some place like that—and would have married him, and would have had a completely different life.

It's not Joe's fault or my fault or anything. It's just the way it is. A mistake. And now, years later, I find everything I want and need—and it's too late. Is it?

I keep having that same dream, giving birth to a baby girl.

Later, as we were walking to the library, I told Dan about the dream. He smiled and said, "That's a female expression of love. When a woman is in love she wants a child by the man she loves."

I smiled too but shook my head. "The last thing I want is a baby, by anyone."

"Well, of course, you don't consciously want one. But your deeper instincts, the real woman in you, comes out this way—in dreams."

162

There was no way to argue with that, of course. I can't prove or disprove what I'm not even conscious of.

Friday, April 20

Today I went to school hopefully. On Friday everyone leaves early. I was half expecting that Dan would have found some place for us to be alone, that we'd get away together early. But he had to leave the minute class was over. He said his wife was sick and he had to get home to take the kids off her hands.

I've let things go this past month. Got to catch up on my work. Pile of reading to do.

But I'm half sick with wanting Dan. It's like the way I felt during those sexually frustrated teen-age years but much worse, somehow. How long has it been since he first touched me? And here we are still fumbling at each other in a car—like teen-agers.

Saturday, April 21

Today I was thinking about the limits of a love affair. I thought that Dan and I would have all the things we had before, but that sexual love would be added. Instead, a lot of things have been subtracted—without even adding complete sexual love yet.

What's being subtracted? Freedom. I used to feel free to go to Dan's office at any time, to sit with him as long as I wanted to in the cafeteria, to walk and talk with him. I knew that some people might gossip about us—there are always rumors of faculty-student romances—but I didn't care. I even felt a little flattered that they might think Dan was interested in me. But now—I suppose it's guilt—I begin to be calculating. I worry about things like, Are we seen together too much? I imagine that people are always watching us. I'm constrained in what I do and say around him. I wonder, How often should I look at him, and with what expression on my face? Is it all right for me to call him by his first name? Or would I attract more attention by switching back to his last name again?

Will I say something that will displease him, disappoint him, and make him love me less? Should I disagree with him? We seldom argue anymore because I just can't seem to say anything contrary to what he says—if I disagree I'm just dumb. I really can't speak. All this uncertainty and unnaturalness has come into our relations. So it seems I see him less often, and I'm constrained when I do see him.

And we haven't even made love! So it's not really "an affair." Is it? Maybe that's why I feel that so many things have been lost—because we haven't really made love. Sometimes I'm even angry with him, probably out of frustration.

This certainly isn't the way it happens in books.

The only person who has gained is Joe. I'm so sexually turned on we make love more often.

There's something obscene about that. Or funny. I wish I could laugh.

Monday, April 23

Today, in Dan's office, I tried to keep my voice casual as I asked, "How's your wife?"

"What?"

"Wasn't she sick?"

"Oh. Yes. She's better." He raised an eyebrow at me. "Curious about her, aren't you?"

I felt myself blushing.

164

He leaned back. "What's my wife like? Talented, temperamental, intelligent. She was a student of mine. My first year of teaching. I started her writing. She just published her third novel." He frowned. "The first time we separated was three months after the wedding. Then she found out she was pregnant. The other two also came after separations. If I had a child for every time we've separated . . . "

"What always brought you back together?"

"The kids? Yes and no. Look, I'm no lone wolf. I need a woman, the right woman. I never found her. But when you leave what you've got, you have to have something to go to. Do you understand that?"

"I've heard it before, but—"

"Someone who really knows you, wants you. Someone who doesn't just use you to work out some foul-up in life; that's what women do, you know; they need, they don't love. At least the women I've known." I'd never heard him sounding so bitter. I opened my mouth to answer him, but a student appeared in the doorway and Dan told him to come in. So I left.

Is that how he sees me? Did he mean me? He thinks I'm playing around and enjoying being a flirtatious, middle-aged, suburban housewife. Needing, not loving. Can't he see how I feel about him? He thinks I'm afraid to go through with it and really be his lover—that's why he's been holding back.

Thursday, May 3

I made up my mind. This morning I told Dan, "Tomorrow, at my house. Tomorrow morning. Everyone is gone by nine, and neither of us has a class until eleven."

"I thought you didn't want to use your house," he said.

He grinned at me and I felt myself go hot, wondering if he thought me coarse and aggressive. Then he growled, "I can hardly wait," with a comic leer that reassured me he was only teasing.

Friday, May 4

By eight thirty everyone was gone. I got ready for Dan. At first I felt uneasy, but I put that aside, like a boring book, and let myself feel happy. We were finally going to be—as one. I shaved my underarms and legs, took a bath, smoothed lotion all over my body and inserted my diaphragm. I took a long time deciding what to wear. Finally I put on a long blue robe that looks like a silk dress. Then I sat down and waited. And waited. I began to think something had gone wrong and he couldn't come.

It was after ten o'clock when the doorbell finally rang.

Halfway through the doorway he sort of grabbed me, pushed me against the wall and kissed me. "Where?" I took his hand and led him to Lulu's room. He looked around. "Your daughter's room. Makes for an easier conscience? Interesting lines we draw." He sat down on Lulu's bed, pulled me down next to him, opened my robe, and pushed me back so that I lay flat, my feet touching the floor. He started kissing my breasts and stroking my legs, kneading the flesh around my hips and thighs.

But then, in a hurried motion, he had pulled off his pants and was pushing his penis into me. I was shivering, absolutely cold and dry. He was hurting me. I made a sound, started to tell him, but he didn't seem to notice.

"Now you're not a virgin anymore," he said, grinning harshly into my face as if he were angry at me. Then

166

suddenly he blinked, moaned hoarsely, then lay still. It was all over.

In another moment he was pulling on his pants, muttering something about his eleven-o'clock class and problems at school, something about the cafeteria, a meeting, a student protest. I don't know. I hardly heard him. Then he was gone.

It was like rape. No, because I wasn't fighting him. It was more like the way a man might act with a prostitute—a very conventional puritanical man who is ashamed of what he is doing.

I just don't understand! All day long I went around with that stupid, clutching diaphragm to remind me of my misery. Well, I finally made it. I finally managed to become an officially unfaithful wife. Finally consummated the great affair. Fine.

Saturday, May 5

I've got to study, that's all. Catch up on my work. Don't think about it. Keep away from his office. Go to classes and come straight home. Catch up on the ironing. Gradually make it up to Joe.

Sunday, May 6

I'm being very cheerful, otherwise I'd scream with shame and misery and disgust at myself. Joe is happy, very happy. He laughs with me, pinches and kisses me until I think I'll go crazy. God, I'm so lonely, so revolted by everything, especially me. Childbirth dream again—I've decided it's guilt, fear I'll get pregnant as punishment for infidelity.

Monday, May 7

Study! Stop feeling sorry for yourself and get some work done! You'll live. You only got what was coming to you After a while you'll forget the whole thing, except the lesson you learned.

What lesson? Is it possible that the old sexual rules still apply, the ones my mother taught me, that men want "just one thing" and, when they get it, no longer respect you?

But he couldn't be that way, not Dan!

Study. Get back to work.

On the way into campus today, I passed students carrying signs—STUDENT POWER. Too absorbed in myself to stop and ask what it was all about.

Wednesday, May 9

Now students are carrying signs that say STRIKE, but no one seems to be striking. Attendance in classes is normal for this time of the semester—thin.

I went up to some picketing students and asked what it was all about. "We want our rights," one girl said. But I couldn't seem to get a straight answer about what the real grievance was. I kept asking until one said the first demand is "integrate the cafeteria." It took me a long time to understand what they meant. I thought they meant to stop sitting in little segregated groups. I'm for that. But they don't have to demand that, just do it.

Then I found out that I had misunderstood. What they mean is they want to eat in the little faculty room that's on the other side of the building.

Ordinarily I'd be talking this over with Dan, sorting out my ideas. But I'm alone now. Really alone.

Monday, May 14

Today I had to go to the library to use a book that was on reserve. I was sitting at a table in the corner. "Where in hell have you been?" The hoarse voice. The dark, bristling face. "Why do you run off the minute class is done?"

I couldn't answer. I just looked at him.

"Your place tomorrow," he muttered. "About noon." He touched my arm with the tip of his finger before he turned and walked away. It was like an electric current. So I'm right back where I started. It's taken me two weeks to begin to pull myself together, and now . . . I don't know. Maybe I misunderstood something. Didn't it happen the way I remember?

Tuesday, May 15

This time I just sat around the house in my jeans and sweatshirt until he came. When I let him in, he stood at the front door a long time looking at me, looking so hurt and unhappy I almost felt as if I owed him an apology.

He took me to Lulu's room and slowly undressed me, kissing and touching every part of me that he uncovered. As he undressed himself, he managed to keep one hand on me almost all the time. I felt so happy, though not really sexually aroused, but gradually relaxing, slowly loosening the tension I'd needed to hold myself together during the last two weeks.

Then he said, "You're not aroused at all. You—often have this trouble?"

"No." What trouble? "I don't think so, I—"

"Relax." But I was relaxed. At least I was until he told me to. Then after a while he said, "I can't wait much longer."

When he finished he lay still and heavy on me as if he had fallen asleep.

Then he rolled over on his back, looking at the ceiling and talking about the "strike." Of course, that's why I haven't seen him. He's been in it up to his neck.

He started to explain it. It was very complicated. Something about the students demanding entry to the faculty dining room. I didn't understand the details. Or maybe I wasn't able to concentrate on them. I kept thinking of what he'd said before about "this trouble."

I tried to act interested. "What do you think will happen?"

"Nothing. Same old pattern. Most of the students who jumped on the bandwagon have been missing a lot of classes and need an excuse. So . . . one of the demands will be passing grades for strikers. It will be granted. Then students who were failing classes before the strike will demand passing grades and get them. So it'll all die down well before final exams without anyone ever having got at the real issues.

"Every time something like this starts I get involved, hoping that some real change is coming. But so far—well, this time, again, it's a tempest in a teapot, everyone content to play around on the surface of the issues. The students most of all."

He went on talking, sitting on the edge of the bed. I'd been starved for his talk, yet I was jealous. He was so much more passionate about this than about me. I really must be an Emma Bovary—narrow and petty and worrying about my "love affair."

Tuesday, May 22

I don't know. I thought it would be wonderful today. But something went wrong again. We kissed and he touched me

170

until I was terribly excited. Then he asked me, "You're doing something about babies?" I nodded and pulled him to me again, but he started insisting on details and before I could figure out what happened, he had gotten me into a long squalid comparison of contraceptives.

Of course, I was embarrassed and . . . cooled off, and our lovemaking wasn't very good. He said something like "Don't worry" again, but he was the one who looked worried.

Then there was just this awful silence between us, and he gave me a sad smile. "Look, it's all right," he said. I was just dumb, waiting for him to go on. But he didn't.

I opened my mouth, thinking I might scream, but it came out in a whisper. "*What's* all right?"

"People can only do what they can do. We mustn't ask of them anymore than that." What was he talking about? About me? Or about him? "I understand that. So don't worry about it."

Then he straightened up and shrugged his shoulders as if everything had been said, all had been settled; and then he left. I felt as if I'd been forgiven for some terrible crime against him.

I don't understand!

I DON'T UNDERSTAND!

I think and think over these past few weeks, and I can't figure out what has been happening. Is this what it's like to be in love? There's nothing, nothing in my life, nothing in the books, to match this up against and figure out what is happening.

What do I want? I want Dan, under any conditions. I want him wholly—want a life with him. Surely he can see that. But sometimes he acts as if I'm just casually using him.

But I feel as if *I'm* being used.

171

And then there's the sex problem. What sex problem? I don't understand that either. It seems to me we haven't made love often enough to give ourselves a chance. Yet sometimes I feel he hasn't wanted to make love to me because of some awful deficiency in me that he's too kind to mention.

Since we've become intimate, we can't seem to communicate.

That would be a very funny statement if I weren't so miserable. Very funny.

Tuesday, May 29

A whole week since I've seen Dan outside class. First he scolds me for avoiding him, and then he ignores or avoids me.

Wednesday, May 30

No point in kidding myself. Dan's avoiding me. All day Friday, all day Monday and Tuesday, I tried to see him. But he rushed off right after class and never seemed to be in his office. Once I saw him talking to another instructor. He saw me, too, but pretended not to. I felt too shy to interrupt—a few weeks ago I'd have walked up and joined right in.

Today's a holiday, and tomorrow and Friday are the last days of classes before finals. I must get to him. I must understand. Whatever is happening, I want to know what it is; no matter what it is, I want to get it straight. If I've let him down in some horrible way, the way he seems to imply . . . but have I? Does he think . . . ?

I'm tired of thinking. I'll just stay near his office the next couple of days and insist that we talk.

Thursday, May 31

No luck today. Not a glimpse of Dan.

Friday, June 1

I must have tried ten times to find him.

Late this afternoon I made one more try. I knocked on his closed office door, not expecting an answer. As I stood there, a woman about my age, but fat and tired-looking, came out of one of the other offices. After she passed me and went out, I heard voices from that office. I thought I'd just walk by the office and listen to the voices, to see if one of them might be Dan's.

It wasn't.

This is what I heard.

"That woman haunts me. I hope she doesn't take my class again next fall."

"Who?"

"Mrs. Amsly. In my English 1A. Another bored suburban housewife. There seem to be more of them every year. They married at twenty—now their kids don't need them, their husbands bore them, they have nothing to do."

"But come back to school."

"And try to resurrect their love lives with one of us."

"I wonder what happens to them."

"Oh, they hang around for a year or two, then drop out. A few turn into good students, go on to the university. Get a degree—along with a divorce decree. I don't want to get involved, and that woman's been in my office, on one excuse or another, almost every day for the past month."

"I know how to get rid of her."

"How?"

"Tell her to take Dan Harkan next semester."

A burst of laughter.

Then one of them talked about how furious Dan's wife used to get, but how she doesn't bother anymore because "it all blows over by finals." And how they could understand it if he went for the young ones, "but what he sees in these worn-out weepers . . . "

More laughter.

Then they started comparing notes on the young girls who were "available."

I didn't hear anymore except their laughter echoing behind me as I ran down the hall.

I still hear their laughter.

Monday, June 4

Got Laura's Berkeley phone number from information.

She was glad to hear from me. I couldn't ask right away, so I inquired about her children. "About the same." But the youngest is starting to feel sorry for her, take her part against the two older ones. "And I'm having such a good time at Cal that they don't really get to me as much—so I suppose they're beginning to give up trying. How are you? How's school?"

"I want to ask you something."

"Go ahead. What can I do?"

"No, not a favor. Just yes or no."

"Fine. Why so mysterious?"

"Did you . . . " I had to clear my throat. "Did you ever have an affair with Dan Harkan?"

There was a long silence, then, "Oh."

"Just yes or no." Silence. "I guess that means yes."

"Look, Ella, it was more a flirtation than an affair. I hardly

174

remember; it was long ago, when I first started school. It never quite got off the ground. It wasn't really what either of us wanted. It . . . it was sort of funny, in a way; you see, Dan probably can't help falling a little in love with—"

"Oh, Laura, I've made such a fool of myself!" And then I really started to cry.

"Why don't you come over here, cry on my shoulder, get it all out." She laughed. "We'll exchange notes, we'll be merciless. God knows, he's exciting in class but hopeless in bed."

I hung up without even saying good-bye.

Thursday, June 14

The hardest thing of all was going to take Dan's final. I thought I'd be calm by now, but as soon as I saw him sitting in the front of the room I started to shake again.

He handed me a test sheet. As I took it, my hand shook. "Oh, come, Mrs. Price, you know by this time you needn't be nervous. You'll do fine." I looked at his face. He was smiling his teeth-bared grin. As our eyes met, his smile changed. It softened; it became gentle, slightly hurt but forgiving. *He* was forgiving *me*. Without intending to, I actually smiled back. I couldn't help it. He was too strong for me. But he's had a lot of practice.

My smile turned into a choked giggle. All through the exam (which was just an evaluation of the class like last semester, only written this time), I fought down hysterical laughter. I felt used, humiliated, rejected. But evidently he also felt used, humiliated, rejected. If each of us were to tell the story of our "affair," would each version come out the same, only with a different victim, different villain?

When I finished I waited until he was busy talking to

175

another student, then put the paper on his desk and got out without having to look at him again.

I feel very old and very tired, as if in the nine months since I started this journal I have lived a whole lifetime. Or nine months' gestation—stillborn. I thought I was starting a new life. I thought I was going somewhere. But I've just gone around in a circle.

And here I am, back in the same place again. Nothing has changed. I thought I had changed, but I guess I haven't. I'm still the same neurotic I always was. And my life is still a bad soap opera.

I thought about telling Joe. Confessing the whole stupid mess, asking him to forgive me and promising to try to be a better wife. He'd forgive. Poor Joe. But it would hurt him. It would relieve me. So I'd really be thinking of myself, as usual. No, there won't be any confession—no more bad soap opera. I'll keep it to myself and learn from it and try to be a better wife to Joe and a better mother to Lulu. They deserve better.

Saturday, June 16

Same dream again—a baby girl.

Tonight I told Joe I wasn't going back to school anymore. I told him I thought it had come between us, and I didn't want anything to come between us again. Then I told him about the peace march and told him that I never wanted to do anything again without him, or without telling him.

"I could tell something was wrong, you had something on your mind," he said. "I only want you to be happy. You can do what you want. Just say what you want me to do, and I'll toe the line."

His words dug into me like a dull knife. But he was

176

smiling. He was happy. Why? I can't imagine. I started to cry.

"What is it?"

I told him I had felt tired again lately.

"Sure, you been pushing yourself too hard, all that studying and all. You should learn to take it easy. Maybe you better see the doctor again." We decided I would.

We made love tonight, but I couldn't feel a thing. I pretended to, and Joe didn't notice anything. I just feel dead inside.

Friday, June 29

Saw the doctor Tuesday. He made an appointment for me to see a psychiatrist today. Joe seems uneasy about it. Why? I guess he feels it's someone between him and me—like this journal. I should stop keeping a journal.

Midnight

My psychiatrist's name is Dr. Redford. He is much younger than I expected. Has a very thin face and black hair. Sun-tanned and hard-muscled, like a surfer. He wears very stylish clothes—light, shiny blue suit. He reminds me not of a doctor but of a model from an ad in *Esquire* magazine.

I gave him a summary of what had happened in the past year, including the part about Dan, which wasn't easy. When I was all through he asked how old I was.

"Thirty-five."

He nodded. "And does your life feel like the closing moves of a chess game?"

"I don't understand."

"Well, when people are young, they see infinite possibilities, many moves to make, as in the opening of the game. But later, as they grow older, there don't seem to be as many moves left—and when they feel themselves to be 'in check' they come for help."

I thought about that. "No. I never felt that way—that there were infinite possibilities. Most of my life I felt there were just a few certain moves, prescribed moves. Then, when I started school, I began to feel—Dan made me feel—that life needn't be like that. I felt as if the whole world were suddenly open to me. But then—I don't know—the doors that opened seemed to open on nothing, emptiness. I made a fool of myself. And then I was right back where I started. Nothing had changed."

"And you want your life to change."

He was looking at me intently, and I didn't know what to say. I felt as if there was a right answer and a wrong answer, and I wanted to give the right one.

"I don't want it to be the way it always has been."

"And why do you think it has always been that way?"

Again he seemed to be leaning forward to catch the right answer if I could give it. "I guess because of me. Because of what's wrong with me."

"What do you think is wrong with you?"

"I don't know. I guess you have to help me find out. And then I'll know what to do about it."

I could see that I had given the right answer. He smiled and said, "Well, let's make some plans."

We decided I'd come twice a week for a while. That'll cost about sixty dollars a week, so as soon as I got home I called the agency and told them I was available. They had an opening, thirty hours a week in an office in Berkeley, filling in for a woman who's on maternity leave. I should clear just about enough to pay Dr. Redford.

Joe still seems uneasy. I told him, "Let's give it three

178

months. That's how long this job will last. Let's see if Dr. Redford and I can get me squared away in that amount of time."

He cheered up, and we drank to it.

Saturday, July 7

First week of work past. No time to write—no energy. The job is routine typing and filing, not hard, but by the end of the day I'm worn out, more from boredom than anything else. The two girls in the office are young, don't talk to me much.

At night I try to read, but my eyes droop and my mind wanders. I feel that I'm getting very stupid.

Dr. Redford's office is in Berkeley, so I can go there right after work on Tuesday and Thursday. This week we mostly talked about Dan. After I got rid of my hostility toward him, I started trying to tell about the feeling I had when I fell in love. "I wouldn't give up having had that feeling for anything, not for . . . " But Dr. Redford sort of looked away, the way he does when I'm not really getting anywhere. So I said, "Well, it's over, and my only concern is how to live this life of mine."

Tuesday, July 10

Told Dr. about Laura today and my determination not to end up alone like her.

Thursday, July 12

Talked about my baby dream, then about babies and why I had only one, and Lulu and . . . exhausting. . . . I have a headache. Joe is always very silent on the days that I come

179

home after seeing the doctor. I think he's afraid we talk about him. But what could we say about him?

Sunday, July 15

Joe and I had a weekend down the coast, just walking on the beaches and relaxing. Honeymoonish. I'm still frigid, but he doesn't know. Is it wrong to pretend?

Tuesday, July 17

Talked with Dr. about being frigid. Then somehow we got onto the subject of my mother, spent the whole hour on her.

Thursday, July 19

More on my mother. Her attitudes toward sex, being called Okies, a lot of other things.

Sunday, July 22

Our seventeenth wedding anniversary. Party last night. Nice but I drank too much. Dear, sweet Joe.

Thursday, July 26

It's amazing the things you can remember about childhood, things buried so deep. I'm beginning to understand so many things about myself, my overseriousness, guilt about sex, my undeveloped maternal feelings. It all goes back to my mother.

I'm really too tired to write it all out here. And there's no need to. My sessions with Dr. Redford take the place of writing in my journal. Besides, there's really no time now, between working and the house and all. Joe has been taking me out a lot too, movies and plays and just for rides. It's like we're teen-agers dating again—but with the sexual freedom we never had as teen-agers. But you'd think Joe was a teen-ager sexually again!

Thursday, August 2

Setback this week. Very depressed. But Dr. Redford says I'm making great progress, gaining insight. And Joe doesn't seem to feel threatened by him anymore. But I feel so tired all the time. Trying to spend more time with Lulu. Not doing too well yet. I'm trying to take greater interest in the things that interest her.

Thursday, August 9

Exhausting session. We talked about Joe. I told Dr. how good he is, how patient. I writhed and sweated with shame when I told him I was afraid I made Joe feel inadequate because of his lack of interest in books and ideas. "But, so far as I can see," I said, "the only purpose of the books and ideas is to lead to goodness and kindness. Joe's already good and kind, and doesn't need the books, so why can't I. . . ? "

Dr. helped me finish the sentence. "Why can't you love him?" We talked about loving, what it was, the ability to love, and why it seems so hard for me. I can see now, we just have to keep going back, back, back, until we find out, dig out all the things that stopped me from being able to love. But that could take years.

Sunday, August 12

Tired. Dread that job tomorrow. Mindless, stifling. Leaves me too tired to think. But I need it to pay Dr.

181

The dream again. This time the baby got up and walked and talked. She said, "Me too. Me too."

Tuesday, August 14

My interpretation of dream: manifestation of stifled feminine part of me, resulting from mother's indoctrination. Dr. said nothing, but I could tell he agreed.

Friday, August 17

Going to Carmel this weekend. Had our honeymoon there.

Tuesday, August 21

Can hardly wait for that martini at five. Work not hard, but tiring. Woman I'm replacing isn't coming back—they want me to stay. Then I can keep up with Dr. Today, talking about feminine roles, I mentioned Ibsen, Lessing, but Dr. hadn't read the books. I tried to summarize but got confused. Too far away from all that.

Thursday, August 23

Dr. says to some degree every woman has the same problem, recapturing the feminine side of her nature, which is left undeveloped because of our society's emphasis on the male. I've always known I wasn't much as a woman, hated being one. Never knew how much it poisoned my whole life.

Monday, August 27

Lovely weekend in Carmel again. But what a hangover.

Thursday, August 30

Had an orgasm last night.

Saturday, September 8

Over a week since I wrote. My journal seems to be dying. There's just no time? No energy? It's as hard to write as it was when I first started—a year ago.

Friday, September 21

Just spoke to Laura. Called to ask me to join a women's peace group she's in. Told her I'd dropped out of things like that. Then she asked, "How's school?" and I told her I'd dropped that too. Then there just wasn't much more to say.
Awfully tired.

Friday, September 28

I can stare at the page for half an hour and still not be able to start. I can't waste time this way.

Friday, October 5

A whole month's entries in a few sentences. Just shows I don't need to do this. Drying up.
I seem to feel depressed after writing, or trying to write. Even seeing this lying in the drawer depresses me. I should get rid of it. Too much introspection. Dr. Redford is enough. Few pages left in this notebook anyway. Time to quit.

Thursday, November 22—Thanksgiving Day

Nearly two months since my last entry.
Joe is out washing the car, getting ready to go to his

mother's house for Thanksgiving dinner. I was hunting for my blue earrings and found this, with one page left. One page to bring this to a neat conclusion—then next week, when I clean out the closets, I'll burn this and the other notebooks.

The rabbit test was positive. I'm pregnant.

Joe is overjoyed. Surprising to see him suddenly so excited about fatherhood. He's already been telling the whole neighborhood. We'll tell the family today.

Lulu thinks it's a little obscene at our age.

Of course, I'm very happy. It's the fulfillment of my recurring dream. A second chance to be a good wife and mother. Last Tuesday was my final session with Dr. Redford, and I quit my job.

And now there's no need to be writing.

In ending this, I remove the last obstacle between Joe and me.

THE END

Notebook

NUMBER FIVE

Friday, November 23

I can't
I CAN'T
I CAN'T

What's wrong with me? I just want to write that over and over again. I want to scream it.

NO
NO

I'm going to die. I'm terrified that I'm going to die and I know what death is, I know what hell is. I know that after I die I'll go to hell and be tortured. And my torture will be this—to go on just as I am, where I am, how I am.

I won't get out of bed. If I get out of bed I'll trip and fall and break my head and die and then I'll never get out of this. Stuck forever.

187

I told Joe I wasn't getting up, and he just said, "You rest, honey, if you don't feel so good. I saw you started looking a little pale during dinner yesterday." And he went off whistling.

He always whistles when he knows there's something wrong and wants to hold me off until it blows over.

I look at these words and I know they're insane, and it feels good to let the insanity out and to think the insanity is really me, and so what? Because I have to let it out. Because it doesn't matter how hard or how often I push it down, that just makes it mad, more mad, and it rages and storms and will eat me alive if I don't let it out.

Oh, God, I'm so tired. Maybe they'll put me away somewhere and I'll get some rest. Clean, white, cool sheets.

No, I must let them put me away only if I'm sure it'll be for good. Otherwise, if I let myself go all the way down, sink all the way down, unless I'm sure I want to stay down there, I'll have such an awful time coming back up because I'll have further to go. But I want to sink. I want to die. But I can't die. Because of hell. Forever.

Write it out. Write it out.

It was the nightmare. The same old having-the-baby dream started. It started out all right. I was in the hospital, I was having a baby. A girl. She was born. The doctor. The doctor was Dan. But he wasn't there. He left just when I was pushing hardest, trying to get her born, and I was calling and calling him. And then it was all over. And Dan came back in and I said, "I had a girl, didn't I?"

And he just looked sort of sheepish and said, "I'm sorry, I did all I could."

"What's wrong? Where is my baby?"

And then Dan was gone again and Joe was sitting by the

bed and holding my hand and patting it and saying, "Just take it easy, hon, just take it easy."

And Dr. Redford was standing behind him, nodding, and saying, "You're doing fine."

"What is it?" I was yelling. "What happened? Did something happen to my baby?"

They were silent and I kept asking, and they said things I couldn't understand, and Joe kept patting my hand, and I said, "You must tell me what happened to her. Is she dead? Tell me!"

Finally Joe said, "There was no baby. It was a sickness, a growth. But the doctor got it all out. You're going to be fine now. Just take it easy."

"Oh." I lay there trying to understand. And then I began to cry and cry. No baby. There never was a baby. I cried and cried, great terrible sobs, with a grief like nothing I had ever felt before. And Joe just kept patting my hand, and Dr. Redford said, "That's it, cry it all out."

And then I saw something. I saw them exchange a look. It was only for a second, a quick look of complicity.

And suddenly I knew. I *had* had a baby girl! I had seen her! They were hiding her from me. They were going to kill her. Joe got up.

"No, stay here," I said.

"I'll be back." He smiled and Dr. Redford smiled and I saw that they were going out to kill my baby.

"No!" I screamed. I tried to get up, but I had no strength. It was as if I were glued to the bed. I watched them leave the room and I screamed and screamed until my screaming woke me up.

And now I'm huddled here as if I were still glued to the bed, completely unnerved by a stupid nightmare. My God, if I'm insane, let me just be insane; stop pulling me back to look at myself and wonder how I can be so crazy.

Why am I so terrified that I'm going to lose this baby? I guess it's because I don't want it so much.

Funny.

I meant to write, It's because I want it so much.

I don't want it so much.

I don't want it.

I don't want to have a baby.

I DON'T WANT TO HAVE A BABY!

The great solution to everything. Get pregnant. Then you don't have to think about anything anymore. You're trapped. Happy trappy. I've seen other women do it so many times. Why didn't I see what I was doing?

4 p.m.

I lay in bed for hours, rereading all my notebooks, following the pattern: me coming out, things happening, learning—and then I stumbled, stumbled over Dan. All right. Pick yourself up. Try again. But I didn't. I gave up.

I thought I wasn't giving up. I thought going to Dr. Redford was not giving up. But why didn't I see through all that junk about fulfilling femininity? Redford is a man. Being a psychiatrist doesn't automatically free him of male prejudice. I thought I was on to all that now.

No, don't blame him. I played along. I'd lost Dan. What was left? I wanted Dr. Redford to help me find good reasons for staying with Joe. I was in a sulk. I was going to quit. A baby. What better reason? What better excuse for quitting?

No. I know I have to build a life with Joe, but this is not the way.

This is not the way.

The sheets on this bed stink of sweat.

5 p.m.

I've taken a shower, gotten dressed and am sitting and waiting for Joe to get home.

Lulu just came by on her way out to a dinner and slumber party. She gave me a strange look. "What are you mad at?" she asked.

"Do I look mad?"

"You look real mean. Poor Daddy, I guess he'll be henpecked tonight."

"What do you mean by that? When did I ever henpeck your father?"

"Gee, don't get mad at me too, just because you're in one of your moods." And she ran off, leaving me feeling in the wrong again.

I mustn't feel in the wrong, apologetic. I mustn't collapse. I'm right about this. I know it.

Stay by me. (Who? I guess I'm talking to you, journal. I'm praying. With no God to believe in, I'm praying anyway.) I must keep you by me. Must keep writing, pouring out whatever comes, looking at it clearly, draining the insanity out of me until what is left is clear thought and I know what to do.

1 a.m.

As soon as Joe got home, I made him sit down and listen to me. He insisted he needed a shower. And I waited. Then he poured drinks, but I didn't touch mine. He whistled. I was right. He does whistle when he's uneasy. Why didn't I ever notice that before?

191

Then I told him. "You were right about headshrinkers. I was a fool ever to go to that doctor. He filled my head full of all kinds of nonsense, got me all confused." Joe stopped whistling and smiled uncertainly. "Joe, I really don't want to have a baby. I don't want to start all that again."

Joe looked at me and shrugged. "Well, I don't see what we can do about that now."

"I could get an abortion. It's legal now."

"It is? How?"

"I don't know. I think you need a doctor or psychiatrist to say it would be bad for your health. Maybe I could . . . Joe, would you feel terrible if we didn't have this baby?"

He was quiet for a minute. Then he put his arm around me. "Honey, I told you a million times, whatever you want is okay with me."

And that was that. So then I had a drink, and Joe and I had a nice, quiet, close evening with television, laughing at the stupid programs. It's all settled, and tomorrow morning I'll call Dr. Redford and see how to go about it.

Saturday, November 24

I tried and tried to get hold of Dr. Redford, but he must be away for the weekend. I left my name with his answering service. I couldn't call it an emergency, but it feels like one. I know I'm right to want to do this, but I'm afraid doubts will creep in and I'll lose my nerve.

Sunday, November 25

Finally got Dr. Redford tonight. He didn't want to see me, said he was too busy next week unless it was an emergency, so I said it was, and I'll see him tomorrow morning. Joe has been very quiet all weekend. I'm afraid he feels bad about my getting an abortion. I hate to hurt him. I've hurt him in so many ways already, even in ways he doesn't know about.

Stop that. No wallowing in guilt, or you'll end up shaking and sweating and hiding under the blankets again, and do you think Joe would like that?

Monday, November 26

I finally got in to see Dr. Redford about twelve thirty. He came back early from lunch to squeeze me in. He looked very impatient and just said, "What is it." It wasn't even a question.

"I think I've made a real breakthrough," I told him. I told him about my nightmare, about the way I felt last Friday. "You see, the dream was telling me that we had misinterpreted something, gotten off on the wrong track. And then it just exploded in my mind. Doctor, I don't want to have a baby. It was just a cop-out. You see?"

"No, I don't see."

"I have a lot of problems to solve, but wanting a baby isn't one of them, and having a baby only temporarily sidesteps the real problems. I don't think my dream of having a baby has anything to do with wanting a real baby. I think it means I'm trying to make a change in myself; you know, we talked about that. It's me I'm trying to give birth to, a new me. You see?"

"No, I don't see."

"I've stumbled and made a lot of mistakes. Yet I mustn't stop now. If I make a mistake I should—like a baby walking—just get up and try again, isn't that right?"

"Right."

Now I really felt encouraged. "And all that stuff about

193

recapturing femininity and all, it doesn't apply to me. That's not my problem, or not my main one. You see?"

"No, I don't see."

I was beginning to feel annoyed at the way he kept repeating that, but then I realized he always talked that way, that flat, objective demand for further clarification, exploration, until finally I said something he agreed with and he'd say, "Right," and I'd be so relieved that I'd gotten the right answer, I'd agree without knowing for sure whether or not I really agreed. I tried to explain this to him. "I'm afraid I often got us off on the wrong track in my eagerness to be agreeable, to give a 'right' answer."

He looked at his watch and frowned. "I have another patient at one. I don't understand the emergency. Are you telling me you want to resume treatment?"

"No. Well, maybe. I'm not sure. But the immediate emergency is my pregnancy."

He just looked at me.

"I mean"—I stumbled—"I want to get an abortion."

He looked at me again for a moment and then picked up his appointment book. "The earliest appointment I can give you would be in late December."

"Appointment? What do I need an appointment for?"

"To explore this question of the pregnancy."

"But that isn't necessary, is it? I mean, don't you just tell someone I should have an abortion? What is the procedure?"

"The law states that you need letters from two psychiatrists stating that bearing a child would be dangerous to your mental health."

"Oh. Well, you could write one letter, and then couldn't you get another doctor to do the other one?"

"We'll discuss all that when—" He held up the appointment book.

194

"Why do we have to discuss it? I want an abortion. It's very simple. That's what I want."

"Is it?" He glared at me with his sharp, intent face. And suddenly I saw something awful. I saw that he didn't like me. That to him I was—what had those teachers said? —another bored suburban housewife, not a real person. He was annoyed. It wasn't a matter of getting an automatic letter from him and getting an abortion. He could make me come back to discuss and explore, to "qualify" as mentally unfit to have a baby. What would I have to do in order to qualify? A couple of days ago I was half crazy. I feel far from strong now. It wouldn't take much to . . .

Suddenly I was terrified. He held this power over me. He could decide whether or not I was to have a baby. I felt rage well up in me, and I swallowed it. I could see by the look on his face, the pout of his lips, that he was enjoying this power. I swallowed again and felt as if I might vomit. I got dizzy and shook my head to clear it.

"Now," he said, "we'll set up a series of appointments, starting on . . . the twenty-first of December."

"You couldn't see me before that?"

"Don't worry, Mrs. Price." He smiled. "Abortion is legal any time up to the twentieth week."

I almost staggered out of his office, out of the building and into the street. Twenty weeks. If he planned to drag this out, I'd never make it. I would begin to feel life by then. Then how could I kill it? He was exploiting a stupid law to make money on my misery. And I was powerless. I needed him and he knew it. I could barely stand to look at him again, and I would have to go back again and again until he was ready to give me what I wanted.

I must have wanted to punish myself terribly to have gone to him for so long without seeing what he was.

I got into my car and started it. My vision kept blurring,

and I blinked and blinked to try to clear it so I could see where I was going. But I didn't really know where I was. I just drove until I saw a sign—Prince Street. That sounded familiar. Yes, that was where Laura lived. I stopped the car and went through my bag until I found my address book. I looked her up; she was only a few blocks away.

The house was one of those funny, broken-down little places with peace signs in the windows, the kind of house you see all over the Berkeley flatlands. It needed paint, and the steps to the front porch slanted dangerously. The bell didn't work, so I knocked on the door.

She was a long time answering, and I began to wonder what I'd do if she weren't home, so that when the door finally creaked open I almost threw myself at her.

"Ella! How good to see you. What's wrong?"

She dragged me into the living room, where I collapsed on a pillow on the floor and poured out the whole thing, blubbering like an idiot and whining, "I don't want to have a baby."

When I was all through, she said in a soft, low voice, "The bastard. The dirty, mean bastard."

It was exactly what I needed to hear. "I should have known he was no good. It's so clear to me now. But I—"

"You don't know how no-good he is. Did he really set up an appointment? Why, that—didn't he tell you?"

"Tell me what?"

She laughed. "Listen. You don't have to go back to him or any other psychiatrist. Last month a county judge declared all abortion laws unconstitutional. It still has to go up through the courts, but ever since then hospitals all around here are doing abortions on demand. Your medical insurance even pays for it."

I couldn't believe it. "Are you sure?"

"Sure? I worked on the campaign. It was in all the papers. Where've you been?"

"Nowhere. I've been really nowhere for a while."

"Welcome back." She smiled.

And I laughed and said, "That son of a bitch." It felt good. We talked for a long time. I was glad that she never mentioned Dan.

By the time I got home, I was so tired I could hardly hold my head up. But I knew I had to write all this down while waiting for Joe, get it all out, see and understand and keep in touch with myself. That's one thing, in spite of everything, that I have to thank Dan for, getting me started on a journal.

Tuesday, November 27

This morning I called my gynecologist and he said he'd see me this afternoon. Then I called Laura, as I promised I would, to keep her posted on my progress. I even felt good enough to ask her how things are with her. About the same. Her children are still not very nice people, and she is very lonely, but she keeps doing things, learning things, fighting her way through. I was a fool not to register this semester at the junior college. Always giving up, that's me. For all the things Dan said about it, for all the betrayal I felt from it and him, that place is still the only one around here where people will let something happen in your mind. It's better than nothing. So I'd better use it. Maybe I'll go out and apply for next semester.

4 p.m.

My gynecologist says he expects no problems. My medical insurance will pay for half. The only problem is getting scheduled at the hospital, which, he says, is swamped. But he felt we could do it during December.

"The sooner the better, please," I said.

He nodded. "Yes, of course, for medical and psychological reasons."

He did understand. He'll make arrangements and call me.

Midnight

Something very bad happened tonight. When Joe came home I told him everything was all set, and he just looked terribly sad. I knew he felt bad about it. And I felt sorry that he felt bad. But I decided that I would have to do it anyway. And later, he would get over feeling bad and forget all about it. Nothing ever bothers Joe for long. So I cooked his favorite supper and pretended that I didn't notice he looked gloomy and drank a lot. I even caught myself whistling a little, the way he does when he knows I'm disturbed and doesn't want to deal with whatever is bothering me.

But then Lulu came in. We sat down to the table. He waited until all the food was on the table and we were sitting there, and then he said to Lulu, "Well, your mother has decided to get rid of it."

"What?"

"Your baby brother."

I just looked at him. Of course, Lulu had to be told, but not that way. He wasn't looking at me, just staring at his plate as he cut big chunks of meat and put them into his mouth.

"Really, Mother? You're going to get an abortion? I thought that was criminal."

"No, it isn't. It's legal," I murmured.

"Well, I wish you'd make up your mind. First you're going to have a baby, and then—"

"I don't want to talk about it."

There was a heavy silence. Then Lulu looked at her father. She looked at him for a long time, and I saw her face taking on that sentimental droop which has nothing to do with real feelings. Then she murmured, "Poor Daddy," and reached out to touch his hand.

"Stop that!" I shouted. "I'm the one who was going to have this baby; now I'm the one who's decided not to."

"Well, I do think," she said self-righteously, "that one has an obligation to—" She sounded and looked like the heroine of a soap opera.

"It's none of your concern. You called it obscene when you first heard." And then I was crying and ran from the kitchen.

Joe followed me, of course, and told me how sorry he was he'd said anything; he just wasn't thinking. "You know me, just stupid," he said. "Come on, honey, smile."

But I can't forget what Lulu said, about not consulting anyone. It isn't just my life, there's another life inside of me. It doesn't just affect me, it's Joe's child and Lulu's brother or sister, and I'm not at all sure I have the right to make the decision alone, even if it is legal now. Lots of things that are legal are morally wrong. And I've made so many wrong decisions in my life, how do I know that this one might not be a decision I'd regret forever?

Maybe it would be better if I had the baby.

Wednesday, November 28

Just a temporary loss of nerve. I'm all right today. I just hope it will soon be all over with. Then I can get things straight in my life. I'll make it up to Joe. How many times have I said that lately?

Thursday, November 29

I know Joe doesn't mean to, but he's tearing me apart. Last night after dinner his mother called. I was doing the dishes, so he answered the phone. I couldn't hear what was said, but he came into the kitchen as I was finishing the dishes. The doorbell rang, and he gave a funny smile. "I bet that's her."

"Who?"

"Ma. She called while you were doing the dishes. And she hit the ceiling."

"Oh, Joe, you didn't tell her about—"

"I didn't mean to. I just didn't think. I mean, she says, How's Ella, any morning sickness yet? You know how she is. And before I thought, I said—well, I told her."

The doorbell rang again, and Joe hung back, looking unhappy and awkward. So I answered it. His mother came in as if she were at a funeral, murmuring something like "You're not going to do this thing." Joe's brother and his wife were with her. It was unbelievable.

For two hours they sat there. Part of the time his mother was crying and part of the time she was yelling. About murder. And Joe just sat there looking helpless and miserable while I tried to explain. But how could I explain? No explanation, no reason I could have would make any sense to her. Pretty soon she was just crossing herself and looking upward.

When they finally left, she went out saying, "Don't do this thing, don't do it. Joe, if you let her do this thing, I can never see you again."

"She doesn't mean that," he said as he closed the door. "Don't worry, hon." He put his arm around me and helped me to bed, because by that time, of course, I was a mess. And I didn't sleep all night. At about four o'clock this morning I decided to call off the abortion, then fell asleep.

But now, in the light of day, I'm all right again, just awfully tired. And I know I must go through with it. If only it would be over with. They'll all forget it. Or will they? No, I guess this will be one more thing Joe's family will hold against me.

I called Laura, hoping she would cheer me up. When I told her what happened, she said, "Well, why didn't Joe just tell them to leave?" I tried to explain how miserable poor Joe was. Then I realized how sick I was of the whole subject. "Let's talk about something else."

Laura told me something about her activity in women's groups. "It's wonderful," she said, "the way I've gotten to know—to love—some women. It's not so lonely now." She's getting involved in campaigns to set up child-care centers and may turn her studies in that direction. "Trying to create a job for myself," she said and laughed.

3:30 p.m.

The doctor just called. It's all set up. The earliest date he could get an operating room is the 26th, the day after Christmas. That means I'll go into the hospital the day before, Christmas Day. I asked if he couldn't do it any sooner, and he said we were lucky to get that date and only got it because hospitals quiet down during the holidays.

Friday, November 30

Last night, as soon as Joe got home, I told him that the date was set. He just nodded.

At the dinner table, I told Lulu. Then I said to both of them, "Now, it's all taken care of, and there's no reason to discuss it anymore. So let's just not say anything about it."

"To anyone?"

"To anyone. Then, after I have the . . . after it's all over, you can tell your friends I lost the baby."

Lulu bit her lip. "I don't usually lie to my friends."

I looked at her for a minute. "That's a nasty mixture of insensitivity and self-righteousness."

"I don't know what those words mean."

"Then look them up! Listen, I don't care what you tell your friends. But I don't want to discuss the subject again."

Joe reached out and patted my arm. "Don't yell, hon, she doesn't mean anything."

And Lulu mumbled, "Well, it sure will mess up Christmas."

"Shh," Joe said to her, but not sternly, just with a sort of silly, clowning grin. She smiled back at him, and then we ate silently while I tried to keep control of myself. Joe was laughing and talking, trying to ease the tension.

But when we were getting ready to go to bed, Joe said, "You know, she's right. We're supposed to go to your folks this year for Christmas, aren't we? It'll be like a wake. You know how my mother will act. And with her knowing about it, I don't see how you can keep it from your mother."

"Couldn't we . . . maybe we could go somewhere, do something else this Christmas?" I suggested.

"Not spend Christmas with the family!" Joe sounded as if I'd suggested a trip to Mars. "That would be even worse."

He was right. Either way it's going to be a mess. "I could always get sick on Christmas Day—that's it," I said. "We'll call in the morning and say I came down with the flu, and you and Lulu can go to Christmas dinner without me. That way I can get to the hospital in the afternoon."

202

Joe was silent. Then he said, "I still think my mother will tell your folks."

"Yes." I thought about that, about the feelings between my family and Joe's, about the way his mother would tell mine, about how my mother would feel hearing it from her.

"I think we've got to tell your mother. Then we don't mention it again."

I knew he was right. I nodded. "I'm just too tired to think about it." But we decided to go over to see my parents tonight.

I hoped a good night's sleep would prepare me, but I hardly slept all night thinking about what my mother's reaction would be. It won't be like Joe's mother, not the Catholic thing. And my mother doesn't especially like children. But somehow I feel so apprehensive, like a little girl again, who's been naughty. Oh, how I wish this thing was over with.

10 p.m.

It was as bad as I expected.

This time it was Joe who did the explaining. When we went in, he said, "Ella has decided to have an abortion."

My mother just sat there white-faced for a while and then said, "Well, that's her decision."

They were talking as if I weren't even there.

And I knew that comment wouldn't end the discussion. It was only the beginning. I could see the anger rising in her and felt scared the way I used to when I was a child. It was only a matter of time before it would all come pouring out.

And it did.

My duty to my family. Shirking my responsibility. Doing something and then trying to escape the consequences. What would all our friends and neighbors say? And Joe's

203

family? What had she done wrong in raising me? I had always been . . . etc., etc.

I can write this calmly now, but when she begins to talk that way, I'm helpless. Before she had talked for five minutes I was paralyzed, unable to answer. Joe did all the talking, but everything he said just made matters worse. "She doesn't want to have another baby, she wants to . . . develop herself." I winced, knowing how my mother would react to that. All my father said was, "This must be something she picked up at that place." He meant the college. He looked angry too, but probably because he knew some of my mother's anger would fall on him and he resented me for making that happen.

So I sat there, and they discussed me, and every defense Joe made of me only enraged my mother more. She said, "Joe, do you want this?" And Joe was silent. Then my mother started crying and for the first time spoke directly to me. "I don't understand you, I don't understand you," was all she said . . . and I could agree with that, but I kept still.

I can write this out now with relief, knowing that no matter what I did she would disapprove. She disapproved when I got pregnant and disapproves of the abortion, but she has always disapproved. That's her, that's just her.

But knowing this didn't stop my emotions from taking over, and it was all I could do to sit there without screaming. On the way home I just fell apart, and Joe kept his arm around me as he drove.

But now I'm beginning to wonder if

Saturday, December 1

Joe interrupted me last night. He walked into the bedroom and said, "Are you writing in that thing again?" I began to put it away, almost guiltily, but then I stopped.

204

"Yes. You don't mind, do you?"

"No, whatever you want."

Again I almost put it away but caught myself and looked at him. "But you do mind. Why don't you say so?"

"What's the point? I don't want to argue with you. Do what you want, hon."

"It doesn't have to be an argument. We could discuss it. You could tell me why you don't want me to write in my journal, and I could tell you why I do it, and maybe . . ."

He put his arms around me. "Why talk about it? You go ahead and do whatever you want."

"But isn't it better to talk about it? If you don't want me to do something, I sense it and I feel guilty. I feel a silent pressure on me to stop doing it. It's worse than an argument, don't you see?"

He just looked helplessly confused. "Gee, no, what can I do? I tell you, Do what you want. That's what I mean. I mean what I say; do what you want. Now you say I'm wrong for what I don't say. What can I do?"

He looked so hurt I didn't know what to say. He doesn't understand that he makes me feel this way. Maybe it's just me.

As we got into bed and turned off the light, I told him, "I'm thinking of taking a couple of classes again."

There was a moment of silence and then he said, "Sure." Then a heavy silence in the dark. But I told myself, The family has been told, we won't discuss the abortion again, and Monday I'll go out to the college and apply for the spring semester. Then I fell asleep.

Monday, December 3

The weekend was pretty bad. Too much time on our hands, I guess. Joe looked sad, and I tried to act as if I didn't

205

notice. I suggested that we get our Christmas tree early, so we went out and got the tree and decorated it.

Then this morning I got really annoyed at Joe.

Just before he left for work, he asked if I was still going back to school and I said yes, I would apply today at the college.

"Then you won't be able to work at all from now on."

"I don't know. Why?"

He was quiet for a minute, as if reluctant to hurt my feelings. "Well, you ran up some pretty heavy bills with that headshrinker, and the abortion won't be cheap."

"But I made enough money to pay Redford, didn't I?" He didn't say anything.

After he left, I went to the drawer where he keeps the checkbook and looked. He hasn't paid even one third of what we owe Redford. He must have used the money I earned to pay other bills. At first I was upset. But I'm not going to worry about it. Maybe I can get a part-time job and still go to school. After all, Laura works and goes to school and has three children, and she manages. There's no reason why I can't work and go to school too.

My breasts feel heavy today. I feel my waist thickening, but it's probably just my imagination. I'm marking off the days on a little calendar and trying to think ahead, trying to think of what I'll be doing a month from now.

4 p.m.

Driving to the campus, all the way, from the moment I got into my car, was such a strange experience. I was thinking of the first time I did it, how frightened I was and how confused about why I was going or what I'd find there; defensive and hostile. Then I thought about other days driving there, days when my head was full of the books and ideas, and other days when my head was full of Dan, and I was as confused as I'd been at the beginning. A whole rush of memories and emotions that seemed to come from a time so long ago. Really only a few months ago, but for me such a long time.

I parked my car and walked to the registrar's office. This time I knew what to do, and it didn't take very long to fill out the forms. One of the instructors walked by, recognized me and waved, just as if I'd never been gone. And I felt as if I were more at home here than anywhere else. Not that I have illusions about the place. The music blasted clear across the campus now—they must have gotten outdoor loudspeakers —and there seemed to be even more people just restlessly milling about.

The sun was bright and the sky a hard blue. I started feeling better than I had in so long, so long—I decided to take a short walk around the campus. I went past the cafeteria and the library, up the slope toward the humanities building, but I veered off before I got there and went over the lawn, behind the science building, and down through the arboretum toward the creek.

I was almost on top of them before I saw them.

". . . and, of course, the minute you open yourself to ideas, they rush on you like a wave that feels as if it's going to drown you."

It was Dan. He was sitting on a rock at the edge of the creek. Beside him, sitting on the grass, looking up at him with wide eyes, was a woman about my age, maybe a little older. She was plump, with tense lines around her mouth, and her hair was streaked where its natural brown and gray was coming through the red dye job she was letting grow out.

207

"But you'll find—Ella!"

"Hello, Dan." My voice sounded quite calm. Warm and friendly. I realized that was just how I felt, warm and friendly and glad to see him again.

"You two have to meet!" he said. "Ella, this is Mary Rugo. This is her first semester."

"Hello, Mary," I said. She nodded at me but hardly took her eyes off Dan.

"Ella was one of my best students. I never saw anyone go so far so fast. Remarkable! Are you at Cal?"

I shook my head. Then I looked at the woman and said, "You're lucky you got into Dan's class; he's a good teacher."

"Sit down, sit down and tell us—"

"No, I'm in a hurry," I said. As I walked away, I heard them begin to talk again, the insistent, passionate, hoarse voice over her soft murmurings. And I smiled because I didn't hate him anymore. And I didn't love him anymore. I just . . . knew him, and was grateful for what he was and what he had done for me, and didn't blame him for not being able to do everything for me. I understood and I forgave him. I understood and I forgave myself.

I understood my mistake. For all the writing I've done in this journal about problems of women, I must have fallen into the oldest, stupidest woman's attitude—seeing myself and my problems and my needs in terms of men. I had realized that I had to make a change. But I saw that change as a change of men, as if I don't exist except as part of a man. But I'm not Joe and I'm not Dan, and I'm not defined by my relation to either of them. They're just a part of my life. I'm myself, although I'm not too sure who that is yet. But I know who it isn't. And what I need to do has to happen in myself. Everything else is just a detour—falling in love, getting

208

pregnant, whatever—just detours away from doing the real job, whatever that is.

That's what I have to learn to do: face things head on; no evasions, no detours, no easy ways out.

On the way home I stopped at the library. I picked up about a dozen books. Gandhi's autobiography, some Tolstoy, *The Way of All Flesh* (that's one of Dan's favorites that I never got around to), piles of Aldous Huxley. No more just marking off the days. It feels so good to get going again.

Tuesday, December 4

When Joe got home he looked at me, then at the pile of books on the sideboard, then got a look on his face that suddenly enraged me. It was as though his look, his presence, just wiped out all the good feeling I'd had all day. I tried to calm myself by looking squarely at him and analyzing the look, trying to understand it. It was a kind of sad, hangdog look, like a mute beaten animal. Then I analyzed my own feelings; that was easy, guilt. I was doing things—I didn't seem to be able to help doing things—that hurt him. It reminded me of my mother, how I never seemed to be able to do anything she could approve of. I opened my mouth to tell him how I felt but then closed it again. It was futile. He'd just deny that anything was wrong. And he'd be right, in a way, because he doesn't realize. . . .

So I pretended not to notice the way he looked at the books, tried not to guess at how much he resented my getting back into reading and school again. I just chattered on about the campus and the books I got and pretended that everything was all right.

But it made me so tired! I can't do that. I can't pretend

things. I just kept looking at the way he was acting, feeling myself getting more tired, feeling that he was trying to wear me down, trying to make me feel guilty, and I was feeling the guilt, but fighting it now and just getting madder and madder.

I guess that's why it happened.

We were watching TV—or, rather, Joe was watching and I was sitting with him, reading a book and half-watching the show, a comedy which showed a father's bungling efforts to take care of a new baby while his wife recovered. I was dimly aware of an image of the father rocking the baby, when Joe got up and turned off the TV. I looked up. He glanced quickly at me, then away, and the hangdog look was so deep and pathetic that it looked like a caricature of itself.

"What's wrong?" Then suddenly I understood. "The TV show. About the new baby."

He just sat down and patted my hand. I jumped as if he'd touched me with a lit cigarette, and he gave me a surprised look. I kept looking at his face.

"I thought," I said, "we were just going to forget it, not talk about it anymore."

"I'm trying to. I didn't say anything."

"You didn't say anything!" I took a couple of deep breaths. "Joe, you can't keep doing this to me."

"Doing what?"

His eyes were clear and innocent. It was amazing. "You really don't know, do you? What you said to Lulu the other night, telling your mother, dragging me out to tell my mother and now this—getting all emotional about a stupid TV program. You're trying to wear me down so I'll give in."

"I'm not doing anything. I can't help the way I feel."

"Joe, how do you really feel?" He tried to get up, but I pulled him back down on the sofa again. I kept saying to myself, No evasions, get things straight. "No, I really don't know how you feel. Does this baby mean so much to you? I can't understand that. When we had Lulu you hardly looked at her for years. You always called children brats and said large families were terrible. You said you didn't want any more children. In all those years you never said you had any interest in another baby. In fact, you were as careful as I was in making sure I used the diaphragm, in never taking a chance if we were somewhere without it.

"Until just lately. It's only been in the last few months that you couldn't wait, you were always at me, let's take a chance this one time, the jelly ruins it, and all that. As if you wanted to make me pregnant. You did. You wanted to make me pregnant. Why? Why does a baby suddenly mean so much to you?"

"Look, hon, whatever you want—"

"Stop that!" I yelled. "We're talking about what *you* want!" I saw the look on his face change. It was still hangdog, but sullen, the way Lulu looks when she doesn't get her way and she knows I'm going to stand firm. I kept yelling. I'd never yelled at Joe before, but I knew if I didn't keep yelling he'd slip away from me again. I had to push him into a corner and keep him there until . . . "You wanted me pregnant! Didn't you?"

"Yes!"

"And you want me to have this baby whether I want to or not! Don't you?"

"Yeah!"

"But why! Why?"

"That should be easy for you to see. So I'll keep you. So I won't lose you."

"Lose me? What are you talking about?" But I felt a kind of shock in the middle of my body. My question, I knew,

211

was some kind of lie. He had hit on something, something true. All of a sudden I felt afraid.

"I'm talking about you leaving me. Don't you think I can see it coming? I'm not stupid." That was the first time he'd ever said that.

"Oh, Joe." I put my arms around him, but I felt strange, afraid, false. "Joe, that's not true. What would I do without you, a silly neurotic like me?"

"You're not," he mumbled. "You were when you married me. You were a mess. But there's nothing wrong with you now. So you don't need me anymore."

"That's not true!" But I didn't know if it was true or not. My feelings were so mixed up, everything was shaking inside of me, and on top of it the guilt came in on me again like a cold chill—guilt that it might be true that I had used him and would leave him when I was through. Haven't I fantasized leaving him? Didn't Dan once accuse me of using *him*? I was so confused and frightened that I just kept talking to drown out the questions in my head.

"It's not true, Joe. I love you. I need you. I'll always . . . " And the more I talked the more uncertain I was, the more hollow the words sounded.

And Joe was silent and just kept his arms around me and patted me. And I asked myself how many times we'd sat this way, with me torn apart and sniveling and him holding me.

Too many times.

And then something clear and cool and logical fell with a thud into the midst of my emotions. I pulled my head up from his shoulder and looked Joe in the face.

"Joe, how long have you felt this way? For a long time?" He nodded. "Then why didn't you ever say anything?"

"How could I say anything?"

"Maybe you're right. But—but Joe. To get me pregnant when you know I don't want that, to do all these things to try to wear me down, to try to make me fall apart, to be so sick I just collapse and give in, out of guilt, and have a baby I don't want. Joe, how can you do that to me?"

He didn't answer.

"It's wrong, Joe. You should have said something, anything. We should have reached some understanding some way, but not this; can't you see how awful it is to do it this way?"

"Right, wrong, I don't know. I just love you. Besides, I can't talk to you. You always beat me with words."

"Beat you? What is this, a contest?"

"See what I mean? You make me feel like a heel for loving you. I just want you. I never wanted much all my life." The hangdog look had come back again. "I just love you. That a crime? Aside from that I'm a simple guy. I don't need anything. I'm happy if I can eat, drink and screw."

"So is a pig!"

The words were out before I had any idea they were coming. I was as shocked as Joe when I heard them. No, I was more shocked. He looked almost as if he had expected this. I was too appalled even to apologize. I couldn't think of anything to say.

After a while Joe got up and went to bed, and I stayed on the sofa all night. When I heard him get up this morning I started to get up to fix his breakfast but stopped. I heard the door open and close and the car start. He left without breakfast.

Lulu got up a few minutes later and did the same thing. I guess she heard us last night.

And now I sit here and think. And think. And hear those

213

words echoing in my head. It's as if when my guilt was gone, when I saw how Joe had manipulated me, when I saw him using my guilt, forcing something on me, when I saw he was just as bad . . . then all at once that came out. As if it had been waiting.

It's the way I really feel, I guess. Yes, that's what I really believe, that a human being shouldn't be content just to eat, drink and screw. That's not being human. I know a lot of people are. I know that for most people in the world, people in misery and poverty, that's their only pleasure. I don't blame them. But for people above the level of bare survival, for people like us, it isn't enough.

Who am I to judge? Joe is happy in the world, he fits, and people love him because he's that way, so why should he change? And I married him because he was well adjusted and I wasn't.

But I guess I didn't love him. I don't know if I ever loved anyone. I was "in love" with Dan, but I don't know if I loved him. I don't know what love is.

Did Joe always know I didn't love him? I guess he did. And he wanted me anyway. I don't know if I think that's wonderful or terrible.

I don't care if most people think you should be unthinking and happy to eat, drink and screw. Thoreau said if you're right you're a majority of one.

That's the trouble with reading books. It's not just a question of me doing what I want and Joe doing what he wants, and each letting the other. In some deep way, we're enemies of what the other wants.

Enemies! What a word. I'm really confused.

There's only one thing I'm sure of. That was the end. Some couples can quarrel and make up, say vile things and forget them, but Joe and I have never been that way. Besides what I said was too . . . too fundamental for him ever to forgive. Too basic to be explained or talked over or resolved.

He won't be back.

I'll be alone, like Laura.

I feel the strangest mixture of relief and terror.

Midnight

Joe came home at the usual time. Everything normal. Cheerful. As if nothing happened. I begin to wonder if anything really did happen.

When we went to bed, he wanted to make love, but I started to gag.

He's asleep. I can't. I can't write either. I sit here and hold this notebook and feel dull and stupid.

Monday, December 10

A quiet week. But I feel nauseated a lot. Isn't it too early for that?

It feels as if Joe and I have just gone around in a circle and we're back where we were before, with Joe being nice, easygoing Joe, and me feeling guilty for having hurt him.

Last night we were lying in bed in the dark and I asked him, "Do you love me, Joe?"

"You know I do."

"What does it feel like? I mean, loving me? What do you feel toward me?"

"I just want you, want to be with you."

"Why?"

"What do you mean, why?"

"I mean, why do you love me? What is there about me that you love? When you fell in love with me, when we were kids, why did you love me?"

He was silent in the dark for a long time. "Oh, because you were different, I guess."

"How different?"

"Not stupid, like me!" He laughed.

"Joe, don't talk that way. You're not stupid. There are lots of people at the college that aren't as intelligent as you. You could run rings around them if you wanted to. You just don't want to. You just aren't interested."

"That's right," he said.

"Then why were you interested in me?"

"Because you're just . . . interesting, that's all. I was always proud I had an intelligent wife. Who wants to live with a stupid woman? I knew you were real smart but not very strong, kind of sick, emotionally."

"You didn't mind that?"

"No, I figured, it goes with the brains. And you needed me."

"But what was in it for you?"

"What do you mean?"

"I mean . . . if I was different in ways . . . if I'm interesting because I'm interested in things that don't interest you, and neurotic as well . . ."

He laughed. "Boy, you sure can get tangled up in words. I figured we make the perfect couple, brain and brawn." Then he began to pinch me and try to make me laugh.

"Don't, Joe." He stopped. "Then . . ." I thought for a while. "I had something you needed too."

"Sure, you might say that."

"Even though what it is doesn't interest you, in fact, bothers you. . . ."

"Huh? Aren't you tired? I am. I got to go to work tomorrow. Let's get some sleep."

And he did. But I didn't.

Tuesday, December 11

Tonight at dinner Lulu said, "Nancy's parents are getting a divorce. That's the third one of my friends."

"Why, what's the matter." asked Joe.

"How should I know?" said Lulu.

"Tolstoy said that happy families are all happy in the same way, but unhappy families are unhappy in different ways," I said.

Silence.

"Well, with so many people splitting up," said Joe, "there has to be a reason."

"Maybe . . . maybe everyone's like the man in your army joke," I said. "Everyone's looking for something, here, there, picking up something and dropping it, not sure what it is. . . . "

"Yeah, all crazy." Joe laughed. "They should be like me. I'm happy if—"

Then he stopped, and I suddenly started gagging and had to go to the bathroom and vomit.

Wednesday, December 12

Every time Joe comes near me I start to gag. It's the cigarette smoke, I guess. It bothered me when I was pregnant for Lulu.

Thursday, December 13

I've got to do something to keep busy. I tried Christmas shopping but that's too awful, makes me feel worse. It'll be such a grim Christmas, it's best not to think about it. Even our tree has started to droop.

Joe's mother calls and says things like "You're twisting a

knife in my heart." My mother isn't speaking to me. That's good.

The sicker I get the more solicitous Joe is, the more tender and loving. It's then that he looks very handsome and strong, no hangdog look, as if my weakness gives him strength. Ten more days.

Took all the books back and got some more.

Friday, December 14

Today I went to see Laura. Her house was so full of activity it made me dizzy. Christmas activities are completely devoted to the peace movement. They didn't buy gifts but put the money into a fund for antiwar groups. So they were making gifts for each other, "Garbage gifts," Laura called them, to be made only from cast-off things. Her son is home from college with some friends. We argued about Tolstoy. It was fun.

"Your children are not so hostile toward you," I said. "I think they like you."

Laura nodded. "It's getting better, with only occasional flashes of hostility."

"You're making a happy life for yourself."

She shrugged. "A busy life, a crowded life. But lonely."

"Everyone's lonely."

I felt so much better after seeing her that I decided to spend my afternoons there next week. It'll pass the time, and I can help with the mailing—there's a huge mailing of gifts and cards to prisoners instead of Christmas cards. That's what I need, to do something for people who have *real* problems, to forget myself and keep busy.

When Joe got home tonight I was busy and lively as I was

218

the day I went to the college. He got quiet as I told him I was going to work at Laura's house this week.

And then it started again.

"There's plenty to do for Christmas here," he said.

"Oh, let's face it, our Christmas this year is shot."

"Yeah, I guess it is."

"Joe, please understand. I've got a few days to get through. I don't know how I'll make it, but if this will help . . . "

"And then after . . . ?"

"After what?"

"You're going to keep going over there, seeing her?"

"I don't know. Why?" There was the old look again. "What is it?"

"Nothing."

"Why don't you want me to see her?"

"A divorcee . . . in Berkeley." I can't even describe the tone he used when he said *Berkeley.* "Running around with men. . . ."

I laughed. "It's not that way at all. I told you. She's very lonely, she's wrapped up in her children—she's a much better mother than I! And she . . ." I stopped. "Joe, do you want to tell me not to see her?"

"Did I ever tell you what to do?"

I just looked at him, and this time he turned away.

"Is it always going to be this way, Joe?"

"What way?"

"Are you always going to be so afraid?"

Then he turned and looked at me, and this time I turned away.

I know what I have to do. Just take him at his word and do what I want. But it's so hard. I don't feel strong enough. And

Joe's very strong. And everyone's on his side. Well, almost everyone.

Sunday, December 16

Two parties this weekend. Everyone asking when we were expecting. We left early. I drove; Joe was too drunk. I've never seen him so drunk. But at least we left early, escaped the boring gaiety.

Maybe there are times when it's best to be out of touch with your thoughts, busy and unthinking. Maybe this is one of those times.

Stop writing, try to stop thinking until the operation is done. Then I'll be able to think straight.

Tuesday, December 25—at last!

Every day last week was the same. I'd go to Laura's house and throw myself into some kind of work there, coming home in time to cook dinner. Lulu had a job in a department store, so she and Joe got home at about the same time.

Joe would start to drink, and Lulu and he would trade stories about their jobs, Lulu talking mostly about the clothes she was going to buy with the money she made. Lulu has stopped speaking to me altogether. Exactly when this happened, I can't recall, but I noticed it last week.

Joe was just the opposite. Every night he came home with some decoration or gift for Christmas. His behavior toward me had completely changed. I steeled myself to withstand his moping and was completely thrown off balance by his slightly drunken good cheer. But I recognized the effects of it on me. It was as if I stood back and watched myself, feeling guilty, thinking what a good person Joe is and—and the part of me standing back and watching was infuriated.

All the little festive things he and Lulu did for a business-as-usual Christmas infuriated me too. I sat quietly trying to read throughout all the giggling and wrapping of gifts. I saw Joe bring home boxes from expensive stores, and I thought, Wait till the bills come. So now I was the sulking one with the hangdog look—no, not hangdog or beaten. Even when I'm beaten I don't look that way. I just look, as Lulu says, mean.

On Saturday night Joe tried to get me to make love. I couldn't. I wouldn't. What does it matter which? After that I stayed on the couch.

"What does this mean?" he said, slurring his words, his face flushed.

"It just means"—I was going to cry but I didn't—"it means leave me alone just until after Christmas."

Yesterday, Christmas Eve, Joe got home at noon. He started right in drinking, and there wasn't much laughing and clowning anymore. My mother called to say she had prayed hard for the strength to forgive me and hoped we would come to Christmas dinner. I told her I had to go to the hospital in the afternoon but that Joe and Lulu could come.

After lunch Lulu left to go shopping. She had been paid and couldn't wait to spend it. Joe hugged and kissed her and said good-bye three or four times.

When she was gone, I asked, "What was all that? She's just going to the store."

"I don't know how much I'll be seeing my daughter from now on." I looked at him. "It's just a matter of time, once you get the abortion and nothing's holding you here. Why kid myself? You want me to go."

I almost begged him to just leave me alone until after the

operation, but I didn't. I said, "I think . . . yes, maybe we should separate for a while."

"Not for a while. You're through with me. I'm in your way. You want to find some guy that you have more in common with, like that teacher."

I guess that was his last weapon. But it didn't work, because I just don't feel guilty about Dan anymore.

"No," I said, "that's not the answer either."

"Then what is, what do you want?"

"I don't know. I have to do something, be something, but I can't do it with you." I was surprised to hear the words coming out of me so calmly. "I'm always in the wrong with you. Everything I think or do seems freaky or frightening. The only time you feel all right about things is when I'm miserable and believing I'm crazy to think at all. Otherwise you're always looking hurt or—"

"I wasn't like that this week. I'm trying . . ."

". . . anything you can to keep me."

"Maybe I'll start reading more, then we could—"

"That would be fine, but if you're just doing it to please me it doesn't mean anything. Besides, it's not just a question of common interests, or brain and brawn, intellectual and nonintellectual."

"It's not?"

"No. I don't know what it is. Maybe it's feelings."

"You think I don't have any feelings."

"I didn't mean that. But you don't like unpleasant feelings. You want to close them off. But there are so many things in life that cause unpleasant feelings. . . ."

"I got my share of unpleasant feelings right now."

"Yes, but that's different. I'm forcing them on you. It's not the same as the feelings that come from—"

222

"Okay, I don't want unpleasant feelings. I want to enjoy life. I should look for suffering?"

"You don't have to look for it. It comes with . . . with being aware, and if you're unwilling to take it, you just keep cutting off and cutting off awareness."

"And you get stupid, like me."

"You're not stupid. When you say things like that, you're very, very clever. Because they shake me, shake my confidence in anything I feel, make me think I'm the one who's stupid and cruel . . . and weird."

"I always thought we were good for each other, that one like you in the family was enough, that we—"

"Complemented each other? That's what we told each other. That was our bargain, like we could split the work, you be unconscious for me and I'd be conscious for you. I think it was a lie. I think we're enemies. I think as long as I'm with you I'll be sick and neurotic because that's the way you want me, because that proves you're right, and yet . . . and yet you want me because you know a person can't live without feeling. But you can't do it this way. Joe, you can't *own* feeling, you have to *feel* feeling."

I can't describe the look that came over his face then. I knew I was right, I knew I was finally beginning to understand, because his face looked for a moment like the face of a man who has lost his balance and is falling from a great height, falling to his death.

Then he caught himself. "Well, I'll need a few things."

"Now?"

He shrugged. "Why wait?"

I was suddenly afraid. What if all this was just talk, what if he was right and I was so sick I couldn't. . . . All this went through my mind as I calmly got up. "All right." I went to the bedroom and started to pack a suitcase for him. He stayed in the living room, and I could hear the clink of a bottle against his glass.

It seems absurd now, when I look back at it, this last scene, with me, like the mother whose boy has said he would run away from home if she would pack a suitcase for him. But I didn't even think of anything like that.

I thought of our whole life together, and of how I had made the bargain too, out of my cowardice, marrying Joe because I too wanted to own something, the love and acceptance he got from people. Because he was what I wanted to be—just like everyone else. And yet, he wasn't just like everyone else or he wouldn't have wanted me.

And I thought of how unsatisfactory a life it had been for him after all, how little he'd asked and how much less he'd gotten. And I thought of his unexciting but rare virtues, how he'd supported us, worked steadily, been a faithful husband, kept an even temper. And I thought of how Lulu would miss him, and how much more she would hate me.

And then I saw that his favorite shirt needed ironing, so I set up the ironing board, and my tears started falling on the shirt while I ironed it, and after a little while Joe came and sat quietly by the ironing board, watching me.

"And look, hon, if you ever need anything, if . . . "

I looked up from my ironing into his miserable face. No one could say he was not suffering now . . . and I just fell toward him.

For a long time I wasn't conscious of anything but my own sobs that seemed to drag all my strength out of me. Then gradually I became aware of his patting my shoulder, kissing my head. I was on his lap, and I seemed to be getting smaller and smaller. "It's all right, hon. Just lean on me. I'll take care of you."

I looked at his face. It was smiling and in his smile was . . . triumph.

"Let go of me!" I tried to get up, but he held me. "Let go!" I yelled. "For God's sake, let go!" I jumped up and began to grab things. I picked up the suitcase, dumped his clothes out on the floor, opened drawers and started stuffing some of my things into it. Then I stopped, threw the suitcase aside, grabbed my coat and purse and ran.

"What are you doing?"

I didn't answer. I was afraid to talk, afraid that words, explanations, arguments would just slow me down, make me unsure again. I knew I had just enough strength to get out, no more.

I drove to Laura's house. When she saw me she didn't ask any questions, and I just lay in the dark in her room for the rest of the day, and most of the night, hearing faintly the Christmas Eve bustle of her children.

Late that night, when she came to bed, I started to talk. I talked all night, not to tell her what had happened but to say it all to myself. To begin, to just begin to understand where I was, what I was doing and where I was going.

"This is the best way," I said. "For me to leave. The house, that life, even our daughter—none of that has anything to do with me. Maybe someday Lulu will . . ." I started to turn cold all over. "I mustn't think about her now."

"No, you mustn't."

"I was a terrible wife to him . . . and that's the only way he could have me, sick and sniveling, but he wanted me anyway. Is that love?"

Laura laughed. "It sounds more like cannibalism."

"Look, I don't want to minimize my part in—"

225

"Of course, of course," she said. "But you can't think about that now, either. You'll have all you can do just getting started, going on with—"

"With whatever it is I'm trying to do, whatever it is I'm looking for." I told her Joe's army joke, but she didn't laugh.

She said, "My back is aching from picking up every scrap I see, but I haven't found anything yet."

"Well, with so many of us looking, someone's bound to find out what we're looking for."

"On the other hand, maybe you'll go back to your husband. This separation may change him."

I thought about that. "I doubt it. I don't think they'll let it change him."

"They?"

"People. He'll be surrounded by pity—his wife left him on Christmas Eve, yet!" That made us both laugh. "Everyone will tell him what a poor abused fellow he is, such a nice guy to be treated this way. They'll invite him to dinner, introduce him to eligible women. . . . "

"That's true. There are plenty of us eager to escape single life."

"He'll be unhappy—no, Joe doesn't allow unhappiness —he'll be uncomfortable for a while. Then he'll find someone else, maybe someone easygoing like him. . . . "

"I'll bet he doesn't. I bet it'll be someone like you again."

We were quiet while we thought about this.

"And what'll I find?"

No answer. She must have fallen asleep.

For a while I thought, wondered what I will find. I don't know. But I think I know what I'm looking for. Something like that feeling I had when I was in love, that first week, when I was high and the world came alive and belonged to me, and I belonged to it. It wasn't Dan, it was something he triggered in me. Something in me.

Maybe I can find it again. If I can, if it's possible to live that way, I don't care how long it takes or how hard or . . .

I slept until noon. Then I came to the hospital and sat in the lobby until they put me to bed.

It's after midnight now, and quiet, except for the old lady in the next room who moans, "Oh, God," in her sleep.

They took samples of my urine and my blood. They bathed me. They gave me an enema. They shaved me from my nipples to my knees. They came to stand by my bed, one after another—my doctor, my anesthetist, a lab technician, and other anonymous green-coated men and women, who talked to me soothingly and ceremoniously about the operation.

I feel like a sacred virgin chosen for an elaborate initiation rite, prepared and purified according to ancient rule.

I feel like a plucked chicken about to be gutted.

I feel

Afterword

THE EDUCATION OF ELLA PRICE

> I feel like a sacred virgin chosen for an elaborate initiation rite, pre-
> pared and purified according to ancient rule.
> I feel like a plucked chicken about to be gutted.
> I feel (227)

Ella Price's Journal ends with an unpunctuated and thus unfin-
ished paragraph of two simple words: "I feel." This phrase and the
dramatic section that precedes it, including the shockingly paired
metaphors of sacrifice and evisceration, mark Dorothy Bryant's first
novel as one of awakening, of becoming, of *rebirth*. The ironies
of Ella being purified and plucked are profound, for at age thirty-
five she is neither a helpless maiden nor a mindless carcass, but
a newly empowered woman about to be anesthetized, to lose feeling—although only briefly and at her own volition. In deciding to
have an abortion and scheduling it on that most celebrated day
of birth, December 25, Ella defies many institutions; in the
process, she claims ownership and control of her body, her life.

That Ella's rebirth depends upon not giving birth is perhaps the most striking irony. While awaiting the medical procedure, she understandably uses language that removes agency, casting herself as sanctified vessel and butchered fowl—passive, helpless, invaded; she underscores, in short, how she has felt for over two decades. Like a phoenix, however, the reborn Ella, truly inspired and testing her wings, can assert a final, unfettered phrase. With that utterance ("I feel"), our initiate completes a series of life-altering decisions that have everything to do with her education.

Loosely organized around the academic year, from college enrollment in mid-September to the Christmas holiday fifteen months later, Ella's five private notebooks show her gradually becoming a critical thinker, an independent woman, and a writer of some promise. For these accomplishments, Ella can thank Bay Junior College. Like most freshmen, she enrolls in English, psychology, and social science, courses which alone might not faze a long-out-of-school suburban housewife, even during the heady days of 1960s activism. But her English class project—to keep a journal—transforms Ella. As she completes assignment after assignment, reading omnivorously and writing frequently, sometimes haltingly and other times with gusto, she discovers interests, examines choices, finds voice, and exults in how writing can beget more writing. Eventually, she also learns that fear and depression abort development.

Still widely used in English and women's studies courses and practiced by countless diarists, the journal format captures well moods and situations; encourages critical thinking, problem solving, and self-analysis; and develops writing and reading skills. Journal keepers document their personal and social histories, keep in touch with "the self," use writing as a learning tool as well as a measure of personal growth, and find what Henry James called "germs" for future pieces of writing.

For many, such notebooks chart patterns of reading and cultivate reader response. Ella's English professor, Dan Harkan, suggests that she read about female protagonists who are troubled, rebellious, conflicted. Through analyzing such works as *Madame Bovary*, *Main Street*, *Anna Karenina*, and *A Doll's House* in her journal, Ella concludes that traits the women have in common are restlessness and boredom. Typically, Harkan suggests only male writers, for in the late 1960s, reading lists included few women. Women's studies as an academic discipline was in its infancy; certainly, most junior colleges were years away from offering courses on women writers or images of women in literature. While the establishment of The Feminist Press in 1970 (followed by others such as Virago) did much to remedy the dearth of women's voices, few works by women, even the journals of Virginia Woolf or Anaïs Nin, would have been available (even had they been recommended) to Ella when she needed them. The only woman writer Ella mentions is Doris Lessing. In *The Golden Notebook*, which her new friend Laura lends her, Ella finds women refreshingly "free, independent . . . who earn their own living, raise their own children, sleep with whoever they want, make their own rules" (88) but whose lives, she feels, are not very different from hers in that they have no influence or power. At this point, in fact, Ella feels superior to Lessing's characters, for at least she is married to Joe, who protects, loves, and cares for her; she is not ready to admit to, much less shed, her life of security and mediocrity.

When she concentrates excessively on her affair with Dan Harkan, Ella equates her reaction, which she calls "narrow and petty and worrying about my 'love affair' " (170), to Emma Bovary's behavior. After experiencing the excitement of intellectual conversation and then finding her trips with Joe to nightclubs boring and depressing (and feeling guilty and somewhat sad about her reaction), she can quote G. B. Shaw's adage: learning always feels at first " 'as if you had lost something' " (111). Ella absorbs and analyzes what she reads so quickly that it is easy to agree with

Harkan's assessment of her as someone who could earn advanced degrees. Ella is a model student: disciplined, perceptive, enthusiastic, needy. But Bryant sensibly balances Ella's abilities with her equally believable naïveté. While Ella shows remarkable skill in self-analysis, for example, she can be exceptionally dense about other people. She takes as painfully long to figure out that Laura also had an affair with Harkan as to realize that he wants only casual sex and is an inept, insensitive lover.

Within the course of a few months, Ella notes aspects of her previously routine suburban life which she now finds annoying and, at times, intolerable. Needing a clear head to read and study, she cannot share martinis every evening with Joe, an activity that used to constitute their most enjoyable moments together. Ordinary shopping trips, Doris Day movies, Saturday nights at bars, and family dinners now seem boring, meaningless activities. Attending college has made Ella selfish with her time, and given her the motivation and strength to make judgments.

Before she begins keeping a notebook, Ella does not know why she feels empty and lost, and cannot perceive that she has choices. By the end of the novel, this woman, once fearful of any transgression, has rejected the major institutions in her white, suburban, lower-middle-class world: family, marriage, motherhood, religion, psychiatry. No longer hesitant and self-effacing, no longer content to accept her invisible and thus marginal status, she has joined what Adrienne Rich calls the "thousands of women asking 'The Woman Question' in women's voices" (25). By the end of her fifth notebook, Ella has also found voice as a writer of promise. Because *Ella Price's Journal* is the first of Dorothy Bryant's dozen published works, we might also say that in it, an actual writer was born.

Known especially for several works set in or near her native San Francisco, where she was born to northern Italian immigrants in

1930, Dorothy Calvetti Bryant attended public schools in the predominantly working-class Mission District. Earning a B.A. in music (1950) and, fourteen years later, an M.A. in creative writing at San Francisco State University, she taught music and English at local high schools and colleges before devoting herself to a remarkably productive literary career in the Bay Area. Disappointed by the commercial book world, in 1978 Bryant and her second husband established Ata Books, which they have developed into a noteworthy and enterprising self-publishing house. With the exception of *Ella Price's Journal* (1972) and her next and largest selling novel, the utopian *The Kin of Ata Are Waiting for You* (1976), all of Bryant's works have been released by Ata Books. In addition to ten novels and two books of nonfiction, Bryant has written four bio-historical plays, three of them produced in Berkeley in the 1990s. She also hosted a popular radio program, "Morning Reading," at Berkeley's KPFA (1980–1994). The novel *Confessions of Madame Psyche* won a 1987 American Book Award, and *Dear Master* (whose subjects are George Sand and Gustave Flaubert) was named Best New Play of 1991 by the Bay Area Critics Circle.

Reluctant to be limited as a writer by labels such as "Italian-American," "working-class," "Californian," or "feminist,"[1] Bryant continues to impress a growing readership with her prescient examination of controversial issues. She was among the first writers to turn a lens, for example, on inner-city schools, AIDS, homophobia, ex-convicts, psychic phenomena, spirituality, ageism, and the intersections of race, class, and gender. Experimental in form (the stream-of-consciousness of one novel covers only a few hours; the "confessions" of another encapsulate over thirty years), varied in point of view, and always eminently readable, Bryant's fiction—whether skillfully spun as fantasy, narrative, epistle, or history—is testament to a sympathetic writer of wide interests 232 and scope.

It could be argued that none of Bryant's work is more forward-looking, more timely, more successful in its smooth blend of form and content than *Ella Price's Journal*. One of the earliest, most moving novels about women's consciousness-raising, the novel slowly, irrefutably establishes how one woman can transform her existence. That Ella (an everywoman) is approaching mid-life, comes from the working class, is only beginning to develop her skills and confidence, and still moves forward, relatively unscathed by an unwise affair and an unsympathetic family, makes her story truly ground-breaking. And that our heroine's survival depends upon something as seemingly mundane and universally available as a few courses at the local two-year college makes her example as provocative, understated, and inspiring today as it was in 1972.

Trying to sell a first novel about a depressed housewife who attends junior college, has an affair with a professor, develops a feminist consciousness, and leaves her husband and daughter required unusual persistence. No wonder it took Bryant's agent four years to find a publisher.[2] But almost as soon as Lippincott issued it in 1972, *Redbook* ran a condensed version, which was greeted with fifty times more letters to the editor than usual for that magazine's fiction.[3] Readers saw themselves mirrored in Ella's struggles, recognized her preoccupations, shared her despair. Like the appreciators of Tillie Olsen, who respond to her so viscerally because, until reading her, they "have not seen their lives fully represented in literature" (Nelson and Huse 11), Dorothy Bryant's readers prized the intimacy and familiarity characters like Ella Price immediately establish. Ella was one of them.[4]

Some *Redbook* readers cheered thirty-five-year-old Ella Price's individualism, raised consciousness, self-awareness, and courage; others cursed her destructiveness, self-indulgence, immaturity, and rashness. (There were subscription cancellations as a result of the story's publication.) One reader wrote that she was repulsed by the work's last sentence, "I feel." She cautioned, "What sense is there to education if women's lives are to be reduced to just a feeling? . . . So much of Women's Liberation today is aimed more at dehumanizing women, which is worse than dewomanizing them" (Horr).

Now that the phrase "women's liberation" has been replaced by various feminisms, we perhaps can gauge how far women have or have not come since 1972, the date *Ms.* magazine was founded and a year before the Supreme Court's landmark decision legalizing abortion. Dorothy Bryant herself notes that by the time the climate was receptive enough for *Ella Price's Journal*, which she wrote between 1965 and 1969, some critics found her heroine's feminist realizations cliché-ridden, too "older-housewife specific." In fact, far from being marred by overworked ideas, Bryant's novel is one of the earliest to document women's consciousness-raising; it predates, for example, Marilyn French's *The Woman's Room*. Novels about feminist issues, Dorothy Bryant argues, "were not common when I wrote the book." And Bryant alone chose a returning community college student as her protagonist. Today, *Ella Price's Journal* still stands as a candid, extremely accessible, and effective document illustrating one woman's experience of what Betty Friedan called "the problem which has no name."

We have to admire Bryant's audacity in writing a novel of initiation about a hard-drinking, sexually frustrated, socially unpopular, unfocused housewife who, although born of working class parents, lives a relatively privileged, if empty life. In a short piece by Margaret Atwood called "Unpopular Gals," the narrator concludes, "You can wipe your feet on me, twist my motives around all you like, you can dump millstones on my head and drown me in the river, but you can't get me out of the story. I'm the plot, babe, and don't ever forget it" (11). While Ella Price would not voice this sentiment—and certainly not in such a cheeky, self-confident voice—we should applaud Bryant for understanding that most of the "plots" in real life have Ellas at their centers. That the book continues to sell well gratifies the novelist. But it also saddens her that the issues she addressed in the 1960s still exist and are perhaps even compounded; because more women today need to earn income without any decrease in responsibility for home and children, they may have even "less leeway to make big changes" in their lives. Bryant regrets, in a way, that the book actually is not "more dated."

Some find Ella's story too plot-driven, too predictable in showing the emergence of a feminist sensibility. Indeed, when the book came out, one reviewer complained that the novel reads "as if the author had based it upon a subject index of Gloria Steinem's speeches" (Sims). Ella's all-too-familiar sentiments might indeed grate, had Bryant not drawn such a believable character, whose unsteady movement toward feminist sensibility, self-actualization, and expressiveness can be witnessed moment by moment from the intimate perspective of reading her private notebooks. In describing the experiences of one particular woman, the author covers, without pedantry and in an admirably comprehensive fashion, the issues that many women have faced—then and now.

Disheartened—but not surprised or as yet angered—by a college community which categorizes her as an "aging Barbie doll," a "female impersonator,"[5] and a "bored suburban housewife," Ella at first reacts defensively. Her journal claims that Joe is the conspicuous consumer, that women must use beauty shop formulas to catch men, that it is impossible to keep up with society's expectations about sexuality. Once women felt ashamed if they liked sex, she muses; now they feel ashamed if they do not demand it (81).

While Ella is not yet capable of arguing against male authority, at least she records examples of chauvinism. One of the jokes in the novel is how contradictory male views about women actually are. Harkan believes, for instance, that America is really a matriarchy where men work themselves to death for women's "useless domestic frills" (23). He accuses women—and, by implication, Ella—of using men to work out their problems. Women "need, they don't love" (165), Harkan pontificates. In contrast, her psychiatrist wants Ella to adjust to the fact that since society is male-centered, women are forced to neglect their femininity. And although Joe misleads her for years into thinking that he respects her intellect, she realizes that husbands allow many things: their wives can drink, gossip, be overly child-centered, and even have an affair; but men cannot tolerate it when their women "start thinking" (107).

In charting Ella's education, Bryant carefully shows her heroine's reaction to two key men—one well-read, liberal, pessimistic; the other cheerfully ignorant, conservative, hopeful. The first is "too smart" for her; the second, "not smart enough." And both, it turns out, are unavailable for what makes a fulfilling relationship: communication, intensity of feeling, shared perspectives, intimacy, mutually satisfying sex. By the end of the novel, Ella forgives each man for his failure to understand and thus please her, and she is poised for another phase of her education. Certainly, she does not want to behave like so many fictional heroines, centering her life on men's expectations.

Initially confused by Harkan's ambivalence, lack of passion, and belief that she is using him for the "growth" that a "bored suburban housewife" particularly needs, Ella finally concedes, "I understood and I forgave" (208). No longer loving or blaming him, Ella looks back at Harkan with gratitude. After all, it is he who initiates Ella's education by encouraging her to write, read, ponder, and converse and by suggesting she keep a private journal. Constantly challenging, opening up radical ways for her to think, he is a notable mentor, one whose goal is to help junior college students—what he calls "the mass man"—become "decent, moral, thinking people" (115).

Readers who accuse Harkan of sexual harassment should

remember that Ella does not show him abusing his authority.[6] The fact that they consummate their affair in her daughter's bedroom also indicates Ella's willing participation. Besides, Ella believes she has found her first real love. But while he is controversial and exciting in the classroom, Harkan fizzles as a lover. He is a withholder, and what incriminates him most is his selfishness in not making clear to Ella the casual nature of his sexual interest. If falling in love with Harkan is unwise, at least it enables Ella to reevaluate her dead-end (and deadened) marriage and, at the same time, realize that sex, even in a potentially torrid affair with one's professor, can be disappointing. Unlike the heroines in *Madame Bovary* and *Anna Karenina*, whose tragic stories Ella has read, and unlike even the more aware protagonist of Kate Chopin's feminist classic *The Awakening*, Ella does *not* end her affair in suicide. Her romance with Harkan initially broadens her passions and her world, and she does not allow its frustrations, both inside and outside of bed, to destroy her.

In Joe Price, Bryant offers a prototype of what has since become a cliché: a husband jealous, fearful, and finally foiled by his wife's return to school. While it takes Joe longer than many men to discourage outright his wife's education, he uses covert means all along: drinking too much, showing disinterest in her studies, planning a surprise Hawaiian vacation for them during final examinations, and, most reprehensible of all, leading her into an unwanted pregnancy.

After realizing he has tried to subvert her education and weaken her growing sense of empowerment, Ella forgives Joe too. To have married this man she initially calls "one of the best human beings I know" (38) was simply a mistake—a simple mistake with complicated consequences. Just before she leaves him, Ella remembers Joe as a good supporter, hard worker, and faithful, even-tempered husband. But she can now also perceive his

238

terrible limitations. Two decades later in *The Test* (1991), Bryant more explicitly outlines the type of man Joe is. In this case the narrator recollects a 1970s family get-together where gender roles are clear-cut.

> Men who drank a little too much or idled between jobs a little too long, or puttered absent-mindedly in a business kept afloat by a wife, or owed a little too much for another new car, or teased the women and children with jokes that were a little too cruel. Easy going men, untroubled by any event or thought that did not threaten their own comfort. Blind to any problem until their wives had solved it. Heedless of the set mouths and flashing eyes of these anxious, difficult women, whose worse misfortune or disgrace would be to lose these men, to fail this relation. (113)

By the end of the novel, Ella has been educated to such an extent that she, despite emotional stress, can try to instruct Joe. Through her persistent and, indeed, painful coaching, he reluctantly admits that he married her partly because of her neuroticism; he begins to regret that he has not tapped his own potential; and he finally understands that he has tried to "own" feelings, simply by controlling Ella. Through Joe, Bryant hints that a woman's liberation can also encourage a change of consciousness in a man (and thus even further chip away at socialized gender roles); nevertheless, for Ella to achieve her fullest growth, she must leave her husband.

In centering her first novel on a woman who enters college late, and in looking at the short-range effects as well as long-range potential of that experience, Dorothy Bryant began a body of work which is perhaps more devoted to formal education than that of any other contemporary writer. Bryant herself taught for thirty years, half of them on the college level, and she peoples her fiction with teachers, professors, instructors, mentors, critics, students, bookstore employees, test takers, readers, and writers. Several of her ten novels offer educators as main characters. *Miss Giardino* (1978), for example, portrays a sixty-eight-year-old retired public school teacher; *A Day in San Francisco* (1982) follows the activities of a history and women's studies professor; and the middle-aged female narrator of The Test (1991) teaches English as a second language.

Dorothy Bryant based *Ella Price's Journal* on her own experiences as a teacher at Contra Costa College in California, where she faced educational barriers firsthand. When hired in 1964, she was only the second female English department member in the school's twenty-year existence. As was too common throughout the country, women basically taught only subjects like domestic science. In the San Francisco State creative writing department, where Bryant earned an M.A., she encountered no women instructors. Bryant says she is relieved that "there are so many faculty WOMEN now, we don't need Dan."

In replying to *Redbook*'s question about how she, while at Contra Costa, arrived at her subject, Bryant recalled:

> I first thought of it while a woman sat weeping in my office, telling me that going to school was the only positive thing in her life but that her development was wrecking her marriage and her relationships with relatives, neighbors and friends. My colleagues confirmed my feelings that there are more and more such women every year and that they are often the best students— aware, intelligent, energetic—but doomed to frustration. No one seemed to care much. I care, so I wrote this book. ("Letters")

Bryant's decision to set the initial part of her novel on the campus of a "junior college" (what today we generally call "community college") was unusually forward-looking, not to mention gutsy. Few literary works of any genre and length concentrate on the much-maligned "commuter" campus, where the most difficult problem is often seen as vying for a parking space. Bryant rightly sees two-year institutions as sites of empowerment, places where

240

one's age, class, ethnicity, sexual orientation, and level of preparation can cause less anxiety than at elite schools. At many community colleges, nontraditional students *are* the mainstream.

When Bryant wrote *Ella Price's Journal*, perhaps it was true that, as Dan Harkan says, nearly 80 percent of those attending junior colleges dropped out and that returning and other unconventional students rarely enrolled. However, as Liza Fiol-Matta's editorial in a special issue of *Women's Studies Quarterly* on community colleges points out, in America's nearly fifteen hundred two-year schools, almost 40 percent of the students now earn associate's degrees. Public community colleges currently lead all higher education institutions in student enrollment, and the fact that they draw from groups disproportionately excluded from elite and other four-year schools underscores their importance. Today, women make up over 58 percent of the community college student body (and more than half of the faculty), and increasing numbers of them are women Ella's age or older (Fiol-Matta 5). Like Bryant's protagonist, many devour books, perform excellently, readily apply their studies to their lives, and bring to the classroom rich experiences. They thrive at two-year colleges, where classes generally are small and attention to student needs generous. Such students, in fact, are themselves transforming life as we know it on campuses around the country. And some of them have read or will be reading *Ella Price's Journal*.[7]

Ella Price's Journal also addresses America's most subtle and overlooked instrument of control: social class. By locating the novel on a community college campus, Bryant gives the issue of class unusual clarity and visibility, placing it—without apology, discomfort, or exaggeration—exactly where proponent of working-class studies Janet Zandy argues it should be, "at the center of educational practices" (3). Bryant herself comments, "The first one-third of the book stands quite well still, because it is not (most of

241

it) older-housewife-specific. It comes from my experience of teaching, as well as growing up with, working-class people."

While the 1980s and 1990s have seen writers such as Bobbie Ann Mason, Sandra Cisneros, Barbara Kingsolver, and Dorothy Allison bring the experiences of working-class characters to the foreground, Dorothy Bryant was one of the few women to tell such a story as early as 1972. Bryant's first heroine is among her most convincing examples of someone who has tenuously and uncomfortably moved from the working class to the lower middle class. She recently noted that middle-class kids take their advantages for granted when they walk into a classroom; women like Ella, in contrast, feel insecure, scared, angry. In capturing the flavor of such a woman's life and consciousness (her curiosity and confusion about student protest, her initial bias against recent immigrants, and her limited experience as someone who has never travelled, reviled authority, or experienced other cultures), Bryant is at her most effective. With a few deft strokes, she presents the milieu from which Ella gradually emerges.

As with so many issues, Ella is at first inarticulate about (although not unaware of) class boundaries. Early in her notebook, she admits being ashamed that the derogatory label "Okies" was applied to her family, and she cringes when her working-class mother repeats the litany that although poor, they are not a family of white trash. During her teens Ella helped out in the family grocery but, to avoid disdain, hid in the back, reading. Because her father, once a farm laborer and then a shipyard worker, wanted a home that he claimed "wasn't so near niggertown"— a sentiment Ella interprets as being about wealth, not race—he finally purchased property "on the hill" (47). Ella herself has internalized the rigidity of class-bound neighborhoods. Her very first journal entry, for example, announces the suburb in which she lives, letting this fact stand as a way of defining herself. Joe had wanted to live "all the way over the hill," but a good, not great,

242

income dictates that they settle in a community of tract houses near the college.

One day Harkan challenges his students, requiring them to attend a film and lecture at Berkeley and asking why none of them takes advantage of the city's museums and its renowned university. First listening to Georgia, an African American student, explain how she does not feel welcome or comfortable at cultural events, Ella, without raising her hand, blurts out: "It's not race. I feel the same way. It's as if you have to be born in it . . . where people talk about books and go to the ballet when they're young" (61). Harkan instructs her that she indeed is referring to class, and Ella admits dreading all her life that someone will at any moment say, "You'll have to leave, you don't belong here, sorry" (62).[8] Perhaps an updated version of Harkan's classroom is what Constance Coiner has in mind when she imagines a reconfigured space which includes multicultural working-class writing, where "students do not get the sense that they have identified with the 'wrong text'— a course in which identity politics is scrapped in favor of a political consciousness capable of decoding the middle-class myth and organizing to give ordinary people better life chances" (262). Of course, there were no opportunities in the late 1960s for Ella to read about her own milieu, but at least, in her notebooks, she is writing that literature herself.[9]

For those who teach writing or, for that matter, who are proponents of active learning, *Ella Price's Journal* holds particular value. Students find the subjects Ella treats accessible and familiar: the self, family, relationships, stereotypes, sexuality, choice, school itself. They can easily chart Ella's gradual education, emotional growth, development of a feminist consciousness, and progress as a writer. For teachers, Bryant provides a model we dream about: a student who takes journal keeping seriously. In entry after entry, Ella illustrates that writing is discovery. She makes frequent statements of varying length and intensity, grapples with reading assignments, comments on classroom discussions, describes observed events, recollects past experiences, questions social institutions and gender roles, records dreams, composes lists, analyzes behavior, and, perhaps most purposefully, confronts the self. She exemplifies the power of journal keeping, which Joan Didion describes in "On Keeping a Notebook": "We forget all too soon the things we thought we could never forget. We forget the loves and the betrayals alike, forget what we whispered and what we screamed, forget who we were. . . . It is a good idea, then, to keep in touch, and I suppose that keeping in touch is what notebooks are all about" (516–17).

Within its five notebooks of relatively equal and substantial length, the novel exhibits exceptional variety of subject and technique. It can truly be read as a primer, a "writer's journal." In including narrative, biography, confession, conversation, dreamscape (both day and night variety), writing assignments, and quotations and notes from her reading, while—at the same time and via the same entries—charting Ella's growth, Bryant counters traditional expectations of how a novel is shaped, situating her work as an early example of what we increasingly view as women's transgressive style.

The "catch-all" quality of Ella's journal permits dramatic, fruitful juxtapositions. In an early entry she shows resistance to revealing herself on the page, denigrating those who, lacking "guts," would expose their problems to a shrink. She chides their action as similar to "vomiting and studying what comes up" (27). Her very next entry, however, is just such a personal revelation: She recounts how, while driving on a boulevard near her home, she became suddenly lost among strips of fast-food stands and furniture stores and then, intentionally and suicidally, swerved toward parked cars.

Ella makes an all-too-familiar beginner's complaint, "I don't see how writing down the things I do every day will help me learn English" (18), and after only a few weeks threatens to drop Harkan's course. Early in her second notebook, however, she admits, "I think I've learned a lot. Just writing in the journal has almost changed my life" (55). As we gradually realize, the practice seems not only to have changed, but actually to have *saved* Ella's life.

After initial resistance and occasional setbacks, Ella eventually finds and practices an authentic, if at times shaky, voice. Near the end of her writings, she berates herself for sounding like twenty different women: "fearful, petty, narrow . . . and getting worse— devious, selfish" (157). Her varying, experimental voice, however, is precisely the process and product English instructors hope for. As she discovers the saving, sheltering, invigorating power of her writing, Ella varies both the style and content of her sentences, moving from exposition in simple, repetitive cadences to more com- plex analysis and syntax; from the poignant, confessional strains of autobiography to the quick-paced punch of eyewitness account. It is in the latter—in her narrative skill at capturing events—that we particularly appreciate Ella as a blossoming writer. Embedded in her journal, in fact, are several ideas for fiction. As Lyn Lifshin reports in *Ariadne's Thread*, an anthology of contemporary women's notebooks, many find, when they reread what they have written, "novels in their journals" (18).

Ella is an assiduous, ardent student, following Dan Harkan's assign- ments and suggestions even while she is annoyed at his criticism, bedazzled by his attention, or confused by his sexual behavior. Harkan demands that his students change, just as the challenging teacher in *Miss Giardino* (1978) does: "For six weeks they feared and hated me because I was attacking them. I was going to make them change, and change is frightening" (119).

Ella does change—perhaps more than Harkan could have imagined—and readers can chart her major changes as well as her emotional swings by the shape and length of her entries and by the dreams and experiences she describes. Noting the concluding phrases of each notebook, for example, is itself revealing: Notebook One ends with Ella's expression of delight and surprise at her prolific output in only six weeks: "It's getting easier"; Notebook Two shows purpose and confidence: "New year, new notebook"; Three establishes her determination to record ongoing experiences: "I want to try to remember it"; Four shows intention laced with desperation: "THE END"; and Five, the only one without terminal punctuation, offers hope: "I feel."

Ella fulfills another dream instructors harbor, that even after the course ends the journal habit will remain. At the conclusion of Notebook Four, Ella decides to stop writing when several events coalesce: she is pregnant, her therapy sessions with Dr. Redford cease, she does not enroll in school, and she quits her job. In resolving not to write, she believes she has removed the final obstacle between her and her husband; the very next day, however, she begins a new and this time pronouncedly frantic series of entries, completing a whole notebook in one month and making multiple entries on particularly distressing days.

Ella's journal is therapeutic, and she knows it. If at first she keeps it as part of her college English assignment and then enthusiastically begins to see it as a "writer's journal"—where she discusses books read, events experienced, memories recollected, dreams recalled—by the time her entries end, Ella realizes she writes in order to remain sane, to keep alive her resolutions about separation from Joe, returning to college, and having an abortion. Indeed, she writes to keep alive, period. Her activity agrees with what Adrienne Rich posits in *What Is Found There: Notebooks on Poetry and Politics*: "*You must write, and read, as if your life depended on it*" (italics Rich's). Rich further explains:

> To read as if your life depended on it would mean to let into your reading your beliefs, the swirl of your dreamlife, the physical sensa-

tions of your ordinary carnal life; and simultaneously, to allow what you're reading to pierce the routines, safe and impermeable, in which ordinary carnal life is tracked, charted, channeled. (32)

At her nadir, during weeks of psychiatric treatment, Ella reads little and worries that her journal is drying up; indeed, she allows two months to lapse without making an entry. Her creativity, expository skill, and engaging style desert her; sentence fragments predominate ("Going to Carmel this weekend. Had our honeymoon there"); entries shorten ("Had an orgasm last night"); description ceases ("Lovely weekend in Carmel again. But what a hangover") (182–83). However, when Dr. Redford steers her toward accepting her role as wife, mother and expectant mother, Ella must write, and often more than one entry per day. Here, she follows Gail Godwin's revelation that in heated times of creativity or crisis, "I often write several times a day. When I am really on edge. . . I sometimes write hourly" (quoted in Lifshin 12). In deciding to have an abortion, Ella makes entries at 4 P.M., 5 P.M., and 1 A.M. In the 5 P.M. account, Ella is most piercing in understanding and accepting her need to write: "Stay by me (who? I guess I'm talking to you, journal. I'm praying. . .). I must keep you by me. Must keep writing, pouring out whatever comes, looking at it clearly, draining the insanity out of me until what is left is clear thought and I know what to do" (191). A few entries later, she admits that despite how confused and angry Harkan has made her, she must thank him nonetheless for getting her to start an activity she now cherishes and finds essential. Over the course of her notebooks, Ella has changed from someone who thinks "there are a lot of questions about life you shouldn't ask" (26) to someone who is actively questioning, searching, taking chances. "With so many of us looking," she writes in her last notebook, "someone's bound to find out what we're looking for" (226).

247

Ella's internal transformation leads to concrete—and dramatic—changes in her life. And her journal helps her not only to think and feel, but to act. Bryant convincingly shows how Ella, through her journal writing, gradually recognizes, analyzes, and then tries to resolve her problems. At first our heroine can only grope with the idea that "there's something wrong with me . . . Inside, things are happening to me" (27). Her reading of E. M. Forster helps her "suddenly admit that all those things [we work hard for] didn't make us happy" (35). An early reference she makes to suicide contrasts powerfully with the final two words of the novel, "I feel." In imagining her own death, Ella says, "Then I could rest. I wouldn't feel freakish or odd . . . bored with all my friends, or ashamed of being bored. I wouldn't feel that I had to work so hard to be normal. . . . I wouldn't feel" (40). But her sense that life is empty and that she has missed opportunities dissipates remarkably when she studies. What she comes to believe is, had she gone to college earlier, she would have met people not afraid of feeling passionately, people who would not have accused her of being neurotic or freakish.

What Ella most hates to feel is fear, and she is even "afraid to admit I was afraid" (43). Her catalogue of fearful things is long. After giving birth to Lulu, she is afraid her baby would "drift off into the world" (70). Eventually she admits to Joe that they both are afraid of knowing things, of facing truths. She is afraid of getting pregnant; once pregnant, getting out of bed terrifies her. Dr. Redford's power over her, his enjoyment in being able to manipulate her, also terrifies Ella. She finally counters Joe's favorite dictum, that all he needs for happiness is to be able to "eat, drink, and screw," with the insult that he is, in that case, strikingly similar to a pig; but after relief in speaking up, Ella quickly feels terror (213). When Ella finally sees that Dan, Dr. Redford, and Joe are her enemies—that they do not even like who she once was or who she has become—she can focus on what to do, not on what to fear.

Ella Price's Journal convincingly shows that writing itself assists action. On her thirty-fifth birthday, she takes stock: "How did I spend the first lifetime? Doing nothing" (120). She immediately corrects this complaint by saying she did produce a child. But now, instead of allowing "outside forces" to decide her course of action, Ella resolves that she will "make it up as I go along" (120). In an effective conflation of thinking/writing/acting, Ella realizes she must resume college, for it is the only place "where people will let something happen in your mind" (197). When a crisis hits, such as an unwanted pregnancy, Ella finds resolution in writing. Right before our eyes her "I want it [another child] so much" becomes, four short lines later, "I DON'T WANT TO HAVE A BABY!" (190). Soon she tells Joe that she needs a separation because, "I have to do something, be something, but I can't do it with you" (222). By this time, her journal has helped her shed, one by one, all the people, things, arrangements that have thus far stymied and deflated her: her extended family, especially her mother and mother-in-law; a challenging and seductive professor; traditional psychiatry; part-time, dead-end jobs; her neighborhood, house, husband, and daughter.

Bryant includes an impassioned argument for putting one's experience into words in *The Garden of Eros* (1979), a stream-of-consciousness monologue that presents a young, blind woman's solitary ordeal the day she gives birth. After delivering her baby alone, the heroine appeals to her frantic husband, whose jeep accident detained him:

> I want to tell you what happened. Everything. Not just the pain and labor. Not just the fear. . . . All the thoughts, new waves rolling over old waves, blending and changing. . . . I knew so many things. I understood everything—everything, so clearly. But now it's beginning to fade. I'm starting to forget all the things I learned. So let me tell you before I lose it all. (169)[10]

At the end of her fifth notebook, immediately after she has left her husband and daughter, Ella records not what she said to Laura, but her need to say it: "I talked all night, not to tell her what had happened but to say it all to myself. To begin, to just begin to understand where I was, what I was doing and where I was going" (225).

Where Ella usually "says it all to herself" first, rehearsing her experience and perceptions, is in her notebooks. In fact, the most engaging and, in the end, important relationship in the whole novel is the relationship between Ella and her journal.

Long recognized as a laudable genre when produced by serious, canonized authors, journal keeping as a popular form worthy of publication sometimes receives short shrift. What Bryant shows is that in the hands of even an untutored writer, notebooks deserve readership. As Holly Prado notes, we need to expand the genre, opening it to include "the current woman, passionate, reflective, exploring. I think we [journal writers] are interested in the process of living, rather than its summation" (quoted in Lifshin 18).

Fortunately, legions of readers for over two decades now have appreciated how Dorothy Bryant's first novel captures their own concerns, and in a form they themselves would like to use, if they do not already—the personal notebook. When Lyn Lifshin sifted through the hundreds of submissions she received for *Ariadne's Thread: A Collection of Contemporary Women's Journals* (1982), for example, she found prevalent the same themes Ella Price addresses: love, divorce, abortion, disappointment, fear, and a growing sense of feminism. Bryant's heroine also essentially avoids those topics Lifshin's respondents do: philosophy, religion, history, economic conditions, activism, current events, and fathers. Major reasons that Lifshin lists for keeping a notebook we could apply to Ella Price's activity: to record emotional growth, to spur a sense of clarity, to pin down an observation, to record events, to talk to oneself, to reduce per-

250

sonal experience to an essence, to keep one's sanity, to heal, to clear out the clutter and then get on with one's work, and to warm up for further writing (Lifshin 8–10).

The most dominant theme Lifshin uncovers also informs Ella's journal: the centrality of change. And Lifshin stresses what readers of *Ella Price's Journal* immediately understand: "how anyone can use a diary, not only for self-understanding and growth, but as a record or a letter to the self, some souvenir . . . like a photograph that can always be touched, gone back to, no matter how far from it one has come" (7–8). What astonishes Lifshin is "the large number of middle-aged women who dreamed about running away from home to begin a new life, or who actually did" (6). Ella's journal provides articulation for and interpretation of a recurring dream: to burn down her house and thus escape an existence which stifles her potential. But until she writes it down, Ella does not confront how unhappy, even to the point of being suicidal, she has become. Far from being over, her life is expanding; writing itself, as Ella increasingly realizes, can bring understanding, growth, and, finally, action.

Ella Price attends college during a time of widespread student activism and near a city known for its campus demonstrations. Protests for social justice even materialize at apathetic Bay Junior College, what Harkan calls "a high school with ash trays" (63). Other students encourage Ella to march against the Vietnam War, Harkan goads her into looking directly at the oppressed —and in so doing seeing herself—and Laura, who eventually moves to Berkeley and enrolls in the university there, invites her troubled new friend to join a women's group. Bryant wisely situates her retiring heroine well on the periphery of any potential upheaval. Ella's rebellion is internal; what action she takes grows out of personal, not public, concerns. Yet as the novel progresses, Ella experiences her first, flickering intimations

251

that the personal can be political.

Students of popular culture, women's studies scholars, sociologists, and historians alike continue to find *Ella Price's Journal* a memorable, immensely teachable, and accurate account of the late 1960s. Such estimation might seem at first surprising, for while Bryant sets her novel near San Francisco, on the fault line of cultural change and upheaval, she does not focus on movement leaders, dramatize historically defining moments, or posit theories about racist, sexist hegemony. What *Ella Price's Journal* does capture, however, is perhaps more powerful and essential, although quieter—a revolution from within, of the kind that took root for so many in the fruitful soil of the 1960s. Our heroine reminds us that an ordinary woman is capable and deserving of the extraordinary.

The longest entry in Ella's journal, and the first sustained passage of marked narrative skill, is a lively account of a late night peace march from Berkeley to Oakland. Weaving nervously in and out of marchers and bystanders, Ella has one grand moment of activism; she joins the ranks. In highlighting her character's intuitive response to the necessity for action, Bryant captures perfectly the way many people experienced the spirited 1960s. At first resistant to marching, Ella realizes she has spent the first half of her life "doing nothing." Once she is in line, her tension, fears, and confusion vanish. Finally calm and peaceful, she is "concentrated, free of distraction and anxieties" (130).

In novelistic detail, including fast-paced action and lively dialogue, Ella dramatically depicts what a woman of her background, experience, and temperament would feel about public protest: fear of recognition, injury, and arrest; foolishness and embarrassment; excitement and, finally, elation. Tentative and nervous at first, Ella eventually warms to the camaraderie and closeness among marchers. She has tapped something she needed desperately, a feeling of "connectedness." Ella captures well this sensation: "I felt right—not self-righteous, not smugly correct. . . . And warm with closeness to the people walking beside me, not physical closeness, something more. Something I had missed all my life without knowing it existed" (130). No longer the outsider, Ella thrills at being part of human movement, not of a particular "movement." In this way, her story is universal.

Ella's seemingly disproportionate narrative (its length more than doubles any other entry thus far) of the march anchors the middle of the novel and ends Notebook Three. Ella begins her fourth notebook by announcing, "I am not the same person anymore. . . . Now I understand the importance of moving the body, walking from here to there or even just standing—maybe that's why we call taking a position 'standing for something'" (139). Being able to move, both literally and figuratively, has changed Ella's life. And in her march for (inner) peace, Ella discovers something further: During her life-transforming experience, she notices some people whose impact quietly spreads out over her remaining pages. Without prediction, gloss, analysis, or, indeed, specific reference to them again in her notebooks, she finds models for her future life: "older women alone, open-faced, matter-of-fact, intelligent looking" (127).

Appropriately, Ella neither theorizes about politics nor debates controversial subjects in her personal journal, and, indeed, we do not know her arguments against United States involvement in Southeast Asia. When she finally volunteers to help the women's group for peace and justice, Ella's motives have more to do with keeping her mind off her upcoming abortion than with wanting prisoners to receive the Christmas cards she addresses. Her halting steps toward connection and community are, however, privately productive. In her case, the personal may be political, but, more importantly, the political is personal. For soon, she will be able to turn a cold eye on her empty life, where she shuffles, browbeaten, from beauty parlor to temporary office work to deadly family get-togethers to shrink. And then she will walk away.

In the suburban sprawl of fast food chains, gas stations, and monotonous shops, Ella has withered, "not dead but not alive" (84). She makes a seemingly unlikely comparison between herself and an upper-middle-class Henry James heroine, Catherine Sloper in *Washington Square*, who is "not really dull, [just] invisible" (84). Catherine is the literary character Ella finds most resonating. While neither overwork, poverty, physically abusive men, nor other obvious forms of oppression overwhelm these two—as they do, for example, the working-class heroines of Tillie Olsen, Meridel Le Sueur, or Anzia Yezierska—Ella and Catherine easily can join the company of characters "cut off from the exercise of their full potential" (Nelson and Huse 3). Clearly, it is stifling mediocrity that Ella struggles to avoid.

In a few connected metaphors, Bryant illustrates universal feelings of helplessness and the need to escape. Since childhood, Ella has had a recurring nightmare of feet walking over her while she is "buried alive" (41). And every Sunday, using apartment ads as her prompt, she daydreams about being "off alone in a room"—a proverbial room of one's own. In her fantasy, she sits high up, almost in a Tower of Babel, "surrounded by a few of my own things, only my very own things, and hearing distant sounds of strange people" (42). Ella has another vision of height, this one actual. She is transfixed by a suburban icon, a gas station statue, over two stories high, whose enameled "Pop-Eye"-shaped arms once must have cradled something. What particularly annoys her about this deteriorating monster is his smile: "happy and menacing and cheerful . . . stupid, willfully stupid. That's what I hate most,…the fixed stupidity of grinning over outstretched, empty arms and hands, the stupidity of permanent good cheer." She ends this angry piece—which, significantly, is her very first descriptive entry—with the strong sentence: "He marks the street that leads to my home" (30). By the end of the novel, Ella has escaped, no longer wanting, needing, or allowing her husband, a human-sized version of the giant, to throw her "off balance by his slightly drunken good cheer" (220).

Although it does not indict the political basis of patriarchy, *per se*, Bryant's work often does excoriate the American family as repressive institution, especially noting how it scars its daughters and leaves them with such negative self-images that they struggle continually to find peace—never, of course, expecting happiness. Bryant depicts joyless, tense, vaguely dissatisfied females whose backgrounds have effectively stymied them.[11]

As anthologist Lifshin points out, journal keepers often fixate on mothers. About motherhood, writers document "the guilts, the ambivalences, the closeness, the desire to please and the feeling one never can" (4). Ella frequently notes how her hardworking, churchgoing, self-sacrificing mother can rarely be pleased. In the long autobiographical entry that completes Notebook One, Ella claims that "all she ever thought about after I was fourteen was that I might get pregnant and disgrace her" (49). Ella's mother found immense relief in her only daughter marrying right after high school graduation.

In Notebook Two, when Ella reveals that she bridled against pregnancy, was traumatized by the pain of childbirth, felt "helpless and vulnerable" as a new mother, and then began to be overly dependent on Joe, she recalls her mother's scarcely veiled glee. Ella translated the message as: "Nobody could ever be as good a mother as I was. . . . Now you must sacrifice yourself as I did" (71). Joe's mother, a staunch Catholic, also contributes to Ella's discomfort. Ella calls them "martyr-mothers," a term reminiscent of Kate Chopin's "mother-women" in "The Awakening." At the penultimate crisis of her life, when Ella decides on an abortion, these women undermine her—crying about and decrying her decision, praying over her, calling her a murderer, and leaving Ella temporarily infantile, weak, and speechless, and thus unable to counter their attacks.[12]

Within Ella's own doors, motherhood becomes fraught with anxiety. Because Joe wants Ella to have a baby against her wishes, their marriage finally disintegrates. In describing their bedroom during this crisis, Ella writes, "There we were, side by side, awake and silent" (161). By day, their daughter Lulu refuses to talk to Ella who, in turn, finds her daughter's attitude "a nasty mixture of insensitivity and self-righteousness" (202).

Sessions with therapist Redford feed into Ella's belief that her mother has made her feel vulnerable, unpopular, unworthy, weak. While she does not recount in detail the meetings between doctor and patient, Ella does summarily report (in some of the novel's shortest entries, only two or three sentences) that her over-seriousness, intermittent frigidity, guilt about sex, undeveloped maternal feelings, and inability to accept or extend love all go "back to my mother" (180). Luckily, Ella does not remain in therapy, where Redford would encourage more unnecessary and misguided fixation on old grievances. What Ella needs is to concentrate on her own rebirth and not let an unsatisfactory affair, her interrupted education, traditional (and sexist) therapy, or an unwanted pregnancy act as deterrents.

If family relations are strained in Bryant's first novel, female friendship is championed. So impaired initially is Ella's vision of life that when she meets the consciousness-raised, familiar-looking Laura, she does not recognize her, does not even consider the possibility that such a woman could live around the corner. Ella's journal rarely captures interiors; however, her exuberant description of an initial visit to Laura, a divorced, politically astute, Berkeley-bound, working mother, shows how rapidly her horizon is widening:

> Her house is exactly the same as ours, of course, but how different! There are books all over, and drawings tacked to the kitchen wall (she draws too, very well), and papers she's been working on spread across the front room—and more than any things a feeling, a spare, clear feel-

256

ing of this being a house where interesting people are doing interesting things. (86)

"Interesting people doing interesting things" partially answers Ella's quintessential question about what her own life needs. When she summons nerve two months later to walk arm in arm with her new friend at an antiwar march, Ella finally feels something that she categorizes as "the closeness, the clear pure rightness" (135) she seeks. Ella appreciates the fact that their friendship is not "based on gossip or girlish confidences" (101), but often includes discussion of books. As the novel progresses, Laura's importance increases, for Ella turns to her not only for intellectual conversation but also as someone who can understand and listen sympathetically. An early reviewer of the novel, in fact, complained, "Only one person stands ready to help Ella at the end when she has left her husband, the teacher, and the psychiatrist, and that is another woman. . . . It is a tortuous journey through these diary entries which sees her finally, safely, established with the truth that men are no good for you" (Burghardt).

For Ella, her friend's situation also serves as a model, for although lonely (and pessimistic about ever finding a partner), Laura commits herself to social action, moves from suburbia to Berkeley, and has a circle of women friends, some of whom she loves. Perhaps Bryant overdramatizes Laura's role as model and superwoman, making us question how someone could so expertly juggle family, college, work, volunteerism, and a new, demanding friendship; but without Laura as idea/l, Ella's march (against war and out of her house) might be a march into the same emptiness she felt when her affair with Harkan failed.

By shining a light into the corners of Ella Price's life, Dorothy Bryant uncovers issues that have advanced further into public discourse during the quarter century since her first novel appeared. She flashes a quick but nonetheless piercing beam, for example, on women's reproductive rights, the chauvinism endemic in traditional psychiatry, the male-dominated literary canon, the shrapnel loosed within nuclear families, and the need for female friendship and community.

In assessing Tillie Olsen's contribution to the American radical tradition, Deborah Rosenfelt makes a comment relevant as well to Dorothy Bryant's fiction. We appreciate, Rosenfelt states, "Olsen's enduring insistence that literature must confront the material realities of people's lives as shaping circumstances, that the very categories of class and race and sex constitute the fabric of reality as we live it, and that literature has an obligation to deepen consciousness and facilitate social change" (86).

Indeed, in showing what shaped her bored, withdrawn, but supremely educable suburban housewife, Dorothy Bryant has helped people recognize and transform their own situations. Most of us, although frightened and leery of change, would like to begin some part of our lives anew, to fill a series of notebooks with what we have learned. Ella bravely embraces what for her is the newness of education—in all its ramifications, which include taking part in class discussions; meeting diverse people; reading and writing about difficult texts; composing and revising papers; becoming frustrated, disillusioned, and ready to drop out; taking part in campus events; being variously goaded, infatuated, and inspired by a professor; changing one's views of family and friends; engaging in self-reflection and analysis; and keeping a journal that examines all of the above and frequently demonstrates good writing. Education enables Ella to make material changes; she cuts right through the fabric of her previous failed life.

In a brief, genre-defying piece called "The Page," Margaret Atwood includes a warning that turners of pages—readers and writers, even novices like Ella Price—might well heed:

Touch the page at your peril: it is you who are blank and innocent, not the page. Nevertheless you want to know, nothing will stop you. You touch the page, it's as if you've drawn a knife across it, the page has been hurt now, a sinuous wound opens, a thin incision. Darkness wells through. (141–42)

There is a price for Ella's journal. While we applaud Ella for her progress in trying to identify who she is and what she feels, and while, in reading her notebooks, we appreciate anew the benefits of education, her example reminds us how perilous it is to read deeply and write passionately. The point of *Ella Price's Journal*, however, is that without the chance to "touch" pages that we might otherwise never have opened, written on, or turned, we face the real possibility of remaining blank.

Barbara Horn
New York City
May 1997

Notes

1. Such categories unduly restrict and, like the thankfully outdated term "regionalist," lead to false expectations, misunderstanding, and a tendency to underrate or simply dismiss. At the risk of yet another ill-fitting mantle, we might apply "issue-oriented" or "issue-driven" to most of Bryant's fiction, which has been exceptionally varied in format. Can a supremely strong, blind young woman survive giving birth alone in the woods? Let's listen to her dramatic monologue on that day (*The Garden of Eros,* 1979). What will happen when an incorrigible ex-convict takes an apartment in the home of his middle-aged, middle-class pen pal and champion? Let's read their letters (*Prisoners,* 1980). Can an aging daughter negotiate her senile father's need to pass a driving test? Let's see what she thinks and does during the seven hours she escorts him (*The Test,* 1991). How will a smart, depressed suburban housewife fare at a junior college? Let's look at her journal. I am indebted to J. J. Wilson, whose entry on Dorothy Bryant in *Feminist Writers,* informs this discussion.

2. Information about the novel's publication history are based on a letter I received from Dorothy Bryant, dated December 31, 1996, and the packet she enclosed containing copies of book reviews from 1972 of *Ella Price's Journal.* Unless otherwise noted, all subsequent biographical information and quoted statements from Bryant are taken from this letter.

3. Dorothy Bryant says that "*Redbook* received nearly 200 letters. One editor told me, 'We usually get about 4.'"

4. In a career noteworthy for its timeliness of subject and its productivity, Dorothy Bryant continues to present a rich circle of variously aged, accessible women. She treats youth in *The Garden of Eros* (1979), *The Confessions of Madame Psyche* (1986), and, to a lesser extent, *Killing Wonder* (1981); middle-aged characters in *Prisoners* (1980), *A Day in San Francisco* (1982), and *The Test* (1991); older women in *Miss Giardino* (1978).

5. Bryant again uses the phrase "female impersonator" in *The Test* (1991),

but coming two decades later and with a protagonist twenty years older, it has lost its sting: "There is no make-up to repair, no alternate female impersonator to consider or plan while looking in the mirror. This face is it, unmasked, uneven, weathered, cracked by lines that split wildly when I laugh" (135).

6. Neither a sexual harasser nor an arrogant chauvinist, Dan Harkan is "a very challenging, hard-working, concerned teacher," Dorothy Bryant argues, who, while arrogant and with feet of clay, kept his affairs with students—"for those days!—minimal." We should allow him his historical context.

7. It is interesting to see how Ella's story can be illuminated by current movements for transforming the curriculum. Several examples can be found in Fiol-Matta.

8. Bryant returns to this type of class shame in *A Day in San Francisco* (1982). The heroine, a noted professor and only child of Italian immigrant parents, recalls a childhood "lived in constant fear of exposure to ridicule and hatred, vaguely threatened by the ever-present danger of being ground up by a machine into which I could not fit, hard as I (to my shame) tried" (46).

9. Perhaps the only other popular work to capture the educational experiences of a woman like Ella is the movie *Educating Rita*. Thanks go to J. J. Wilson for making this point in a conversation we had about *Ella Price's Journal*.

10. This sentiment, the fear of losing what one has learned unless it is articulated, permeates Bryant's work. Whether through conversation, personal papers (*The Confessions of Madame Psyche*, 1986), letters (*Prisoners*, 1980), essays and other "published" materials embedded within the fictional framework (*Killing Wonder*, 1981, and *A Day in San Francisco*, 1982), or notebooks, her characters' hard-won knowledge, especially of the self, requires documentation, lest it too quickly be lost.

11. For example, the blind, twenty-one-year-old, pregnant narrator of *The Garden of Eros* (1979) harbors at times paralytic bitterness toward both her parents: an abusive, tyrannical father, who even mis-

appropriates her insurance settlement, and a mother who, while thinking her kindness will protect her three daughters, fails to be assertive. *The Confessions of Madame Psyche* (1986) presents an alcoholic, neglectful father, who was once a learned, brilliant man, and an older sister who so imprisons the title character, insisting that she remain a reclusive "medium," that Madame Psyche, a grown woman with a child's experience, finally runs away.

12. By the time she writes *A Day in San Francisco* (1982), Bryant can look more understandingly at the inevitable discomfort between generations. In referring to her parents, the middle-aged narrator of this later novel realizes, "Hating and craving you as they do, they also love you. . . . And the pain of it makes you stammer that you love them, then increases as you realize you really do" (60). Pat, the narrator of *The Test* (1991), written over two decades after *Ella Price's Journal*, recalls her mother's "fear of blame and shame, fault and failure. Whether it was a dirt spot on the floor or a daughter's divorce, it was her disgrace" (112). A woman in her fifties, Pat laces her criticism with more wisdom and generosity than Ella can understandably claim: "Nothing we [two sisters] did or became could satisfy my mother's own deprivation. No one ever lived through her children, least of all one who thought she should" (28).

Books by Dorothy Bryant

Fiction

Ella Price's Journal. New York: Lippincott, 1972; New York: NAL-Signet, 1973; Berkeley: Ata Books, 1982; New York: The Feminist Press at CUNY, 1997.

The Kin of Ata Are Waiting for You. New York: Random House, 1976.

Miss Giardino. Berkeley: Ata Books, 1978; New York: The Feminist Press at CUNY, 1997.

The Garden of Eros. Berkeley: Ata Books, 1979.

Prisoners. Berkeley: Ata Books, 1980.

Killing Wonder. Berkeley: Ata Books, 1981; London: Women's Press, 1986.

A Day in San Francisco. Berkeley: Ata Books, 1983.

Confessions of Madame Psyche. Berkeley: Ata Books, 1986; London: Women's Press, 1988; New York: The Feminist Press at CUNY, 1998.

The Test. Berkeley: Ata Books, 1991.

Anita, Anita. Berkeley: Ata Books, 1993.

Nonfiction

Writing a Novel. Berkeley: Ata Books, 1979.

Myths to Lie By: Essays and Stories. Berkeley, Ata Books, 1994.

Plays

Dear Master. First production 1991.

Tea with Mrs. Hardy. First production 1992.

The Panel. First production 1996.

The Trial of Cornelia Connelly.

Works Cited

Atwood, Margaret. "The Page." *Good Bones and Simple Murders.* New York: Doubleday, 1994.

———. "Unpopular Gals." *Good Bones and Simple Murders.* New York: Doubleday, 1994.

Bryant, Dorothy. "Letters." *Redbook.* December 1972.

Burghardt, Robert A. Review of *Ella Price's Journal. World.* August 29, 1972.

Coiner, Constance. "U.S. Working-Class Women's Fiction: Notes Toward an Overview." *Women's Studies Quarterly.* 23.l—2 (Spring/Summer 1995): 248–267.

Didion, Joan. *The White Album.* New York: Farrar, Straus & Giroux, 1979.

Fiol-Matta, Liza. Editorial. *Women's Studies Quarterly.* 24.3–4 (Fall/Winter 1996): 3–15.

Friedan, Betty. *The Feminine Mystique.* New York: Norton, 1963.

Horr, Mrs. James. "Letters." *Redbook.* December 1972.

Lifshin, Lyn, ed. *Ariadne's Thread: A Collection of Contemporary Women's Journals.* New York: Harper & Row, 1982.

Nelson, Kay Hoyle and Nancy Huse, eds. *The Critical Response to Tillie Olsen.* Westport, CT: Greenwood Press, 1994.

Rich, Adrienne. *What Is Found There: Notebooks on Poetry and Politics.* New York: Norton, 1993.

Rosenfelt, Deborah. "From the Thirties: Tillie Olsen and the Radical Tradition." *The Critical Response to Tillie Olsen.* Ed. Kay Hoyle Nelson and Nancy Huse. Westport, CT: Greenwood Press, 1994.

Sims, Barbara W. Review of *Ella Price's Journal. Chattanooga Times.* March 4, 1973.

Zandy, Janet. Editorial. *Women's Studies Quarterly.* 23.l–2 (Spring/Summer 1995): 3–6.

Wilson, J. J. Entry on Dorothy Bryant. *Feminist Writers.* Ed. Pamela Kesler-Shelton. Detroit: St. James Press, 1996. 76–78.

CONTEMPORARY WOMEN'S FICTION FROM AROUND THE WORLD
from The Feminist Press at The City University of New York

Allegra Maud Goldman, a novel by Edith Konecky. $9.95 paper.
Bamboo Shoots After the Rain: Contemporary Stories by Women Writers of Taiwan. $14.95 paper. $35.00 cloth.
Changes: A Love Story, a novel by Ama Ata Aidoo. $12.95 paper.
Ella Price's Journal, a novel by Dorothy Bryant. $14.95 paper. $35.00 cloth.
An Estate of Memory, a novel by Ilona Karmel. $11.95 paper.
Folly, a novel by Maureen Brady. $12.95 paper. $35.00 cloth.
Miss Giardino, a novel by Dorothy Bryant. $11.95 paper. $32.00 cloth.
No Sweetness Here and Other Stories, by Ama Ata Aidoo. $10.95 paper. $29.00 cloth.
Paper Fish, a novel by Tina De Rosa. $9.95 paper. $20.00 cloth.
Reena and Other Stories, by Paule Marshall. $11.95 paper.
Sister Gin, a novel by June Arnold. $12.95 paper.
The Slate of Life: More Contemporary Stories by Women Writers of India. $12.95 paper. $35.00 cloth.
Songs My Mother Taught Me: Stories, Plays, and Memoir, by Wakako Yamauchi. $14.95 paper. $35.00 cloth.
Truth Tales: Contemporary Stories by Women Writers of India. $12.95 paper. $35.00 cloth.
Two Dreams: New and Selected Stories, by Shirley Geok-lin Lim. $10.95 paper.
What Did Miss Darrington See?: An Anthology of Feminist Supernatural Fiction. $14.95 paper.
Winter's Edge, a novel by Valerie Miner. $10.95 paper.
With Wings: An Anthology of Literature by and About Women with Disabilities. $14.95 paper.
Women Working: An Anthology of Stories and Poems. $13.95 paper.

To receive a free catalog of The Feminist Press's 150 titles, call or write The Feminist Press at The City University of New York, City College/ CUNY, Convent Avenue at 138th Street, Wingate Building, New York, NY 10031; phone: (212) 650-8890; fax: (212) 650-8893. Feminist Press books are available at bookstores, or can be ordered directly. Send check or money order (in U.S. dollars drawn on a U.S. bank) payable to The Feminist Press. Please add $4.00 shipping and handling for the first book and $1.00 for each additional book. VISA, Mastercard, and American Express are accepted. Prices subject to change.